CROWN OF MAGIC

WHITE HAVEN WITCHES
BOOK SEVEN

TJ GREEN

Crown of Magic

Mountolive Publishing

ISBN eBook 978-1-99-004709-1

ISBN Paperback 978-1-99-004716-9

ISBN Hardback 978-1-99-004787-9

Cover design by Fiona Jayde Media

Editing by Missed Period Editing

To my ex-work colleagues, the fabulous nurses in the Communicable Disease Team at Regional Public Health.

You are all amazing xx

Contents

Fullpage image	VI
One	1
Two	11
Three	22
Four	29
Five	39
Six	51
Seven	61
Eight	68
Nine	75
Ten	84
Eleven	94
Twelve	104
Thirteen	114
Fourteen	122
Fifteen	129
Sixteen	141
Seventeen	150

Eighteen	165
Nineteen	180
Twenty	189
Twenty-One	199
Twenty-Two	213
Twenty-Three	224
Twenty-Four	234
Twenty-Five	242
Twenty-Six	251
Twenty-Seven	264
Twenty-Eight	272
Author's Note	279
About the Author	281
Other Books by TJ Green	283

One

Avery Hamilton and the watching crowd cheered as the maypole was finally secured into position in the small square in the centre of White Haven.

At the top was a colourful crown of flowers, and for the next couple of weeks until Beltane, or May Day as the non-pagans called it, Greenlane Nurseries, Reuben Jackson's business, would be making sure the flowers remained fresh.

The bright ribbons that were fixed to the pole unfurled in the breeze, making Avery feel as if summer was getting closer. The sky was pale blue with a few scurrying clouds, and although it was mid-April, it was warm.

Reuben stood next to her, keeping an eye on proceedings, and she turned to him. "Your flowers look really good!"

Reuben, like Avery, was a witch, and one of her best friends. Despite the fact that he was here in an official capacity, he was still wearing his t-shirt and board shorts. He winked at her, his blue eyes bright against his tanned skin. "Nothing like having a huge phallic symbol in the middle of the town to get everyone in the Beltane mood."

Avery whacked his arm playfully. "You are terrible!"

"But it's true, you know it is," he said, laughing. "I can feel it in the air! It's like everyone's woken up feeling frisky."

"I'm not so sure it's friskiness, as just a general air of excitement, Reuben! You just like to think that everyone is obsessed with sex," Avery said, as she looked around at the excited locals and tourists who had gathered to watch the official start of the Beltane celebrations. The traffic had been diverted for a few hours for the maypole to be put in place, so it lent an even more festival air to the proceedings. And yes, there was definitely an air of goodwill and teasing.

"Nothing wrong with liking sex, Avery. You've got a spring to your step now that Alex has moved in." He raised an eyebrow. "I like to feel that Greenlane Nurseries is adding some cheer to the town!" He pointed at the hanging baskets and pots that his nursery had already positioned outside the local shops, making the streets look bright. "I've made sure that there are a few flowers in there to help spread feelings of love, with maybe a little spell or two to help things along."

Avery shook her head. "You're incorrigible. I don't know how El puts up with you." El was another witch, and also Reuben's girlfriend.

He looked at her, mock-outraged, but before he could answer, Stan, White Haven's pseudo-Druid who loved to officiate at their pagan celebrations, stepped away from the crew who had raised the maypole and addressed the crowd.

As usual at these pagan events, Stan was wearing his long, woollen cloak and carried a wooden staff, and he grinned as he looked around. "I am pleased to announce that our Beltane celebrations are officially open!" The crowd cheered again as he gestured to Reuben. "Thank you to Greenlane Nurseries for providing the wonderful flowers that are decorating White Haven. For the next couple of weeks, we will keep plants around the maypole and the ribbons tied out of the way, until the dancers are ready to perform on Beltane. This coming weekend will also see the start of the play, Tristan and Iseult!" He beckoned to a young couple that stood at the edge of the crowd, and they smiled and waved at the onlookers as they reached Stan's side. They were both in their twenties, and the young woman was slim with shoulder-length blonde hair, and the man was of average height, with light brown hair and a deep tan. "Let me introduce Emma Whitehall and Josh Atkins, who are playing the leads! I'm sure you'll love the show, which was last performed in White Haven in the sixties! In the meantime, our very own Morris Dancers are here to start the festivities!"

A group of men were clustered on the edge of the square, dressed in traditional costumes. As they moved into position, the bells that were wrapped below their knees jingled. A lone accordion player started a tune and the men raised their sticks and started to dance as Stan joined Reuben and Avery, bringing Emma and Josh with him.

"Excellent job on the plants," Stan said to Reuben, his voice low. "White Haven looks magnificent."

"Thanks Stan, always happy to help!" Reuben nodded towards the maypole. "This afternoon, when the dancers have finished, a few of my staff will be back with the pots to go around the base."

Stan rubbed his hands together and repeated, "Excellent, excellent. Have either of you met Josh or Emma before?"

"No," Avery said, smiling and shaking their hands as Reuben did the same. "Are you ready for opening night?"

Josh looked nervously at Emma. "As usual, it doesn't feel like it, but I'm sure we will be."

Emma nodded. "It always feels like this in the week before the show. You feel like you keep forgetting important lines and that the costumes won't fit and you'll miss your cues, but it will be fine."

Stan refused to be worried. "You'll be fantastic! And the costumes are perfect." He looked at Reuben and Avery. "It was the White Haven Players who performed it last time, so it seemed only fitting they do it again. And of course it's a Cornish story, all about love that cannot be withered by time or circumstance—perfect for Beltane! And what perfect star-crossed lovers you are!"

At the mention of love, Josh and Emma seemed to look determinedly away from each other, and a pink flush started up Emma's cheeks.

Stan, however, was too busy talking to notice. "I'm not sure whether I enjoy Beltane or Samhain more! Have you decorated your shop yet, Avery?

"Of course! Sally has been working hard, as usual."

Sally was Avery's friend and the manager of Happenstance Books, and was responsible for making her shop run smoothly. Sally had already roped Dan, another friend who worked for her, into helping her decorate the shop with flowers, garlands, and lights.

Stan bounced lightly on the soles of his feet, making him seem younger than his fifty-odd years. "I didn't doubt it, my dear."

"How are the plans for the procession going?" Reuben asked. "Have you chosen a May Queen yet?"

Stan shook his head. "No. There have been, as usual, lots of applicants, and also for the Green Man, her consort. But they need to have a presence!" He sighed. "You may not know this, but we encourage the drama students at the local college to apply. They will need to follow a certain direction, because you know the whole thing is tightly organised, and the events manager has been arranging this for months!"

"Isn't this short notice for them, then?" Avery asked, surprised.

"Hence the need to choose wisely! We're close to selecting who it will be, and will make our decision in the next day or so. They need to have the final fitting for their costumes, and they'll spend the next week rehearsing. Next Tuesday we'll have the first street procession. That's when we'll officially announce them. "

Avery nodded. "And where will the play be performed?"

"White Haven Little Theatre," Josh answered. "The first performance will be on Saturday night, and the final performance will be the following Saturday afternoon in the castle grounds, in the open air—as long as the weather's good."

"So much to do!" Stan exclaimed. He held his hand up, and ticked off his fingers, one by one. "The fire is being built on the beach, ready for the celebration on the evening. The small arena for the performance of the play is almost complete, the maypole is up, the performers in the procession are also rehearsing, and the girls who'll be dancing around the maypole have been practicing, too—they're all from the local school. And obviously the May Queen and the Green Man will be part of the main Beltane procession through the town."

Reuben's eyes met Avery's over the top of Stan's head. "That's quite a list, Stan!"

"I know. Such a busy time of year, but the town is full of visitors and we must put on a show! I love it, and wouldn't want it any other way. Now, you must excuse me, I have to get back to the council!"

Without waiting for a response, Stan headed back into the crowds.

"We better go, too," Emma said, smiling at them. "Will you be coming to the play?"

"I must admit I haven't got tickets," Avery said apologetically. "But I would like to see it."

Josh frowned. "You may have trouble now. I think it's sold out."

"Wow," Reuben said, with a shake of his head. "That's great!"

"I know." Emma's eyes widened with a mixture of excitement and worry. "That makes it more nerve-wracking, but better than performing to an empty house!"

"Sorry," Josh said, smiling. "We really do have to go. Nice to meet you."

They walked away, and Reuben looked at Avery. "There really are a lot of events going on!"

"You know Stan, he lives for these celebrations. And he missed Samhain, thanks to your spell," she reminded him. They had to make sure Stan left White Haven on the previous All Hallows' Eve, worried that he would be sacrificed to the Wild Hunt by his girlfriend, Suzanne, the time-walker witch and one of Avery's ancestors. "And Stan is right—the town is already getting busy with visitors!" Avery checked her watch as she felt her stomach growl. "I'm heading back to the shop for lunch. What are you up to?"

"On a glorious day like this? Must be time for a surf!" Reuben was obsessed with surfing.

"It could be raining, and you'd still go!"

"Because it's brilliant! You should try it someday, Avery," he said mischievously.

Avery shivered. "Sounds far too cold. Shall I see you later in the pub?"

"Yes, you will. Nothing like a pint and some of Alex's excellent pub grub following a surf." He winked. "See you later."

Avery laughed to herself as she walked up the winding streets of White Haven, admiring the decorations as she went. Beltane was one of the biggest pagan celebrations in modernity. It was a fire festival that celebrated the sun, the peak of spring, and the arrival of summer. It was also a celebration of fertility, when the Maiden Goddess attracted the attentions of the Green Man, sometimes called the Young Oak King.

She hadn't just been massaging Reuben's ego when she complimented the flowers. Hanging baskets and pots of all shapes and sizes lined the streets, filled with late spring plants. Some shops liked to provide their own displays, but on the whole, Greenlane Nurseries supplied them, and they looked bright and cheerful. The shop windows were full of flower garlands, and images of the May Queen and the nature spirit jostled for space. There were sculptures of both of them in the window of her own shop, fashioned out of twisted willow, and artfully woven to resemble faces.

Avery halted before she stepped through the door, admiring Sally's handiwork. It seemed there was no getting away from the Green Man now. Ever since the night they had defeated the Empusa with his and the Raven King's help, the mischievous spirit was always in White Haven. He'd given them Ravens' Wood, the ancient forest that had grown magically in hours, and had given Briar, the earth witch, a wildness she'd never had before. Now that Beltane was approaching, Avery felt his energy rise again, and with the potent arrival of the Goddess, magic was once again swirling through White Haven, stronger than ever.

Avery stared at them both, muttering under her breath. "You two had better behave!"

She jumped when Dan's face appeared next to them, peering at her with a frown. "Talking to yourself now, Avery?" he said, sounding muffled through the glass.

She poked her tongue out at him and then headed inside, the bell jangling overhead.

Dan continued to talk as he walked to the counter, shaking his head with mock concern. "I think you might need a break."

"I'm perfectly fine, thank you! I was just telling those two not to make trouble."

He patted her arm affectionately. "That's exactly what I meant."

She ignored him and looked around at the shelves filled with old and new books, and various occult objects. Fresh spring flowers were tucked in available spots, filling the air with a lovely scent. Avery inhaled deeply and sighed with pleasure. "It smells divine in here!"

Dan followed her gaze. "While you were out, Sally filled a few more vases, because clearly there weren't enough. I may have to fight my way out of here tonight."

Avery laughed. "It's not that bad! You should have a walk around White Haven. The whole place looks amazing. I watched the maypole go up. The Morris Dancers were there to celebrate."

"And Stan was in his Druid costume, I suppose?"

"Of course."

Dan eyed her bag. "Where are the cakes?"

"What cakes?" she asked as innocently as she could.

"Don't do that to me, Avery!"

She grinned. "Kidding." She slid out the bag with a selection of pastries, and Dan's face lit up.

"Thank the Gods!" he said as he reached for one.

"Take your lunch break now if you want," Avery suggested. "I can wait. Where's Sally?"

"In the back room, doing the accounts. And yes, lunch sounds great." He weaved through the stacks, and called to her over his shoulder. "I'm in the back room too, if you want me."

Avery settled herself on the chair behind the counter, nibbling on a pastry as she watched pedestrians wander down the street. She saw several couples stop to kiss and giggle; it seemed the Beltane spirit was already strong. It made her think of Alex, her boyfriend and the fifth witch in the White Haven Coven, and she felt a warm glow inside. Since he had moved into her flat after they had defeated the Empusa, they had settled into domestic bliss, and she hadn't felt so content in years. It was good to share her magic with someone who understood, and even better when they made spells together.

Her reverie was broken when she heard a wailing sound at the back of her shop, and she quickly followed the noise to the romance section.

A young woman stood with a book in her hands, tears pouring down her face. Avery looked around perplexed, but there was no one else in sight. Avery gently took the book from the woman's hands, and offered her a tissue. "Are you all right? Has something happened?"

What a lame question. Of course she wasn't all right.

The woman blew her nose and sniffed, looking at Avery through red, swollen eyes. "Sorry, I'm being silly. I felt I needed something to cheer me up, and thought I'd find a nice romantic book, but—" she stopped talking as she started to cry again. "Sorry," she repeated, through gasps. "It reminded me that I'm going to die alone, and that Brian will never love me!"

Avery's mouth opened in shock. "What? I'm sure you won't die alone! Of course you won't," she corrected herself. "Who's Brian?"

"I work with him. He's so handsome, but he never looks at me. Barely ever a smile!"

She burst into tears again, and Avery felt compelled to keep talking.

"Have you known him long?" she asked sympathetically.

"No. He only started at work last week."

Avery frowned. The woman had started sobbing again, almost hysterically. This was not normal. Who cries over someone they'd barely known for a week?

"Forgive me for asking," she said tentatively, "but you really didn't know him at all before last week?"

"No! But he's the perfect man for me, I just know it!"

Avery leaned closer. Was magic at work? Or was this woman just lonely and had become worked up over nothing? "It is quite soon though, isn't it, to think that something will or won't happen just yet? Perhaps you need time to get to know him?"

"Maybe." The woman sniffled. "I don't normally get like this, but this feeling just came over me! We're meant to be together. I think it's destiny. I know it—right here." She thumped her chest over her heart, and burst into tears again.

Avery realised that something was very wrong. Most lonely, lovelorn women didn't plunge head over heels for a man they barely knew. She sent her magic out, gently easing around the woman, trying to detect some kind of spell. Yes, there was something subtle; she could feel it. The woman looked up, her eyes wide, and Avery noted that her pupils were dilated.

"Have you been anywhere odd, or done something different recently?" Avery asked, suddenly suspicious.

The woman frowned. "Why are you asking that?"

"Just humour me," she said gently.

"I went to a party on the weekend in a pub. It was a birthday party for a friend, and lots of people were there that I didn't know."

"Was it a good friend?"

"A friend of a friend, really. It was a good party though!" She smiled weakly. "Lots of drinks and fun. There was a punch too, very fruity."

Avery tried not to show her concern, but what if something had happened that night? Some kind of love spell, possibly. If it was a spell, had it been directed just at this woman, or lots of people? And if so, how many others could be affected? Love spells could be dangerous, like any spell that endangered free will.

"Nothing else unusual?" Avery asked.

"No, just work," the woman answered, sniffling into the tissue.

Avery frowned. She couldn't cancel the spell—if it even was one—but she could soften the effects. "Maybe it's just the party that has you feeling like that. Let me give you a hug."

"Yes, please," the woman said, tears once more pouring down her face.

As Avery pulled her close, she whispered a spell to calm the mind and soothe the senses. Within seconds, she felt the woman relax.

Avery pulled away. "I have just the thing to cheer you up." She headed to the shelves where she kept a selection of coloured candles, picked up a blue one and gave it to the woman. "This is a present from me. Light it when you get home, and leave it burning all evening. It will cheer you up."

She looked surprised. "Oh no, I can't just take it!"

"Yes, you can. Promise me you'll light it!"

She smiled. "Yes, of course. I feel better already. Maybe talking to someone helped."

"It always does," Avery reassured her, as she walked her to the door. "What pub did you go to?"

"The Flying Fish. You know, the one on the road that leads out of town, overlooking the sea."

Avery nodded. It was one of the pubs they had investigated for mermaids the year before. "I know it. It's big, isn't it?"

"Very! The party was in the room on the first floor, with the balcony." She smiled shyly. "Anyway, I must go. Thanks for the candle."

With a jingle of bells the woman headed outside, leaving Avery wondering if someone was casting love spells, or if it was just the season of Beltane.

Two

When Avery arrived at The Wayward Son, Alex's pub that was close to the harbour, it was already busy with people dropping in for after-work drinks.

As she sat down on a stool at the far end of the bar, Alex headed to her, a broad smile on his face. His long, dark hair was loose, and as usual stubble grazed his cheeks and chin.

"Hey, gorgeous." He leaned over and kissed her, and quickly poured her a glass of wine, sliding it in front of her. "How was your day?"

"A bit weird, actually. How was yours?"

He frowned. "Just the usual for me. What happened?"

She sipped her drink appreciatively, and then told him about the woman in the shop who had burst into tears. "I'm pretty sure I detected a spell on her."

"Really?" Alex looked puzzled, and he leaned across the counter, lowering his voice. "That sounds odd. I mean, who would do that? None of the Cornwall Coven, surely?"

The Cornwall Coven comprised of thirteen different covens from across Cornwall. As far as they knew, there were no other witches in White Haven. There was a coven in Harecombe, the town closest to them, headed by Caspian Faversham, and it comprised of other members of his family. The next closest town with a coven was Mevagissey, and there were only two members, Oswald and Ulysses, neither of whom would be casting love spells.

Avery shook her head. "I doubt it. Maybe someone has been dabbling in magic, or perhaps it's just Beltane?"

"I guess either is possible," Alex said thoughtfully. "Let's face it, anyone could try to cast spells...there are enough spell books around. Have you sold any recently?"

Avery had an occult section in her shop that included books about magic and the arcane, but White Haven was filled with occult and new age shops, and lots of other people sold books about magic, too. "I'm always selling that type of book, but tarot books are my biggest seller."

Alex shrugged. "Maybe that woman really was a bit lonely. I think it's more likely to be the Beltane spirit. Emotions are pretty heightened right now."

"I'm pretty sure I didn't imagine that whiff of magic, Alex. Although, I know what you mean. The festival is enough to make anyone who's single feel alone."

"I can feel *him* again, can you?" Alex asked, smiling softly. "The plants in the courtyard garden are going nuts!"

"I feel him everywhere. But if I'm honest, he never really left."

Alex laughed, but he looked worried. "True, but earth energies are rising. Things could get a little weird around here—weirder than normal, I mean! I must admit, I've been having some odd dreams." He paused, thinking, and then said, "They're quite intense, actually—almost visionary."

Avery's mouth fell open in shock. "What? You haven't said anything!"

He shrugged. "I know. I just thought that with all the Beltane build up over the last week or so that it was just playing on my mind, but now I'm not so sure."

A few months before Alex's visions had been threatening to overwhelm him. With the aid of Nate, a witch who lived in St Ives and whose mother had the gift of sight, he had managed to control them.

She voiced her worries. "Are you losing control of your psychic abilities?"

"I don't think so. They don't appear at any moment, like they used to—you'd surely see *that* happening! But I think they're finding another way to manifest, in my dreams. And like I said, I think it's just the recent circumstances."

"Go on, then," Avery prompted. "What did you see?"

"Just a jumble of images, really. I see Ravens' Wood a lot—well, ancient trees and forests, it could be anywhere. The vegetation is thick and strong and it tangles around me, so that I can't see where I'm going. I feel lost, confused, and a bit scared. And then I see people arguing, dressed in old-fashioned clothes—just glimpses of them in the trees. The air is thick with tension. And passion." He nodded to himself. "Yes, I feel passion, power, lust—not me, you understand—but around me." He focussed suddenly on Avery again. "And then I get jumbled images of White Haven, suffocating beneath a tangle of branches and vines, and the feeling of wildness and uncontrollable chaos."

"Wow." She sipped her wine, lost for words for a moment, and then said, "That sounds pretty intense. How often have you dreamt that?"

"Three or four times over the last week or so. But you know how it is with dreams...they become something else, and don't make sense."

"But dreams don't usually repeat like that, not really," she pointed out.

"No, they don't." He leaned on the bar, looking into space again, and it was clear that since he'd voiced his dreams, he was worried.

"Maybe you should start writing them down," Avery suggested. "You might be forgetting important details."

"True, I will. Remind me to put a notebook by the bed tonight."

She nodded, her thoughts now flying to Briar. She felt the Green Man's energy more than anyone else, especially after allowing him to possess her on the night they defeated the Empusa. "I wonder how Briar's feeling."

"You can ask her yourself. She's here."

Avery looked toward the pub's entrance and saw Briar arrive, with El and Reuben behind her. Avery waved, and they made their way to her side, pulling stools close together.

"Wow, Briar, what's going on with you?" Avery exclaimed. There was something more primal about her, an uncanny wildness.

Briar ran her hands through her thick, dark hair, smiling ruefully. "I look a little wild, don't I?"

El winked. "I think you look cool. You've got this amazing vibe going on! It suits you."

"That's good, because I can't do anything about it!" She lowered her voice. "My hair is growing thicker than ever, and my magic feels like it's bubbling up like a well. Now that spring is really here, I can feel the earth so strongly! I only have to reach for its energy, and it's there." She looked confused as she looked at their bemused faces. "You must feel it, too?"

"I do," Avery agreed, "but not like you, I'm sure. The ring of green around your irises has got stronger!" The colour had appeared just after they had defeated the Empusa.

"I know! And I can't control that, either!"

"I agree with El," Reuben said, raising his pint in salute. "You look awesome! I can feel you crackling with magic."

"I'm trying to subdue it," Briar told them, "because I'm getting a few strange looks. I think some people do detect something, but they don't know what it is." She sighed. "It's not easy."

Alex smiled sympathetically at her. "Me and Avery were just saying that the Green Man feels stronger in White Haven in general."

Briar raised an eyebrow. "I really didn't think he'd get any stronger than after Imbolc, but that was stupid of me. Of course he'll be stronger at Beltane. It's when he joins with the Goddess. And she is most definitely here, too!" She looked around to make sure they weren't being overheard. "As you know, Eli is very popular with the women in White Haven. They flock like birds around him, and he loves it! But it's getting worse now, and not in a good way."

Avery felt a rumble of disquiet. "Why, what's happening?"

"There are little spats between the women who visit the shop. You know, petty jealousies, put-downs, and snarky comments. Gaggles of women are in and out of the shop all day, and while I'm selling lots of stuff—because let's face it, it's a good excuse to be there—I feel I'm working in a harem!"

"Lucky bugger," Reuben exclaimed. "All that female adoration."

El smacked his arm playfully. "Er, you have me!"

"Well, of course, but it's nice to be admired by many."

Briar shook her head. "It's really not. Eli looked amused at first, but not anymore. He's trying to keep them all happy, but he's failing. I've put a calming spell on the shop, which is helping, slightly."

"The energies of the Green Man and the Goddess are too strong," Avery acknowledged with a frown. "That must be what I felt earlier, rather than a spell."

Briar's eyes widened with surprise. "Has something happened to you, too?"

"Not to me exactly," she explained, and went on to tell them about the woman in her shop. "She was so upset! I was sure I felt magic around her, but maybe it wasn't a spell. Maybe it was just Beltane magic."

The witches glanced at each other nervously, and El suggested, "Maybe it's a bit of both?"

"Oh shit," Reuben said, looking sheepish. "I did tell Avery I'd enhanced the hanging baskets and tubs with a few mild love spells. Do you think that was me causing her to be upset?"

Briar shook her head. "I doubt it, Reuben. I've walked past your plants on the way here and couldn't feel anything too strong."

"But that's not the case with all love spells," Alex said. "They can be dangerous. They subvert normal willpower and play havoc with relationships. And people can get crazy, jealous, and violent!"

"Or depressed and tearful!" Avery reminded them.

"Crap!" El started playing with her rings, turning them around on her finger. "I'm starting to get a bad feeling about this. I haven't seen anything odd yet, but I'll keep watch."

"We all should," Reuben said, looking reassured that it wasn't his fault. "Even if it's just the Green Man's magic, it could get dangerous enough."

"I've been having weird dreams, too," Alex told them. "I'm beginning to think they're visions—or at least a psychic awareness manifesting in my dreams."

He told them what he'd been experiencing, and the witches glanced nervously at each other.

"That's never a good sign," Reuben said. "I trust your visions."

"Thanks," Alex told him. "I do, too."

Avery sipped her drink. "I wonder whether it might be worth visiting The Flying Fish, the pub where the party was."

Alex nodded in agreement. "Let's go for a meal there tomorrow night, Avery. I'm not working in the evening."

"Great," she said, pleased to be doing something practical.

"Anyway," Alex glanced down the bar to where some patrons where waiting, "I better go and serve some customers before my staff get overwhelmed."

"And I should go home," Avery said, finishing her wine. "I can't wait to start reading my grimoires."

"Has anyone seen Shadow recently?" El asked, still with half a pint of beer in her glass. "I wonder what she's making of our rising earth magic problem."

"Not for a few days," Briar told her. "Haven't you?"

"About the same. She's been busy since that business at Old Haven Cemetery with the zombies and the fey necromancer," El admitted. "She told me that she and the Nephilim have had an interesting proposition from the Orphic Guild. I think it's keeping them all busy, actually."

"Really?" Avery felt like she'd missed something. "I wondered why she hadn't been in the shop recently. What kind of proposition?"

El leaned forward conspiratorially. "I'm not sure, but it concerns the

Nephilim's past—I think."

Reuben grimaced. "She's being very cagey, which makes me more intrigued." He looked at Briar. "Has Eli said anything?"

She shook her head. "No, other than saying his brothers are busy."

"Mmm, interesting! Ash says the same."

Ash was another Nephilim, and he worked for Reuben at Greenlane Nurseries.

"I thought he was cutting down his hours?" Avery asked.

"He has, but I still see him regularly. We've been flat-out lately—you know, with spring gardening and preparing the plants for Beltane—and he's been great." He looked pleased. "He's a good laugh, actually. Not anywhere near as quiet as he used to be. Quite the gamer, I gather. Loves to tease Shadow!"

"I'll invite Shadow for dinner," El said, brightly. "With Gabe! Sound good? We can ask about the Green Man *and* the Orphic Guild."

"Sounds great," Avery said, sliding off her bar stool and gathering her bag. "Do you think we should tell Newton about our concerns?"

Briar groaned. "Not yet! What's to tell? He'll only get all grumpy and shouty."

"He's not that bad!" Avery said, laughing.

"You know what I mean!"

"Let's hope the festival cheers him up," Avery said, laughing. "Is Hunter coming to visit soon?"

Briar smiled shyly. "End of the week."

"Oh, goodie!" Reuben said, with a cheeky grin. "Let's see what some wild Beltane magic does to the shifter. You could be in for a good weekend, Briar!"

Briar just looked at him. "Is your mind always in the gutter?"

"I watched a large, phallic symbol being erected in the town square today. That's where my mind is naturally going to be for the next couple of weeks. You may as well get used to it!"

When Avery arrived back at her flat above Happenstance Books, she passed through her open-plan living and dining room that were on the first floor, and headed to the kitchen to collect some cheese, crackers, and a glass of wine before heading to the attic on the floor above, her favourite room.

The attic stretched the length of the house. A third of it comprised her bedroom and en suite bathroom that she now shared with Alex, separated from the rest of the space by a fireplace that was set into the thick wall. The rest of the attic was a spell room, and now that Alex had moved his magic equipment in too, they used the space together.

The evening was already chilly and it was growing dark, so Avery lit a fire before doing anything else, and spelled her lamps and candles on with a flick of her magic. Her cats, Circe and Medea, came to greet her, stretching from where they had been sleeping in the throws on the sofa.

Avery stroked their soft fur and then headed to the table, pulling her grimoires towards her and greeting them like old friends. She sat for a moment in quiet contemplation, pondering the events of the day. Magic was rising in White Haven. All the witches could feel it, and that was troubling. It hadn't felt like this last year, but that was before they had found their old grimoires and released the magic of their ancestors across White Haven. And, of course, before the Green Man had arrived with the Crossroads Circus and never left.

Avery pulled Helena's grimoire towards her, her hand sliding over the still soft leather cover, and she opened the pages reverently. Helena was her witch ancestor who'd been burned at the stake, and her ghost remained in Avery's flat, appearing at unexpected moments. She was generally a force for good, but Avery remained wary of her—not enough to banish her though.

Avery turned the pages, scanning the spidery handwriting that was difficult to read. These spells were arcane and powerful, and just looking at them made Avery feel connected to her magical roots. There were spells in here she hadn't seen anywhere else, and some she wouldn't dream of using. They were cruel and dark, and she wondered what her ancestors had been thinking. She hoped they were spells that were recorded but rarely used. The other witches had expressed the same concerns about their old family grimoires, too.

The other important thing about this grimoire were the notes her ancestors had written in the margins of old ceremonies and Sabbats, and she knew there were pages of information about Beltane in here, spread through the book, recorded by many different witches over time. But that wasn't what she was looking for right now. She needed spells to use on the whole town, to bewitch some calm and peace—if they had to.

Avery sipped her wine, grabbed a pen and paper, and started to make some notes as she read. She shook her head and frowned, hoping this would be a last resort. To cast a spell so big as to encompass the town was one thing, but to maintain it for a period of time would be something else. And actually, she reflected, it would be no better than casting love spells. It would still influence someone's willpower.

Her phone rang, disturbing the silence, and picking it up Avery saw it was Genevieve's number, the High Priestess of the Cornwall Coven.

"Hey Genevieve, how are you?" Avery greeted her.

"Worried," Genevieve said, forgoing niceties. Her soft Irish voice was surprisingly abrupt.

Avery's heart sank. "Why?"

"Beltane bloody magic. Can you feel it?"

"Yes, we can actually. We were just talking about it today, but thought it was just White Haven—you know, because of the Green Man." Genevieve knew all about their experiences with crossroads magic.

"Well, unfortunately, it's pretty strong here too, and the other covens are reporting it as well." She sighed heavily. "While normally I love Beltane, of course—it's a brilliant time of year, things just feel—" Genevieve paused, and silence fell.

"A little odd?" Avery suggested.

"To say the least. Emotions seem a little heightened. There are petty jealousies and arguments between couples, or overt and desperate flirting among strangers. It's all very unnerving. "

Avery leaned back in her chair and gazed through the windows to the night sky beyond. "Same here." She told her about what Briar had reported, Alex's dreams, and about the woman who had cried in her shop, and then Avery summoned her courage and told her what she and the White Haven witches had been debating for weeks. "By the way, Genevieve, I'm not sure if we'll join the coven celebrations for Beltane. We might celebrate here, instead. We thought we'd observe it in Ravens' Wood."

Avery was expecting a complaint, but instead Genevieve sounded disappointed. "I expected as much, and that's okay. But it would be good if you celebrated the solstice with us—please think about it."

"Of course, I'll talk to the others."

Genevieve rushed on. "I've decided to hold a coven meeting to discuss some of this Beltane oddness that's going on. We're meeting on Wednesday at Oswald's place. I know it's short notice, but can you make it?"

"That sounds great, I'll be there," Avery assured her, and after another few minutes of chatting, Genevieve rang off, leaving Avery thinking about what else had been happening in White Haven, and whether she'd missed anything.

She saw her tarot cards on the shelf next to her pots of dried herbs and roots, and picked them up, shuffling them as she sat back at the table. The cards were warming already to her touch, slipping alongside one another easily, and Avery focussed only on the feel of them beneath her fingers while trying to decide her question. Should she ask if someone was casting love spells? Or if Beltane meant trouble? She decided to keep her question broad.

Would the Green Man and the Goddess bring problems to White Haven?

As she placed the cards out in the Celtic wheel, she felt a shiver run through her. Major Arcana cards were everywhere—reversed cards, royals of the suits, and finally a reversal of The Lovers dominating the whole reading. It was a powerful spread that she needed to analyse. But one thing was clear. Passions were running wild, and would only get worse.

Three

When Avery walked into the shop the next morning, Sally, as usual, was already making coffee in the small kitchen, which also served as a stock room and meeting place. She turned to greet Avery, trying to plaster a smile on her face.

"Morning, Avery!"

Avery frowned. Sally was normally bright-eyed and cheerful, but today she looked flushed and her eyes were swollen. "Sally! What's wrong? Are you upset?"

Sally quickly turned away. "I'm fine, sorry, just ignore me!"

Avery rushed over to the counter and turned Sally around, her hand resting gently on her back. "You are *not* fine. What's happened?"

Sally started to cry again, tears welling up and pouring down her cheeks, and she whipped a tissue out and wiped them away. "I had an argument with Sam, that's all." She shook her head. "It was so silly! I don't know what came over me."

Sam was Sally's husband; they had been married for years and had two small children. They were childhood sweethearts, and Avery had never heard of them having cross words before, at least nothing significant.

"This is so unlike you two," Avery said, voicing her concerns. She tried to reassure her. "You're my role model for happily ever after! I'm sure it can't be anything really bad."

"It was! I got so jealous last night, and we had this massive argument this morning! It was just the way he looked at her—as if I wasn't there!"

Sally burst into fresh tears and Avery hugged her close, feeling Sally trembling against her. A horribly slow, insidious fear began to creep though Avery, and she stroked Sally's hair.

"You two are the happiest couple I know! This doesn't make sense, Sally."

Sally pulled away, sniffing. "I know!"

Avery directed her to a chair at the table, poured coffee for both of them, and then sat next to Sally. "Tell me what happened."

"We went out for dinner last night with friends—old friends, really good friends—and everything was fine at first. And then Sam just seemed to be flirting with Laura—and she flirted right back!"

Avery frowned. "But friends do flirt, it's harmless! Reuben flirts with me constantly, and it doesn't mean anything. Alex flirts, too. He flirts with you!"

Sally met her eyes. "I know. It's usually just harmless fun. But this didn't feel harmless, and I couldn't brush it off. I got home and it ate away at me all night. I barely slept! So I brought it up this morning, and he told me I was overreacting and we had a massive row! He stormed out, and I got the kids to school and came here."

Avery fell silent while she watched Sally sip her coffee in between sniffs and tears. *Was this Beltane magic? Or a spell?* Two women crying in two days in her shop was unusual. Especially since one of them was Sally. *Or was it really just an argument? People had them all the time...*

"How do you feel now?" Avery asked her. "I mean, are you still jealous? Do you look back at last night and think you overreacted?"

Sally thought for a moment. "Yes, I still feel jealous. Like I have this twisting knife in me. But I know it's irrational, too. I trust Sam—I really do. But he did seem odd last night, both of them did."

"What about Laura's husband?"

"I think he was fine." She covered her hands with her face. "I don't know! I feel like an idiot now."

Avery sipped her coffee and came to a decision. "Sally, I don't think this is entirely normal."

"What do you mean?" Sally asked. Her hands dropped and she looked at her wide-eyed.

"I think Beltane magic is playing with people's emotions. The Green Man and the Goddess are rising, their energies are spilling over into everything. At least, I hope that's it. My other sneaky worry is that there's some kind of love spell going around."

"This is what love spells do?" Sally looked horrified.

"Love is a strong emotion. If you subvert it, or try to replicate it, all sorts of horrible, unforeseen things can happen."

"Who would do such a thing?"

Avery shrugged. "I don't know...and I could be wrong. It could be Beltane magic on overload."

"But if it isn't, is this spell directed at me? Is someone trying to break up my marriage?" All of a sudden, Sally had gone from tearful to furious. "I'll kill them!"

"Slow down! There'll be no killing! I don't think you've been targeted deliberately—at least, I hope not. I did a reading last night, and the tarot certainly suggested heightened emotions, and Alex is having strange dreams. I spoke to Genevieve last night, and it sounds like this unusual behaviour is happening all over Cornwall—arguments, jealousies, and exaggerated flirting. The coven is meeting tomorrow, and I'll know more then."

Sally sighed and leaned back in her chair. "That actually makes me feel better. I've never felt like this before. It's sort of uncontrollable, but to know it's a fake emotion helps."

"It's not a fake emotion," Avery warned her. "It's very real, though the reasons behind it are fake. But you and Sam are amazing. You'll work it out."

"How are you and Alex?" Sally asked. "Anything weird going on with you?"

"Not at the moment!" Avery grinned. "It's awesome living together—even if he makes me tidier than I want to be. And he's a great cook."

Sally smiled, and Avery saw her shoulders drop as the tension seeped out of her. "Good. He makes you all glowy." She pulled her phone out of her pocket. "I'm going to phone Sam."

Avery stood up and carried their cups to the sink. "Good luck. I'll leave you to it."

As Avery entered Happenstance Books, shutting the door to the back room firmly behind her, she sighed and leaned against it with relief. *What a start to the day!* She took a few deep breaths and then walked through the shop, spelling on lights, burning incense, and reinforcing her spells. She paused at the window, admiring the bunting that was hanging across the road. There were only a few pedestrians at this hour—it wasn't even nine o'clock yet—but they stopped to admire the decorations, taking photos and posing together. The tourists were filling up the town, and the cafés would be full later.

Maybe she should add another spell to the shop, something to provide calmness and serenity. It would protect the staff, as well as the customers. Avery nodded to herself as she unlocked the door. She'd do that later.

It was a busy morning, and it was almost time for lunch when Avery, Dan, and Sally were able to pause and share a coffee at the counter.

Sally pulled out a packet of shortbread biscuits from a drawer and handed them around, and Avery was pleased to see she looked more like her usual self. Avery was reaching for her second biscuit when the door swung open and Shadow walked in, gazing around imperiously before finally settling on the three of them.

Shadow was the fey who'd been stranded when the Wild Hunt had broken through the veils between worlds at Samhain the year before, and she now lived with Gabe and the six other Nephilim. She headed towards them with a broad smile, as usual clad in skinny jeans and boots, and as usual Dan smiled dreamily as his eyes travelled over her enviable figure.

She helped herself to a biscuit. "How are you three in these wild and unusual times?"

"Wild and unusual?" Dan asked, puzzled. "Why? What have you done?"

"Me? I never do anything!"

Her violet eyes challenged them to disagree, but Avery wasn't buying it. "You're always up to something. I hear your new business is proving interesting."

Shadow's lips twitched. "It's certainly given us some interesting ways to earn money."

Avery leaned forward and lowered her voice. "Are you stealing things?"

"We call it liberating things, actually."

Sally laughed. "Same thing!"

Shadow tossed her long, caramel-toned hair that was likely to change colour frequently due to her fey ability to add glamour to herself. "Actually, it's not. We are hoping to find things that have been lost for a long time. And yes," she conceded, "some of those may have been lost in certain dusty collections."

"I knew it!" Dan said, narrowing his eyes. "You've been a very bad girl."

"But that's what you like about me, Dan!" She flashed him her biggest smile, and he wilted.

Avery interrupted their flirt fest. "What were you saying about wild and unusual times? Do you mean Beltane?"

"I mean many things! Our new employer is very unusual, and yes, Beltane as you call it, has given the town a restless energy."

"You mean the Green Man and the Goddess?" Avery suggested.

Shadow nodded. "I must admit, their wildness is coursing through my veins acutely. Do you feel them?"

"Them?" Avery asked, alarmed. "We can feel *him*! Do you feel the Goddess, too?"

"Oh yes! She has to meet him with her own strength and power. They are equals. If you can't feel her yet, you will."

Shadow said this with such a tone of finality that Avery didn't doubt her. And actually, it made perfect sense. But it was unnerving. "Briar tells me Eli is having trouble with his harem."

"Lucky bugger," Dan said.

"Not lucky!" Shadow told him, laughing. "It's his own fault. He's being stalked by one of them."

"What?" Sally said, shocked.

"I know!" She leaned forward to share her gossip. "She hangs around the shop all day, and tries to follow him home. I offered to scare her off, but he refused." She looked disappointed.

"Probably wise," Avery told her. "Any suggestions as to what we can do about this rampant energy?"

Shadow crunched on her biscuit as she thought. "Not a lot, actually. As spring rises, so do they. He's a nature spirit who's reaching his zenith and feeling very sexually charged, and so is the Goddess! They are reaching their sexual peak together."

Dan sniggered at that, and Sally smacked his arm. "This isn't funny!"

"Yes, it is! I might actually get laid."

Sally smacked his arm again. "*Dan*!"

"What? I can feel my blood stirring, too!"

"By the great Goddess," Avery muttered. "That's all I need! A randy assistant. You're as bad as Reuben. He keeps talking about phallic symbols!"

"That's what the maypole is! He's quite right about that."

Shadow looked intrigued. "We have such symbols and celebrations in the Otherworld. Our traditions have obviously mingled. We celebrate our spring with more magic, though, and it's when many fey choose to wed under the eyes of the great Goddess—in the open, you understand, under the sky. We don't have churches."

Avery frowned. "Do Gabe and the others feel the change in energy?"

"Of course. Although, as you know, they have a little more resistance to magic than most. El has asked us to come to dinner, so me and Gabe will see you on Friday night."

"Great!" Avery felt relieved. It would be good to get their perspective on things, and it would be good to see more of Gabe. He was always so elusive.

"Anyway, I need a few books," Shadow said brightly, "on John Dee."

Sally frowned. "Who's that?"

"The Virgin Queen's magician!"

History wasn't Avery's best subject, but the name did seem familiar. "Didn't he talk to angels?"

"Amongst other things!" Shadow said, raising a speculative eyebrow.

Dan was already making his way around the counter to her side. "Interesting! Let me take you to the history section, Madam. Any reason why you're researching him?"

"Just brushing up on my history," she told him as she followed him into the stacks and their voices faded.

Sally snorted. "Brushing up on history, my ass! That woman never does anything without good reason."

Avery had to agree. Shadow was surely up to something.

Four

Avery sat across the table from Alex, sipped her wine, and looked around the room at the crowded pub.

"I don't get why this place is so popular," she said. "Your pub is much nicer!"

Alex grinned. "Oh, I don't know. It has its charms. There are hordes of women here!"

She pretended to be outraged. "You shouldn't be looking!"

"To be honest, I can't help it. They're not wearing much, either!"

Avery had to concede he was right. They were in The Flying Fish, and it was well known for being a place where singles went looking for action. The women were dressed in strappy dresses and heels, or skin-tight jeans and plunging t-shirts, and the men were showing off their muscled arms and wearing very well fitting jeans. And the whole place smelt strongly of perfume, aftershave, and hormones.

"It all feels a bit obvious, though!" she said, wrinkling her nose.

"Just think," Alex joked, "if you hadn't rescued me from singleness, this could be me, desperately trying to find a woman so I wouldn't die alone."

"I think it's less about dying alone than having to sleep alone!" she pointed out. "The real question is, though, can you sense any magic?"

"Only yours, my love." He picked up her hand and kissed it.

Avery laughed. "You really are full of it tonight."

"I mean it! You are more beautiful than any other woman here." He held her gaze with his dark eyes that were starting to smoulder with desire, and

Avery felt heat radiate from his touch, sending a shiver though her. "Maybe we should skip food and just go home."

"We'll be home soon enough," Avery said, fighting a strong urge to lean across the table and snog Alex. She fanned herself. "You're making me hot!"

"Good. But you're right. Business before pleasure. What do you suggest?" They were on the upper floor, and he nodded towards the bar. "I could ask the bar staff about their recent bookings."

"Would they tell you?"

He shrugged. "I know a couple of them, but not well. But if not, a little glamour wouldn't hurt."

She'd already told him about her phone call with Genevieve, and she asked, "Have you felt anything in your pub today, or seen anything strange?"

Alex frowned. "I guess everyone does seem a bit more flirty than usual, but that could be because I'm looking for it now. One of the customers was coming on a bit strong to Kate earlier. I was going to intervene, but she set him straight quickly enough. Of course, that could have been anything, though."

Kate was one of Alex's bar staff, and was very capable of looking after herself. "Was he a local?"

"No. I didn't recognise him, but that's not surprising. There are lots of visitors at the moment, and the town will only get fuller over the next couple of weeks." He pushed his chair back from the table. "I'll go and order the food and see what I can find out."

She watched Alex walk to the bar, and then glanced around the room, feeling with her magic for anything odd. However, after several minutes, she had to conclude that she couldn't detect anything especially different. But why should she? The party that the woman in her shop had attended had been several days ago now. She shook her head, perplexed, and then saw Alex heading back to her.

He sat down, looking disappointed. "The party was for a woman's thirtieth birthday. The place was packed, apparently. Unfortunately, the guy behind the bar didn't have the name. The bookings are taken downstairs."

"Did anything odd happen?"

"Nope. Just the usual, drinking and eating. It got pretty loud, but nothing out of the ordinary from what he could remember."

Avery huffed. "Oh well, I suppose it was a long shot. And even if we find out who booked it, doesn't mean we could ever find out if someone had cast a spell."

"He did say though that it had been a busy couple of weeks, and that although they cater to the younger crowd who are always rowdy, there had been a few more arguments lately. Girls getting catty, and men getting possessive or pushy." His fingers tapped his beer glass. "The bouncers have had to step in a couple of times."

"Really? That's interesting!"

"And worrying. Maybe we're not imagining things. I'm going to ask downstairs about the booking anyway, on our way out."

Avery leaned her chin on her hand, idly playing with her wine glass with the other. "Shadow can feel magic rising, and she said the Goddess is here, too!" She updated him on their conversation, and then said what had been worrying her all day. "Do you think it will affect us? Will we start overreacting with exaggerated feelings of lust or jealousy?"

Alex took her hand in his. "It might. But we should be strong enough to resist it, especially as we'll understand where it's coming from."

"I hope you're right. I'm enjoying what we have right now. You know—us, together at my place." She squeezed his hand, enjoying feeling his warmth. "I don't want it to change."

"It won't," he reassured her. "But let's increase our protection spells anyway. Even if emotions start to affect us in the town, we can be safe at home and at work. Besides, Beltane energies might mean we get even more loved up, and won't want to leave the bedroom!" Avery laughed as he winked at her, and he added, "I'm hoping for the latter!"

Before she could comment, his phone buzzed and he pulled his hand away to take it from his pocket, scanning the text. He looked up at her, his cheeky grin vanishing. "It's Newton. He'd like to meet us for a pint, at my pub."

"Did he say why?" Avery asked, already imagining the worst.

"No. I said we'd be there once we'd eaten."

Newton was perched at the end of the bar with a pint in front of him, watching a football match on the TV that was mounted on the wall in the corner. The volume was low, but he was completely absorbed, not seeing Avery and Alex until they sat next to him.

"Hey Newton," Avery said, noting his jeans and sweatshirt, which meant he hadn't come straight from work. "How are you?"

He turned to her, his grey eyes distracted, but he focussed quickly. "Hey Avery, Alex." He nodded at both of them. "Sorry, I was watching the footie. I'm fine, mostly. How are you two?"

"Worried about Beltane," Alex answered. "And you. We're hoping this is a social call."

Newton wagged his head. "It sort of is, but you might have answered my question anyway. Why are you worried about Beltane?"

Alex explained about the heightened emotions they'd observed. "We think things can only get worse as it gets closer."

Newton grimaced. "Damn. I was hoping I was imagining it, but maybe not. My colleagues have been dealing with more fights in recent days, and increasing domestic violence. Some of it's from our usual suspects, and other incidents have been unusual."

"Domestic violence?" Avery exclaimed. "You think that's caused by

Beltane?"

"Maybe. Domestic violence is about control and power, but sometimes it's triggered by jealousy—and I don't mean just men attacking women, either. We've had a fair bit of women attacking men, too." He shrugged. "It could just be a coincidence, but I have to consider these things, and the timing is suspicious."

Avery slumped against the bar. "You're right. It is suspicious. We're having a Witches Council meeting tomorrow. Everyone is reporting heightened tensions."

"We've also had—" Newton started to laugh. "Sorry, it's really not funny. We've also had a lot of very lusty behaviour. We've caught a few couples having sex in parks, down alleyways, and in cars at the side of the road. They didn't even look that sorry at being caught!"

"Wow! Well, that sounds like a lot more fun than jealous arguments," Alex said, also laughing.

"Are Beltane babies a thing?" He looked between them, amused.

"Actually, I think it used to be," Avery admitted, "before contraception was so widely available."

Newton nodded. "Well, I predict a baby boom in nine months! And maybe some broken marriages, too."

"No one's dead though, I hope?" Avery asked.

"Not because of this yet, as far as I know. There are a couple of deaths we're looking into, but nothing to concern you."

"How's your new DS getting on? Inez, was it?" Alex asked.

Newton nodded. "Inez Walker. She's good! I like her. Efficient, clever, gets on with Moore, too. She's an in-law of an officer who works in London, actually—on another paranormal team." He looked at them over his nearly empty pint glass with raised eyebrows as he finished his drink.

Avery and Alex exchanged cautious glances. "What's going on?" Avery asked, suspicious of his expression.

Newton smirked. "A certain DI Milne has been asking questions about

Shadow and the Nephilim—and you, actually. Her DS is Inez's brother-in-law."

"Why is she asking about us?" Avery asked, alarmed. She shot a quick glance at Zee, the Nephilim who was serving customers further along the bar.

"Shadow and the Nephilim are working with the Orphic Guild, which you probably know, and Shadow ended up killing someone—while defending herself," he added quickly. "Milne decided to look into their background, and contacted me." He watched them both carefully as he said, "I told her about everyone, of course. I had to, she's a colleague. But don't worry, she'll be discreet. It was those guys she was more interested in."

"I get it," Alex said to Newton. "Shadow told us some of what happened in London, and Harlan stayed here, actually, but they didn't ask for our help—well, not much anyway. They didn't want it. Gabe said he was sorting his own crap out."

"Good for him," Newton said, gesturing to the bar staff for another pint. "Now, tell me some more about Beltane. I have a feeling the more I know, the better."

"I met my mate down the pub last night," Dan said to Avery the next morning, while they were restocking shelves. " He had some interesting news."

Avery paused with book in hand, and looked up at him from where she was kneeling on the floor. "Is it bad?"

"Yes. Well, weird actually."

She groaned. "Go on."

"He's in that play that's on next week—Tristan and Iseult." He looked around and then squatted next to her, lowering his voice. "He says that the atmosphere in rehearsals is tense, and there are rumours that the leads are having an affair."

"I met them yesterday morning," Avery admitted. "In the town square, with Stan. I must admit they both looked awkward when Stan was talking about love than cannot be tamed!" She moved closer to Dan. "Are they in other relationships?"

"Yep. They're both in long-term relationships. They're being discrete, but let's just say their performances are really good!"

Avery frowned, trying not to leap to conclusions. "Does that happen sometimes though, with actors? All that time spent together being intimate?"

Dan shrugged. "I guess so, but my mate said that it is unusual for those two, and I wondered if this could be Beltane stuff again? I didn't say anything to him," he added hastily.

"I guess it's possible. Has your mate been in the group long?"

"The theatre group? Yeah, a few years. He's had a few lead parts, but not in this one. Of course, there are three main parts really in that play—Tristan, Iseult, and King Mark."

"What's the group called?"

"White Haven Players. They perform in a few different venues, but this one will be at the Little Theatre."

"So Stan said," Avery told him. "They're lucky to be performing there."

"The town council arranged it—it's all part of the Beltane celebrations, so it has to be good. Their first dress rehearsal is on Friday night. But," Dan looked awkward. "I must admit, my mate didn't seem his usual self, either."

"In what way?"

"He was a bit intense, and Harry is normally pretty laid back." He shrugged. "Maybe it's the pressure of rehearsals."

"I'll bear it in mind," Avery said, knowing better than to ignore Dan. He was calm and rational, and wouldn't have mentioned it if he didn't think there was something in it. "You never know, I guess."

Sally stuck her head around the shelves. "There you are! What are you doing down there?"

They both stood up, and Avery said, "Dan's sharing gossip about the theatre company."

"You'll have to fill me in," Sally said to him. "But you've got a visitor, Avery."

"Who?"

"James."

James was the vicar at the Church of All Souls, and they had developed a friendship and mutual respect over the preceding months, although for a while he was suspicious of them. He knew about Avery and Alex's magic, but they hadn't told him about the other three witches. James often shared any concerns he had about the strange activities in White Haven, and with a sinking feeling, Avery realised he had more to share today.

Avery left Dan to finish stacking the books and headed to the window, where she could see James admiring the display.

James was in his late forties, Avery estimated, and wore a jumper and casual trousers, his jumper not quite disguising the white collar at his throat. He turned to greet her with a smile. "Hi, Avery. What an interesting window decoration."

"Our Green Man and the Goddess. They are good, aren't they? Sally found them."

"Very rustic and seasonal. White Haven is certainly putting on a show for May Day."

"Don't we always?" she said, laughing. "Is the church decorated?"

"Not yet, but we'll start filling it with flowers next week." He glanced around, noting the customers browsing the shelves, and said, "Any chance we can chat privately?"

"I had a feeling you were going to ask that. Of course, follow me. Sally has brought a coffee and walnut cake in, and it's amazing!"

Avery led the way to the kitchen and put the kettle on. When she turned around, James was already at the table, idly looking through some books stacked in the centre. "You have some books on Beltane," he said, looking up at her. "These are nicely decorated."

The books were hardbacks with cloth covers, and there were beautiful illustrations throughout. "They are! They'll be going next to the window display later. We like to keep things seasonal, and these should sell well."

James nodded, but his expression was vague and Avery could tell his thoughts were already drifting elsewhere. Before asking him anything else, she filled the teapot, and placed it on the table with cups, plates, and the cake.

He smiled wanly as she sat at the table with him. "Sorry, I always seem to sit here with worries on my mind."

"I sometimes feel that's what this room is for, and that's fine. We all need a chance to offload sometimes—including me. What are you worried about?"

He glanced at the pile of books he'd moved to the side. "I've had a few parishioners coming to me with marital concerns—worries about infidelity, jealousies, or feelings for other people that have struck them out of nowhere. Some people are really concerned they might cheat on their spouse because their feelings for someone else are so strong. They're bewildered because they can't explain it." His hands gripped his mug as he asked, "I'm concerned that this is Beltane-related, and I wanted to know if you've seen or felt anything strange?"

Avery sighed heavily and broke off a piece of cake, crumbling it into pieces. "Unfortunately, yes. We've all noticed odd behaviours. Even Sally had an argument with her husband, and that rarely happens! I'm hoping it will settle down, but..."

James nodded. "It's unlikely isn't it? In fact, it will probably get worse."

"Two weeks until Beltane, and yes, undoubtedly passions will get stronger, wilder perhaps. It's not just happening here, either—it's all over Cornwall."

James swallowed a mouthful of cake, his dark eyes serious. "I'll ask around the other churches, see what they think." He grinned suddenly. "Of course, it's not all doom and gloom. I have some very loved-up couples, too. Several locals have announced they wish to set marriage dates. They are positively glowing with love, so that pleases me."

"That's the thing though, isn't it? I've noticed extremes of behaviour, too. I wonder why some people are affected more than others. I mean, I feel fine now. What about you?"

James looked into the distance while he pondered the question. "I'm okay, so is my wife...I think. Let's hope that continues. But what I'm also wondering is, why now? I don't remember this happening in previous years."

Avery appreciated James's honesty, so she felt she should reciprocate, as much as seemed reasonable anyway, so she shared about what had happened with the Green Man and the Crossroads Circus.

James's eyes widened slightly with surprise. "Oh. So, he's here, a nature spirit, roaming around White Haven?"

"Sort of," Avery said with a smile. "And he's beyond our control, I'm afraid—he's wild and mischievous. The Goddess is coming, too—they will only make each other worse. I must admit that I am concerned that someone is casting love spells, as well. I can't completely blame the Green Man, but I have no proof as yet."

"Love spells? Who's doing that?" James asked, looking alarmed.

"I have no idea, and as I said, I might be wrong, but trust me, I'm looking into it."

Five

Avery decided to use witch-flight to attend the coven meeting at Oswald's house, Crag End, just outside Mevagissey.

She arrived on his leafy driveway about thirty minutes before the meeting was due to begin, knowing there would be a chance to talk informally first. The evening was already darkening, the sky thick with clouds that promised rainfall. Avery shivered in the chill air, and pulled her woollen wrap around her shoulders as she stepped out from beneath the trees.

Oswald's house was a turreted affair set within extensive grounds, and very private due to the high walls, trees, and shrubs that surrounded it. It looked inviting in the gloom with its many windows glowing with yellow lamplight, and smoke drifting from the chimneys. She was looking forward to catching up with the coven members, despite their ominous reason for meeting, but had to confess to feeling a little niggle of worry about seeing Caspian.

The last time she had seen him was on the night they had defeated the Empusa, when he had used witch-flight to take her to the crossroads. Avery couldn't forget his expression as he'd looked at her with such longing and regret, confessing his feelings for her. Even now she felt inextricably guilty, as if she'd encouraged him somehow, and she hadn't seen him since.

Avery had barely walked a few steps when a swirl of black appeared to her left, and she realised someone else had arrived using witch-flight. She paused, waiting, and in seconds Caspian stood there, quickly hiding his surprise at seeing her. For a few seconds, neither of them spoke, and then

Avery said, "Hi, Caspian. It's been a while."

"It has," he said, walking to her side, his eyes sweeping over her. "You look well."

"I am, thanks, are you?" She felt awkward and hated it, and her heart was fluttering with nerves.

"I am, although work has kept me busy. Tonight will be a welcome distraction."

She laughed, determined to appear as if nothing was wrong. "I'm not sure it will be. Beltane madness appears to have arrived."

As soon as she'd said it, she felt the wind in the trees and smelled pungent blossoms, thick and cloying as they wrapped around her, making her giddy. This wasn't the Green Man. It was the Goddess, flush with power and desire, and she brushed by Avery, filling her with an unexpected virility. She became painfully aware of Caspian's height and heat as they stood together. She looked up at his face, noting his clean jaw and lips parted slightly, and something in her stare must have caught him by surprise, because in a split-second he grabbed her and pulled her under the trees.

Caspian's eyes were wild, his arm wrapped around her waist, his hand tangled in her hair. Cradling the back of her head he pulled her close and kissed her with unexpected tenderness. For a second, Avery was stunned, and then became horrified as her sense returned, she pulled back, her hands on his chest as she pushed him away. "Caspian, no!"

He blinked, his eyes focussing, and he stepped back. "I'm sorry, I shouldn't have." He took another pace back, his arms falling to his sides, but his eyes held hers. "I can't say I didn't enjoy it, though."

Avery felt incredibly flustered, and she backed away, feeling the trunk of the tree behind her. "It was the Goddess," she said, slightly breathless. "She's messing with all of us."

He shook his head, his eyes still intently on her. "Maybe. Or maybe she pushed me to do what I've wanted to do for months."

"Your eyes looked different," she said, wind stirring around her with annoyance, and still aware of the feel of his lips on hers. "She's playing games."

He continued to watch her. "I went away, you know. I thought it would help."

"Help what?" She wanted to go inside, but equally felt she couldn't move, caught within this moment.

"Help me forget about you."

"You have to. Nothing has changed."

Caspian gathered himself together, smiling ruefully. "A man can hope."

She forced herself to make light of it. "You're incorrigible, and delusional." She turned to walk to Oswald's front door. "I'm going in."

He followed her onto the drive, and together they walked to the wide porch. Caspian rang the bell that sounded deep within the house. A million things seemed to race through Avery's mind as she thought of what to say to break the awkward silence that had fallen, and Caspian also looked as if he was about to speak, but in the end before either of them could say anything, the door swung wide, and Oswald welcomed them in.

Oswald was in his sixties, tall and gaunt, with slightly unkempt grey hair. As usual he wore an old-fashioned velvet jacket and trousers. Tonight his jacket was a rich shade of plum, and his shirt beneath was a pale pink. Oswald was quite the dandy.

"Lovely to see you both," he said, smiling broadly. "Plenty of time for a G and T. Come on up."

He led them up the stairs to the drawing room on the first floor that overlooked the gardens at the back of the house, chatting about the weather and their health, and Avery composed herself, hoping Oswald had no idea of what had just happened. He headed to his drinks cabinet, saying, "Make yourself at home!"

The room was decorated with bold wallpaper and thick carpet, and a fire burned merrily in the grate. Avery automatically drifted to the window, distancing herself from Caspian to admire Oswald's magnificent gardens, and decided she really needed to spend time in her own walled garden. "Are we the first ones here?" she asked, tearing herself away from the view and finding Caspian's dark eyes on her.

"No, Genevieve is next door." Oswald gestured to the double doors leading into the room that housed the long oval table they had their meetings at. "She's just taking a phone call." He handed Avery and Caspian their drinks, and rolled his eyes as he picked up his own. "The Goddess is causing trouble this year—I presume you've noticed."

"We have," Avery said, nodding and studiously avoiding looking at Caspian. "If I'm honest, I'm quite relieved we're not the only ones, counterproductive though that may be."

"I know what you mean," Oswald agreed. "It's always nice not to feel singled out. I must admit though, she is certainly playing havoc with Ulysses's half-Siren blood."

Avery knew that Ulysses had a mermaid mother and human father, which made his magic a little different to the other witches, but had completely forgotten the consequences of what his Siren blood may cause. "Of course!" she exclaimed. "Is Beltane magic affecting him?"

"I'm afraid so. It is making him very attractive to everyone, regardless of their normal sexual orientation, *and* has elevated his sex drive to a high degree!" Oswald looked both appalled and gleeful at the same time. "He's trying to control his urges, but with little success. I fear there may be many little Ulysses offspring running around in a few months."

Avery almost dropped her glass and had to suppress a snigger, but Caspian was openly smirking. "Really?" he said in his characteristic drawl. "Lucky Ulysses!" He didn't look at Avery once, but she felt sexual tension roll off him.

Oswald carried on regardless. "Not lucky! Almost two weeks until Beltane, and it's already like living in a Roman orgy! Mevagissey is a hotbed of lust, sidelong glances, and open flirtation." He pulled his collar loose as if he was getting hot. "The thing is—as you well know—that Siren blood has an effect on everyone. I don't know what's worse—Siren blood or Beltane—but either way, things are magnifying in Mevagissey very quickly!"

"Are you saying it's affecting you?" Caspian asked, a smile spreading across his face.

"It certainly is! I'm having thoughts I haven't had for years!"

"You're not that old!" Avery said, laughing.

"And surely you're never too old for *that*," Caspian said, glancing at Avery.

Avery looked determinedly at Oswald. "I take it that Beltane doesn't normally affect Ulysses like this?"

"Not this strongly, certainly. He always gets a little—" he paused, considering his words. "*Frisky*. But I haven't seen him this bad before."

Avery had an odd vision of Ulysses frisking along like a goat, which was all the more unnerving, considering he was enormous and looked an older version of Aquaman.

"Which raises the question—is someone casting love spells, too?" Genevieve said from behind them.

No one had heard her come in and they turned to look at her. Genevieve was imperious with long dark hair, and was every inch their lead witch. She could be grumpy and impatient, but generally radiated calm decisiveness, though now she looked flustered.

"That is a concern," Oswald acknowledged with a frown, "but it would have to be a big spell."

"Or lots of little ones," Caspian suggested.

"And I would dearly like to think that no one in our coven would do anything so foolish!" Genevieve said grumpily.

The deep *clang* of the doorbell resounded throughout the house, and excusing himself, Oswald disappeared.

Genevieve carried on. "If I find out that one of our witches is responsible, there will be consequences!"

"Are things bad in Falmouth?" Avery asked. Genevieve was the sole witch there, and lived with her husband and children.

"Well, we haven't got a huge half-Siren stirring things up, but as I explained to both of you on the phone, I can just feel sexual tension in the air."

"And we won't be immune, either," Avery admitted, thinking of the event just minutes before. "I'd like to think our magic would offer protection, but—" She trailed off, her meaning clear.

"Of course it will affect us," Caspian said. "A spell will play on our fears and strengths as much as anyone else's. Natural Beltane magic will do the same."

Before Avery could comment, the door opened, admitting Eve, Claudia, Rasmus, and Jasper. There were a flurry of greetings, and within minutes the other five members of the coven entered too, and Oswald hurried to fix them all drinks.

Avery nodded at Zane and Mariah, two of the coven she didn't really like, mainly because they had always sided with Caspian when he was clearly against the White Haven witches joining the Cornwall Coven. However, considering Caspian's change in attitude, they had grudgingly needed to acknowledge her.

Once Eve had a drink in hand, she headed to Avery's side and hugged her. "It's been too long, Avery! We should have met before tonight."

"I know. I guess life gets in the way sometimes." Eve looked well. Her thick, dark hair fell in dreadlocks, and as usual it was bound back with a colourful scarf. She wore patched jeans, old combat boots, and a hippy t-shirt, and Avery loved her unconventional appearance. "How are you and Nate?"

Eve rolled her eyes. "Busy. I've been doing lots of painting, and am selling quite a few. It always picks up with spring. Same for Nate."

Eve was an accomplished artist who lived in a studio flat full of light and views of the ocean. She was also a weather witch, capable of drawing power together over a huge area. She had helped them defeat the mermaids on Spriggan Beach in the summer of the previous year, and Avery was still astonished when she thought on her abilities. Nate was as unconventional as Eve, and was a skilled metal worker who made sculptures.

Eve continued. "And like everyone else, we're worried about Beltane."

"What's been happening in St Ives?"

"The same as what everyone is reporting. Heightened emotions, overt flirting, rising petty jealousies, and I feel it, too! A surge of desire that I can't control." She looked worried.

"Really? Desire for who?"

"Anyone! The feeling comes over me, and then goes again. I can see it for what it is," she said, reassuring herself as much as Avery, "but it doesn't make it go away."

Avery was really worried now. If Eve, who Genevieve had once told her was strong enough to lead the Cornwall Coven, could be affected, it didn't bode well for the rest of them.

Now that they were all present, Genevieve didn't give them long to chat, and summoned them to start the meeting, her voice rising over their conversations. They all filed into the adjoining room to sit around the long, wooden table inlaid with arcane symbols.

Avery sat next to Eve, and Jasper, the witch from Penzance, was on her other side. He nodded in greeting as he sat next to her. Jasper was a skilled witch whose family was from the West Indies. He was also skilled in research and knowledge about myths and folklore, and had teamed up with the White Haven witches to help defeat the vampires. He met her eyes, a glint of intrigue deep within his own. "I think we're in for a rough time," he murmured softly to her as he made himself comfortable.

"Welcome all," Genevieve began from where she sat at the head of the table. "I wish we were meeting in better circumstances, but current events are already spiralling out of control. In a moment, we'll go around the table so that we can share our experiences, but I'll summarise what I know first.

Beltane is approaching, and magic is rising. The Goddess and her consort, the Green Man, are gaining in strength and power." She gazed at them one by one. "I feel her even now—her desires, her magic, and the earth's fertility that rises with her. It makes my blood sing, but it's also terrifying. She is far more powerful than any of us, and while she is generally a force for good, we cannot ignore the consequences of such wild magic on human emotions. And combined with the Green Man—well, emotions are running wild indeed."

Jasper leaned forward, his elbows on the table, his hands steepling together. "But you also fear someone has cast love spells. Why?"

"Because Beltane happens every year, and it never feels like this," she explained bluntly.

Caspian spoke next, his dark eyes on Avery briefly before he addressed Genevieve. "The arrival of the Crossroads Circus in White Haven just after Imbolc had long-term implications. It brought the Green Man and the Raven King, and the Green Man never left. Right, Avery?"

Avery nodded nervously as all eyes fell on her. "Caspian is right. The Green Man and the Raven King helped us to defeat the Empusa. The Raven King took her and her two accomplices to the Underworld to face justice. The Ring Master, Corbin, became him for a short time, and he left ravens in Ravens' Wood. But it was the Green Man who had the greater consequences. He raised Ravens' Wood from nothing, and he's never left. He's a part of Briar now. Forevermore, it seems."

A stunned silence fell upon the group, and then a clatter of conversations started all at once. Jasper and Eve both leaned towards Avery, and Eve asked, "Is that true? Why didn't we know?"

Before Avery could answer, Genevieve shouted, "Silence!" When she had everyone's attention, she said, "Avery, perhaps you could elaborate so that everyone is satisfied."

Avery described the events around the Crossroads Circus, and Caspian helped, but there were many doubts when Avery explained about Ravens'

Wood.

"That wood has been there for as long as I can remember," Claudia, the older witch from Perranporth said, perplexed.

Avery sighed, knowing no one would believe her, and was suddenly very grateful that Caspian was there to support her. "It really hasn't. Before, there were only fields around the castle. The wood grew that night—ancient, majestic, magical. Only the people who were there at the time can remember it happening. For everyone else, it just appeared in their consciousness."

"And you were there, too?" Jasper asked Caspian, a crease dividing his forehead.

"I was. It was astonishing. Briar, the White Haven earth witch, helped harness his power. The Green Man has never left her, or White Haven." He hesitated, and then added, "It was the single most amazing night of my life."

Caspian glanced at Avery again, and she knew he was referring to more than just the rising of Ravens' Wood and meeting the Raven King.

"Well, you've changed your tune," Zane said, his sharp face pinched with annoyance as he glared at Caspian.

Caspian gave him a withering stare. "You would rather the Empusa be on the loose? That would be foolish. I have long since overcome my father's prejudices against White Haven, and so should you."

Avery swallowed nervously, and felt Eve staring at her. When Avery turned to look at her, Eve just looked puzzled.

"Well said," Rasmus agreed, his growling voice cutting through the murmurs that had once again sprung up. "I am very grateful you helped them when needed, Caspian." Rasmus had a shock of white hair, and although appeared gruff, was actually a pussycat. He turned to look at Avery. "White Haven handled things admirably, and I am grateful you now get on with your neighbours. It's good for the whole coven."

"It is indeed," Genevieve said. "But it doesn't answer whether or not we have someone casting love spells. It certainly explains why you feel Beltane Magic quite strongly in White Haven, but what about elsewhere?" She turned to Oswald on her right. "Let's start with you, Oswald, and events in Mevagissey."

One by one they recounted their experiences across Cornwall. Everyone reported that they had witnessed exaggerated emotional responses, and it seemed that on the whole, lust and love were prevailing over jealousies—for now.

"Are we sure of our own covens?" Claudia asked. "If there is a witch casting love spells, surely it must be one of our own, although I hate to think that!"

"I'm sure of mine," Avery said, immediately. "No one would be so foolish."

"I'm fairly certain of mine, too," Jasper said, and then he frowned. "Except Mina, maybe. She's very young. To be honest though, Samhain scared her so badly, I can't see her messing with Beltane magic." Mina was the young witch who'd been trampled by the horse of the escaping fey on the night of the Wild Hunt, and had spent days recovering in hospital. "I'll speak to her when I get home."

Claudia broke the silence that had fallen while everyone thought about their covens. "I doubt my youngest witches would, but I will question them."

"I'm pretty sure I can rule out my family," Caspian said, surveying the room confidently. "But I'll ask, of course."

Avery wondered if he would really question Estelle. His sister was a powerful witch who treated everyone else with disdain. It wouldn't surprise her to find that she might be stirring things up for the pure fun of it.

The meeting had been long, and everyone began to stir, eager to be gone, despite the fact that nothing had been resolved. Genevieve was clearly aware of that, and she rapped the table with her knuckle, drawing everyone's attention.

"All right, settle down, I know you're all anxious to be off. I suggest we continue to monitor situations closely, and try to work out if we think a spell is adding to the problem. Anything untoward must be investigated. If you're in need of help, let me know, but I fear we need to manage our own problems, as we'll all be busy with our own issues." Everyone nodded, exchanging worried glances with each other. "And finally, we come to our own Beltane celebrations. Rasmus has once again offered the woods behind his house, but Avery had said her coven wish to celebrate in Ravens' Wood."

"Sorry," Avery said to the council in general. "It seems the perfect place for us. It's not to say you can't join us, but obviously it's not as private as Rasmus's place."

Rasmus agreed. "Far too risky to have the whole coven there."

Zane piped up again, his tone aggressive. "Too good for the rest of us, Avery?"

"Not at all," she shot back before Genevieve could intervene. "Ravens' Wood is very special to us. It's a good way for us to mark its arrival."

He was relentless. "As if a wood could just appear out of nowhere!"

"If you doubt the magic of the Green Man," Jasper said, leaning forward, "then you're more of an idiot than you look." Jasper had clashed with Zane before and had zero patience with him. "If you understood magic at all, you'd know that some forces are well beyond our control. You're just making yourself sound young and foolish!"

"How dare you!" Zane started, until Caspian intervened.

"He's right. Cut it out, Zane. I was there, too. I saw it. Are you accusing me of lying?" Caspian's voice was low and dangerous, and an unpleasant air of tension had risen.

Zane flushed and could barely look Caspian in the eye. "No, of course not. It's Avery I doubt."

Avery dearly wished to bind his tongue, but she seethed quietly instead. And besides, she didn't need to do anything, because Caspian said, "If you doubt Avery, you doubt me. *I was there.* Understood?"

Zane met his gaze defiantly. "Yes."

Genevieve had watched the exchange with narrowed eyes, and her voice now rang out clearly. "You speak out of turn again, Zane, and Bodmin will have to find a new representative to the council. I will not have rudeness and intolerance here. Debate is fine, but I will not tolerate such baseless accusations."

Zane was obviously furious, but he shut up and nodded, and as soon as Genevieve called the meeting to an end, he left immediately, Mariah next to him. With regret, Avery realised that Zane's enmity hadn't improved, and if anything had only grown worse, despite Caspian's defence. But there was nothing she could do, other than acknowledge that Zane and Mariah would never welcome White Haven to the coven, and she was fine with that.

Six

Avery used witch-flight again to take her to The Wayward Son, where she'd arranged to meet the other witches after the meeting.

She arrived in Alex's uninhabited flat above the pub, slightly disorientated, as the room was in near darkness, illuminated only by the street lights which slanted in through the blinds. It was strange to be here again, without Alex's personal items. Her old sofa stood in place of Alex's tan leather one that was now in her flat. A couple of prints were still on the walls, and a few books in the bookcase, ready for if he decided to rent the place out. As yet, he wasn't sure what to do with it.

Avery headed downstairs to the pub, noting that it was after nine o'clock. No wonder she felt drained. El, Reuben, and Briar were already sitting around the table under the window in the quiet back room, and Avery slid into a seat next to them.

"Hi, guys!"

"Long meeting?" El asked, pushing a glass of red wine in front of her. She nodded at the drink. "We got you one in."

Avery reached for it and took a long sip. "Thank you. I needed that! Yes, it was very long." She looked around. "Where's Alex?"

"At the bar, helping Zee," Reuben said. "It's been a bit tense in here tonight."

"What? Why?" Avery looked at their faces, finally observing their grim expressions now she'd gathered herself together.

"A couple of guys started to argue over a woman," Briar explained.

"Zee reacted really quickly and stepped in, and they asked one guy to leave—well, told him to leave." She shook her head. "The woman was really shaken up, actually. It was a bit unpleasant."

Avery couldn't believe that Alex's normally relaxed pub had seen such an incident, and released a flurry of questions. "Was she hurt? I mean, did it get violent? Was the woman even with them?"

"The woman was with her boyfriend, or maybe husband," Briar told her, "and this guy at another table just got up, came over, and hit on the woman when her partner went to the bar. She basically gave him the brush off, but he became insistent, well, persistent is probably the better word. She raised her voice, telling him to leave her alone, but—"

"It was like he had no control," El finished as Briar floundered. "Her partner came back from the bar, but the guy still wouldn't back off, and the next thing you know, Zee is in his face and had propelled him out the door, along with his mates."

Reuben nodded. "I followed them outside, and questioned one of his friends while they were trying to calm him down. Apparently, this is really unlike him. I sent a little calming spell his way, hopefully it will work." He stood up. "I'm going to get another round, and I'll get Alex while I'm there."

Reuben headed to the bar, leaving Avery looking at El and Briar, stunned. "Wow!" She leaned forward, intrigued. "What kind of things was the man saying to her?"

Briar rolled her eyes. "'You're the woman of my dreams,' 'please go out with me,' 'I'm better than that loser,' 'I can't live without you...' You get the picture. Well, that's how it started. Then he got nasty. Started accusing her of toying with him and leading him on. His mates tried to intervene too, and had no luck."

El laughed, despite the events. "You should have seen Zee! He literally picked him up by the collar, like actually lifted him off the floor, and just carried him across the room like he was a kid. It was seriously impressive!

Everyone was watching, and there were quite a few checking his ass and pecs out on the way."

"More fans for Zee!" Avery said, trying to brush off the feeling of impending doom, and hoping that this was not going to be a regular occurrence for the next few weeks. "You weren't tempted to step in and hex the annoying dickhead, then?" she asked El and Briar with a wry smile.

"Very tempted," Briar said, a fire burning behind her eyes. "I hate to see women treated like that. But I was slow to react compared to Reuben, Alex, and Zee." She sipped her white wine, still annoyed, and then looked beyond Avery's shoulder with a nod. "And here's Alex!"

Avery looked around to see Alex and Reuben enter the small room together, both carrying drinks. Alex's expression was tight, but he sat next to Avery, planted a kiss on her cheek, and put down a pint and another glass of red wine. "Here you go, Ave. I thought you'd need a second. I gather you've heard our news."

"I have. Sounds awful!"

"Could have been worse," he said, shrugging. "The girl's boyfriend was annoyed but wasn't about to start swinging punches, and as you've heard, Zee just took the other bloke outside." He sipped his pint and leaned back with sigh. "I gave them drinks on the house."

"Nice move, mate," Reuben said, approvingly. "Just wondered, are they all regulars?"

"Yeah, I recognised all of them. Don't know their names, but they come in reasonably frequently. And no, that guy has never caused trouble before," he said, guessing Reuben's next question.

Avery hardly dared asked the question, but she swallowed and said, "Beltane magic, or something unrelated?"

Alex shook his head. "You're going to think I'm mad, but over the last couple of days, things have been feeling distinctly off in here. Not Beltane, something else." He held his hand up to ward off the questions. "I can't explain it any other way, so let me think on it. I presume you don't feel anything?" They shook their heads, worried, and he smiled wanly at Avery. "Anyway, that was our fun night. How was yours?"

"Well, it was great to catch up with everyone, but I guess the good news is that we are not the only ones affected." Avery repeated the evening's discussions, saving the news about Ulysses until last. She knew Reuben wouldn't stop laughing, and she was right, but his laughter was infectious, and soon they were all giggling.

"You are kidding, right?" El said, her eyes wide with surprise.

"No! Mevagissey is a hotbed of lust—I think those were Oswald's exact words!"

"That's the best thing I've heard all day! No, all year!" Reuben exclaimed. "I wonder if all the old people in the rest homes are affected." He sniggered again, and almost spat out his pint. "I can see the headlines now. 'Unknown affliction turns Mevagissey into the porn capital of Cornwall!'"

"But this really isn't funny," Briar said, trying to control her own giggles. "This could break up peoples' relationships!"

"Or start them," Reuben pointed out. "This isn't all bad, Briar."

"But it's unnatural," she persisted. "No good can come of it."

"It's not like Ulysses can control his Siren blood," Alex pointed out. "Well, not completely. But, yes, it's worrying." And then he sniggered, too. "I'd love to see Oswald having sweats about his erotic thoughts, though."

That set Reuben off again, and they were both giggling like schoolboys.

"This is going to be an intense two weeks," Briar said with a wry smile at El and Avery. "What if Hunter is affected? His libido really doesn't need any help!" And then she bit her lip as if she'd said too much.

El's mouth fell open. "Briar! You little minx."

"Well, I may as well be honest," she said, shrugging it off, and knowing it was pointless to deny what she'd said. She glanced up at Avery, and it seemed as if the ring of green around her pupils flashed like emeralds.

"Do you think we're already affected?" Avery asked, worried. "It's like we're in a Carry On film," she said, referring to the series of classic English comedy films filled with double entendres. "Look at us! All we need is for Sid James to walk through the door."

"No, of course we're not affected," Reuben said, sobering up. "We're just seeing the funny side of what could turn into a nightmare. So, what was Genevieve's suggestion?"

"Be watchful. Investigate for spells cast by whoever it may be. The other covens will ensure any young witches haven't got carried away, and in the meantime, try to negate the effects of the Goddess and Green Man in their ascension." She paused, wondering what she'd missed, and then said, "I should tell you about Zane, too."

She related what he'd said about Ravens' Wood, and the general reactions of the council.

"That weasly-faced little bastard will always cause problems," Alex conceded. "You say Caspian backed you up?"

"Yes, of course."

Alex merely nodded in response, giving Avery the faintest flash of concern. She hoped his antagonistic attitude toward Caspian had subsided, but maybe not.

"Where's he been?" Briar asked. "Eli tells me he's been travelling for business."

"I have no idea," Avery admitted. "We didn't really chat." She pushed all thoughts of the kiss to the back of her mind.

"At least we can plan our celebrations for Beltane," El said, pleased. "Beltane Eve is Thursday, which is perfect. The town's celebrations won't be happening until two days later, on the following Saturday. We should have the wood to ourselves."

"I wouldn't bet on it," Reuben said, draining his pint. "I reckon quite a few people from the town will head up for their own private celebrations. Ravens' Wood is perfect for it. The good thing is that it's pretty big, and densely planted. We could spell ourselves into our own protected space. No one will see us."

Alex finished his pint too, looking tired. "Let's hope you're right. At this moment, next week feels like a long way away, and who knows what will happen in between now and then."

Avery noticed that Alex was subdued on their walk home, and she snuggled under his arm as he pulled her close.

"What's wrong?" she asked. "Are you worried about that fight?"

"A bit," he admitted. "It's weird how that man was singled out. I mean, why was he affected, and his mates were fine? And as I said earlier, something feels a little off in the pub, but I can't quite place why, and neither can Zee."

"Maybe the guy was just being a jerk," Avery suggested. "Some men are."

Alex shook his head. "But his mates said he wasn't normally."

"Some mates don't always tell the truth."

He looked down at her, and kissed her cheek. "You're right, but I have this feeling they weren't lying. They genuinely looked shocked."

"Well," she said resolutely, "I've decided to head into my garden tomorrow. I have some hawthorn I'm going to cut and put in the shop, for protection. I'm going to cut some for you too, to put in the pub. Briar told me tonight that she's put some in her shop, and I think it's a good idea. The more I can do, the better. I want my shop and our home to be a safe haven."

"It is a safe haven," he said, pausing and turning her to face him, his arms encircling her. "You're there."

"You say the sweetest things," she told him, feeling a wave a both contentment and desire sweep over her.

Alex leaned in, kissing her until she was breathless. As he pulled away, Avery had the strangest sensation of being watched, and she looked around suspiciously at the other people who were leaving pubs and restaurants, filling the air with a high-spirited chatter. They were in the square where the maypole was erected. A colourful collection of containers filled with spring plants were placed around it, and the long ribbons for the dancers were tied beneath the crown of flowers at the top of the pole. The air smelt sweet, like honey, and it felt as if there was promise in the air, a sense of expectation; but the promise of what?

"Did you feel that?" she asked him.

"The aching in my pants? Yes," he said, grinning.

"No! I meant like being watched!"

"Let them watch," he teased.

"I don't think it's people I can sense. It's her—the Maiden Goddess."

As soon as Avery said her name, a wave of longing seemed to intensify around them, and it affected everyone. Couples and groups paused, confused, and the heady scent of honeysuckle became stronger. The night had been still, but now a breeze eddied around them, making the hanging baskets in front of the shops sway, and ruffling the plants. Avery felt her hair lift, as if someone was caressing the back of her neck, and a wild passion bubbled up inside her. Avery's arm was still wrapped around Alex's waist, and she felt him shudder as the feeling gripped him. She met his eyes, dark as night, and for a moment felt lost in them.

Alex grabbed her hand, and pulled her up the street towards home. The primal desire the Goddess had left burning within her was blazing now, and she knew Alex was experiencing it, too. By the time they reached the door of their flat, they were running. They had barely stepped inside when they started tearing each other's clothes off, falling onto the floor of the living room in an effort to slake their desire, both of them lost in wild abandon.

Alex's skin felt hot, as if he was going to burst into flames, and his corded muscles felt like steel. As her hands slid over him, gripping the hard planes of his body, she was aware only of his touch stoking the flames of her desire, and she lost herself, completely.

When Avery woke the next morning, it was with a sense of confusion, as if she was emerging out of a deeper than normal sleep. Her head was groggy, and her limbs felt heavy, and she tried to recall how much alcohol she had drunk the night before.

And then she remembered: the Goddess had filled her with a wild passion she had never experienced before.

Avery turned to look at Alex who slept next to her, lost within a tangle of blankets, and felt another wave of elation flash over her. She flopped back on the pillow, trying to sort through her memories of the night before—the sense of the Goddess in the town square, and then the race home. Alex's groan broke into her thoughts, and he turned to look at her, blinking.

"What the hell happened last night? Did I get drunk?"

She rolled over, her hand on his chest. "No, the Goddess happened."

He was silent for a moment before he said, "Holy shit! I remember. How could I forget last night? That was incredible!"

She laughed. "It really was. I'm just glad we managed to hold it together before we got home."

He rolled onto his back and looked up at the ceiling that was brindled with stripes from the pale grey light filtering through the wooden blinds, and Avery propped herself up on her elbow to watch his face.

"That was the most intense feeling I've ever had," he exclaimed. "Terrifyingly so, in fact. I'm not entirely sure I had control of myself last night." He looked at her, his dark eyes serious. "Did I hurt you?"

"Of course you didn't," she answered, surprised. "You would never hurt me!"

"But I had no control. I acted out of pure, blind lust."

"We both did. Trust me, I enjoyed every second of it—what I can remember, anyway. Things are a bit foggy." Avery still couldn't really remember details, except for the fact that they seemed to have had sex for hours, starting in the living room, and working their way upstairs, finally.

Alex pushed himself upright, stacked pillows behind him, and leaned back, still looking perplexed. "But that's it, Ave. I can't remember much at all, except this absolute need to have sex. I'm not sure I could have stopped myself if you would have said no!"

"There was no way I'd have said no," she said, laughing. "You're worrying too much!"

"What if I hadn't been with you?"

A slow, insidious curl of fear started coiling in the pit of Avery's stomach. "I'm presuming we felt that way because we were together."

"But what if we weren't? What if I'd been with Briar or El—or even Sally? Or if you'd been with Newton or Reuben...or Caspian?" His eyes hardened for a second.

The memory of Caspian's kiss flooded her mind. That was the Goddess, but she'd been able to resist that—she'd pushed him away, and he'd accepted it, too. But she couldn't tell Alex. Not now, at least.

"I think," she said cautiously, "that we abandoned ourselves to it, because we were together. We had no internal brakes...since we didn't need to have them. I am not about to have sex with Reuben, Newton, or Caspian! Or Dan, for that matter," she added, reflexively.

Alex relaxed and grinned. "You're probably right. It will be interesting to see if anyone else had the same experience, though."

"It will! I'll ask Sally and Dan later."

Then Alex's face fell again. "I had another weirdly vivid dream again, too."

"The same as last time?"

"Yeah. This feeling of being smothered by vines and branches, and people wearing strange clothing, as if I'd gone back in time. And then," his face creased with confusion, "I was looking at the sea, and this mist was thick over it, as if something was there."

"Is the dream of the sea new?"

"I think so."

"Was it a dream or psychic vision, though?"

"I'm not sure. It doesn't feel like my normal visions, but I don't normally get recurring dreams, either."

"Well, I'd better head into the shower," Avery said, turning to get out of bed, and trying to dispel her worry about Alex's dreams. "I need to get to work."

But before she could go far, Alex pulled her back to him. "Oh, no! We've got time for round two before work."

And with a squeal of pleasure, Avery allowed herself to be pulled back beneath the sheets.

Seven

Avery and Alex found Sally and Dan already in the kitchen at the rear of the shop when they arrived downstairs.

"Morning, you two," Sally said, breaking away from her conversation with Dan. "How are you, Alex? Haven't seen you for a while."

Alex normally stayed in the flat when Avery went to work, popping in only occasionally. "I'm very good, thanks! We had a fun time last night."

"I know what that means," Dan said knowingly. He leaned back against the kitchen counter looking pleased with himself. "You must have had as good a night as us."

Avery sat on a chair at the table, feeling like she knew what they were going to say already. "Really? What happened?"

"Sex! Lots of it." Dan sighed, looking into the distance, and Avery tried not to think about what he might be seeing.

Alex helped himself to a cup of coffee, and as he fixed it, asked, "So who was the lucky lady?"

"Her name is Caroline. We've been out a couple of times, she's a friend of a friend, but well, last night, things just took off!" Dan grinned again. "I'm seeing her again tonight!"

"And what about you, Sally?" Avery asked, pleased that she and Sam appeared to have resolved their differences of a couple of days ago. "Dan said, '*us*.'"

She laughed. "Sam and I also had a night of unbridled passion such as we haven't had in years! Thank the Gods he's had the snip, because I don't want any more kids!"

Alex glanced at Avery, his eyebrows raised, and then asked, "Do you think it felt like normal passion, or something else?"

"Why?" Sally said, looking between them suspiciously. "Oh, wait, the Green Man?"

"The Goddess, actually," Avery said, accepting a cup of coffee from Alex, who was now making a drink for everyone. "We were walking home from the pub, passing through the square, when she swept through—and wow, just *wow*! We both experienced absolutely blinding, primal passion, and literally ran home. I wonder what the other people felt there."

"True," Alex said. "I didn't even stop to look. Where were you two?"

"We'd just got to her place," Dan said, frowning. "She lives in a flat at the top of town. Now that you mention it, it did seem to happen really quickly, you know, that flare of desire. At the time I put it down to me being absolutely charming, but now I'm not so sure."

"We were at home, already in bed," Sally admitted. "I was knackered, and so was Sam. The kids had been playing up, and all we wanted to do was sleep. And then, we didn't! And I think that's all I need to say," she said, her cheeks dimpling as she smiled.

Dan sighed heavily. "Damn it! Does this mean my charm was not the reason for my great night?"

Avery tried to reassure him. "I'm sure it was part of it."

"I wonder if this is going to happen more frequently over the next couple of weeks," Alex mused. "I'll ring the others before I go to work later. I want to know what they experienced last night." They all knew he meant El, Reuben, and Briar. He headed to the door that led to the stairs and Avery's flat. "In the meantime, I'll see if there's anything interesting on the news."

After he left, Avery said, "I'd like to get out to the garden today. I want to put some hawthorn in the shop, for protection. I think it might be wise. As long as we're not busy, of course." She glanced out of the tiny window that looked onto the lane at the back of the shop and the high wall of her garden beyond it. Above was only bright blue sky. "It's going to be lovely today—perfect gardening weather!"

"Head out there now," Sally suggested. "The first couple of hours are always quiet. Just cover us for lunch. And then you can tell us what happened at the council meeting!"

Avery grinned. "Will do, thank you!" And without waiting another second, she headed outside.

The morning was bright and fresh, and for the next few hours Avery worked tirelessly, weeding the garden, clearing leaves, and pruning, pleased to see the garden busting with life.

She didn't stop until Alex appeared with a cup of tea and a tin of biscuits. "I saw you from upstairs," he said, smiling. "You've made good progress. I would have helped, but I've been doing the pub's accounts."

"That's fine," she said, accepting the drink gratefully, and taking a cookie. They sat at the wooden garden table in a patch of sun, and she asked, "Any news from the others?"

"They experienced the same thing as us, as did Reuben's employees up at Greenlane Nurseries. Hot, unbridled lust swept over White Haven last night! Although," he added, dunking his biscuit in his tea, "it sounds as if the intensity of those feelings varied, depending where you were. The centre of town sounds the most intense. I think we were at the epicentre!"

Avery nodded as she gazed around at the verdant lushness of the garden, unable to forget the heady and overpowering feelings of the night before, although it had a dreamlike quality now. "I think you're right. I almost feel that by naming the Goddess—recognising that she was there with us—I set it off. Is that nuts?"

"Maybe?" Alex gazed absently around the garden, too. "Although, I'm not sure we really influence her actions."

"No, I guess not," Avery admitted.

"And there's more," Alex said quietly. "I watched the news this morning. That reporter, Sarah Rutherford, you know the blonde one? She's been in town interviewing Rupert about his ghost-come-occult tour. He's starting it next week, Monday morning actually."

Alex was referring to Rupert who owned the House of Spirits in West Haven. They'd investigated it with the three paranormal investigators before the winter solstice the previous year, finding that it was linked to a vampire. Rupert had no idea about the vampires, but he did know all about the house's occult history and that it had been owned by a medium. It was the reason he'd bought it. None of the witches really liked him, or his wife, Charlotte.

Avery groaned. "I haven't seen him for a while and I'd hoped his bloody tour had blown over."

"No such luck. According to the report he had a few things to do before it got approved, but the council have signed it off now." He rolled his eyes. "Stan, of course, is all for it, and they were interviewed together. They reckon it's perfect timing with Beltane only a few days away."

"I suppose they're right. Did he say where the tour will go?"

"It will focus on a couple of things." He paused, watching her carefully. "Helena and her history in the town, her burning at the stake, of course, and the general history of witchcraft in the town. And the ghost walk that happened after Samhain last year."

Avery knew she was worrying unnecessarily, but she hated the fact that her ancestor would be the subject of interest for other people, and she knew it would draw unwanted attention to her. She chewed her lip, trying not to swear, but failed. "Shit! I'm so annoyed about this, but if I complain it will look weird!"

Alex leaned forward and squeezed her hand. "It will. It's best to let it play out, and just go along with it."

"Did he say what his itinerary would be?"

"He'll be running evening and daytime tours, so I think it varies. Essentially, it will start up at Old Haven Church because of Suzanna's weird witch signs that appeared there at Samhain—Rupert's got a van, apparently! Then they go to the castle, and then it will work its way down the street, a walking portion, stopping outside Penny Lane Bistro, the town hall where Helena and the other women were tried for witchcraft, past your shop at some point, and then ending up at the witch museum. I think the grand finale will be the House of Spirits." Alex sighed. "He's done his homework about Helena—where she lived, got married... Oh, and of course, he'll be going past all the new-age shops too, though that's more for his daytime tour."

"I suppose at least my shop won't be singled out, but I still don't like it," Avery admitted.

"It won't be. I think Briar and El's shops are included, too. Think of it as good publicity. Maybe you should capitalise on Helena. I know you don't like to advertise your relationship with her, but at least you get to own it that way."

Avery shook her head. "It feels cheap. I don't like to think of her as an attraction."

"And she's likely to turn up in your shop for revenge." Alex grinned, and she knew he was trying to cheer her up. "That *would* put your shop on the map!"

"Don't even suggest that as a joke!" Avery finished her tea, and reached for one more biscuit. "I haven't seen Helena for a couple of weeks actually, have you?"

"No." He frowned. "She's suspiciously quiet. I wonder if she's affected by Beltane magic?"

"Who knows what affects Helena." Avery stood up, feeling unexpectedly rattled, and suddenly the bright spring morning wasn't as cheerful as it had been. "I'm going to carry on, because I said I'd relieve the others for lunch."

Alex gathered the cups and biscuit tin and stood, too. "I'm heading down to the pub soon, but I'll see you about seven hopefully. Fingers crossed for a quiet night."

"Let's hope. I'll cook." Avery kissed him goodbye and returned to her gardening.

When Avery entered Happenstance Books at lunchtime, she was laden with hawthorn branches, and she placed them in a large vase full of water to keep them fresh before finding Sally and Dan in the shop. They had already heard the news about Rupert's occult tour of White Haven, and Sally was seething.

"How dare he try to make a profit out of those women's misery," she said, referring to the women who had died as a result of the trials.

"And the men," Dan pointed out. "It wasn't all women who were accused by that madman, the Witchfinder General."

Avery leaned on the window frame and gazed out at the street beyond, watching the bunting bob in the breeze. "Alex said I should take advantage of it and reclaim Helena, but I'm not so sure."

Sally walked over from behind the counter and stood next to her. "What do you mean by reclaim? Like clear her name of black magic? That might actually be a good idea!"

Avery looked at her, confused. "I don't think he meant that. I think he meant just to embrace her as my ancestor, seeing as I normally keep it quiet. But," she paused as an idea began to form, "that might not be a bad idea!"

Sally began to look excited, too. "Happenstance Books is already seen as an occult bookshop as well as just a normal one, but I could do some kind of display—you know, something that highlights what witchcraft really is, display books on the cunning folk, talk about herbal remedies and healing, the role of those people in the town before doctors were so widely available and cheap. That would be a really positive thing to do. You could still have the tarot cards and all your other occult books, but just try to demystify the whole thing."

By then, Dan had joined them, and he also looked intrigued. "That's a great idea! Layman's books on witchcraft. They'd probably sell really well. And now I've had an even better idea!"

Avery and Sally both turned to look at him, and Sally asked, "What?"

"We'll do what we did at Christmas and Halloween. I'll set up a reading corner and use an afternoon next week to talk about Beltane, as well as witchcraft. I'll put up a poster, try and coincide it for either the same day as Rupert's tour, or the days after it. What do you think?"

"I'm thinking why the hell didn't we think of this before!" Sally said, her excitement infectious. "Avery, are you happy with this?"

Avery grinned. "Yes I am, actually! It will be a really positive thing to do."

"Great." Sally grabbed Dan's arm. "Come with me, and let's scope out an area of the shop we can use. I think we should use the occult section, of course, but we could move the bookcases, maybe put everything under the window with the Green Man and the Goddess..."

Sally's excited chatter faded as she and Dan were swallowed up in the shop's interior, and Avery breathed a sigh of relief, wondering for the umpteenth time what she'd do without them.

Eight

When Avery and Alex arrived at El's apartment on Friday evening, they found it filled with candles and dramatic arrangements of flowers, and with music playing loudly. The windows were open, allowing in fresh evening air, and the table was decorated with elegant plates and glassware.

"Wow!" Avery said as she stepped through the door, shrugging off her jacket. "This looks amazing!"

"Thanks," El said, beaming at her. "Sometimes I really enjoy going a bit nuts for dinner!"

Reuben was in the open kitchen, wearing an apron over his board shorts and t-shirt. "She's had me slaving over a hot stove all day!"

"Liar!" El said, rounding on him. "You've only been here for an hour!"

He groaned. "It feels like all day!"

"Men," El said to Avery, rolling her eyes, before turning back to Reuben. "At least get our guests some drinks!"

Alex had joined him in the kitchen, already putting some beer into the fridge, and Reuben grinned at him. "Women!"

Avery accepted a glass of wine from Reuben, and leaving Alex and Reuben chatting, headed to the window to look at the view. "You're so lucky to look onto the harbour, El." El's apartment was on the fourth floor of a renovated warehouse on the quay.

The tide was in and the harbour was crowded with sailing and fishing boats. The street lights were already on, brightening the twilight, and the shops and restaurants on the street next to the quay were still doing brisk business. Avery could smell the sharp tang of brine cutting through the aromatic scent of food.

El joined her, smiling as she looked at the people milling around below. "It's lovely, but as you know, it costs me a small fortune."

"It's worth it!" Avery nodded at the people below. "It looks pretty normal out there tonight," she observed, hoping that wouldn't change. "Any after-effects from Wednesday?"

"Our visit from the Goddess?" El said, laughing. "Wow! That was something, wasn't it? No, I don't think so. We spent the night at Reuben's last night, so of course we're a bit out of town there."

Reuben lived in Greenlane Manor, originally a medieval building that had been added to over the years. It was just out of White Haven, positioned on the hills above the town, and his gardens ran to the cliff edge, affording him a spectacular view of the coast. His nursery business was set in the grounds, but accessed by the lane, allowing him to keep his privacy. Reuben and El migrated between his house and her flat.

"I can't wait to see if Shadow and Gabe experienced the Goddess," Avery admitted, feeling both a wave of excitement and dread wash over her. "I still feel this sense of expectation in the air. I don't know whether to be excited or not."

El pointed down to the street. "You won't have to wait long. They're here."

Gabe and Shadow were strolling along the harbour, and within a few minutes they were at the door, and Hunter and Briar arrived with them.

For a few minutes, there was a flurry of greetings while everyone shed coats and received drinks.

"Hunter!" Avery exclaimed. "I didn't know that you would be here tonight!"

Hunter enveloped her in a hug, and Avery detected a wave of Alpha-ness rolling off him. He was a wolf-shifter who lived in Cumbria with his pack, and although he wasn't the pack Alpha, his wolf nature meant he always seemed predatory. He was dark-haired, lean, and muscled, with a swagger that refused to be tamed. His dark eyes smouldered with a yellow glow when he was aroused or angry, but right now they looked mischievous.

"I've been driving all day to get here," he told her as he sniffed appreciatively. "I couldn't miss out on El's cooking! Do I smell steak?"

"You certainly do," El said, turning as she heard her name, "but it's raw right now! I won't cook it until we're ready."

"I like mine blue," he instructed.

"No surprises there!" Avery said, laughing. Gabe was standing just behind Hunter, taking in his surroundings. "And how are you, Gabe? It's been a while!"

Gabe's bulk filled El's flat, making everything seem smaller, but there was a lightness to him that Avery hadn't seen before. His dark brown, almost black hair had grown, softening his military manner, and he looked more relaxed.

"I'm pretty good, Avery," he said with a nod and the hint of a smile. There was no hug from Gabe, which wasn't a surprise. He wasn't really a touchy-feely kind of guy. "This is a cool place."

"I presume you haven't been to El's home before?"

"No. I'm intrigued as to why I've been invited now, to be honest."

"Because we haven't seen you for a while," Avery explained. "It's nothing sinister. You're as suspicious as Shadow!"

"Did you call me?" Shadow said, turning around and dazzling Avery with her smile and unusual violet eyes.

"I was saying that Gabe is as suspicious as you are."

Shadow cast Gabe a knowing glance. "He can't help it! Neither of us can. It's a natural predator's state. I bet he's the same!" She nodded to Hunter. "The wolf can't help it, either!"

Hunter looked at her, amused. "So says the famous fey."

She raised an eyebrow. "Famous? I like that." She took him by the elbow and steered him across the room, and Avery heard her say, "Now, tell me about your wolf side. I feel sure you're part fey."

Gabe rolled his eyes at Avery. "Some things never change."

Nearly two hours later they were sitting around the table, having finished starters and the main course, and they were relaxing before dessert.

Avery felt deliciously full, and she sipped her wine slowly, savouring its richness. So far they had all had a great evening, chatting about everything and nothing. Gabe was charming, and she'd watched him and Shadow banter all evening. They insulted each other more than anything, but they both seemed to enjoy it, feeding off one another. Whatever relationship they had seemed to work. Avery was pretty sure it wasn't romantic, but there was something there. They'd talked a little bit about their work with the Orphic Guild, and had elaborated on the events at Old Haven Church, the night the dead had risen from their graves, summoned by the fey necromancer. Within days of it happening, Shadow told Reuben about seeing his brother, Gil, in the mausoleum, and although it had upset him at the time, he had now accepted it, and seemed grateful to hear that at least Gil's body hadn't been desecrated.

Hunter had told them about the pack in Cumbria, chatting about how the new Alpha had settled into this role, and it seemed Briar had made plans to visit, arranging that Eli would cover the shop, with help from Cassie when she had time between studying for exams.

Everyone had held off discussing the events of Beltane, but as the group relaxed, the conversation naturally turned to the upcoming celebrations, partly prompted by mention of Eli.

"Is Eli still being stalked by one of his fans?" Reuben asked, with a mischievous grin.

"Yes, unfortunately," Gabe said bluntly. "It doesn't seem to have stopped his flirting, though."

"It's great for business," Briar said, repeating what she'd said to Avery only days before. "Although, there are times it feels like I'm running a dating agency."

"Are you sure you don't mean a knocking shop?" Reuben asked, baiting her.

"Is that the same as a house of ill repute?" Shadow asked, looking between them. "I'm unfamiliar with the term 'knocking shop.'"

Avery inwardly groaned. They were back to Carry On innuendos again.

El smacked Reuben's arm. "Behave! Yes, that's exactly what it means, Shadow."

"And, no I do not mean that!" Briar said, glaring at Reuben. "But, wow, I think emotions are getting more heightened. Eli said he felt that wave of primal passion on Wednesday night. He happened to be out with one of his girlfriends, and he said it was intense. He didn't elaborate, thankfully!" She looked at Gabe and Shadow. "We've been wondering if you felt it too—especially you, Shadow."

For once, Shadow didn't answer glibly. "I can feel the Goddess and the Green Man. They are circling each other at the moment. It's like some kind of courtly dance. Wednesday night was a tease on her behalf. The Goddess was suggesting how things could be once they meet at Beltane. It was a promise...and a warning."

"A warning?" Alex asked. "Why?"

"The Goddess's emotions are not to be trifled with. Their meeting is the fulfilment of spring and the promise of summer. He must come to her, pure of heart and intent. If he does, she will be his willingly. If he fails her, she will have her vengeance." Shadow looked at the men around the table, a smile twitching at her lips. "Do not take the women in your life for granted, for we are full of fury and might." Her eyes flashed and her glamour flickered, showing her fey nature clearly, and a wave of both fear and wonder rolled around the room. And then she cloaked her Otherness again, sipping her drink demurely.

Silence fell as Alex, Reuben, Gabe, and Hunter looked at each other nervously, and then Reuben said, "More alcohol?"

It was close to midnight when they all made to leave. Avery had finished her wine and was wishing she didn't have to walk up the hill toward home when Alex's phone rang, and he glanced at it and frowned. "It's Newton."

He headed to the far side of the room, talking quietly, while the others glanced nervously at each other, straining to hear what he was saying. Within minutes Alex returned, pocketing his phone. "There's been a stabbing at the Little Theatre. Newton says things are very weird, and he wants us to go."

"All of us?" Hunter asked, clearly eager to be a part of it.

"You're allowed, surprisingly, and us witches, but not you two," Alex said, looking at Shadow and Gabe.

Shadow looked disappointed, but Gabe shrugged. "I am more than happy to be left out of a police investigation, but what's at the theatre?" he asked, looking confused.

"The dress rehearsal for the local production of Tristan and Iseult."

Avery remembered the conversation she'd had with Dan and frowned. "One of Dan's friends is in that show. He told me that he's a little more intense than usual, and that the leads seem to have taken their roles to heart."

Reuben nodded. "I remember them. Emma and Josh, wasn't it?"

Avery nodded as she grabbed her jacket. "I must admit, I thought they looked a bit guilty. They were trying too hard to avoid each other's eyes."

Hunter groaned. "That sounds very ominous."

"A stabbing always is, mate!" Reuben exclaimed, looking at him like he'd grown two heads.

"Not for that, you tit," Hunter replied. "The play! You know what it's about, right?"

"Some girl and some bloke?" Reuben's knowledge of the arts was poor, and he didn't really care.

"It's about a love triangle, and jealousy, and love spells—just a little bit topical, don't you think?"

"What are you? An English major?" Reuben asked, baffled.

"Yes, actually! Years ago, admittedly."

"Oh!" Reuben looked taken aback.

By then, the room had stilled and everyone was looking at Hunter expectantly, so he explained, "Tristan and Iseult is set in Cornwall. It's about King Mark, his nephew, Tristan, and his wife, Iseult. It's a very old tale and is thought to be what the King Arthur love triangle was originally based on. I won't elaborate now, but essentially the nephew, Tristan, and Iseult, King Mark's intended, accidentally drink the love potion meant for her and King Mark, and they fall in love—cue a weird love triangle, angst, jealousy, etc. Do you get what I'm saying? We're in the throes of Beltane passions, and now this happens. Coincidence? I think not."

Nine

White Haven Little Theatre was a Victorian building set on a road just off from the main street, and not far from the beach.

It had originally been a busy theatre in its heyday, but had fallen into disuse during the early part of the 20th century. There was talk of turning it into a cinema, until the public petitioned the council and they bought it and renovated it. They had kept the original Victorian decor, and it was now used by local amateur dramatic groups and touring companies. There was also a small café and bar at the front entrance, and it was popular with locals and visitors alike.

Tonight it was also busy, but for very depressing reasons. A few police cars and an ambulance lined the road in front of the building, and lights blazed inside, despite the late hour. A group of bystanders stood down the street, watching the activities in gruesome fascination.

Avery and Alex phoned Newton, as he'd instructed, and they waited across the road. Within a couple of minutes, DS Inez Walker appeared, and as soon as she saw them, beckoned them to the narrow passage that ran down the right side of the building. They ducked under the police yellow tape, and when they reached her, she escorted them to the side entrance and into a corridor beyond. Walker was dark-haired and olive-skinned, an indication of her Spanish ancestry, and she looked perplexed as she halted just inside the entrance. She had been working with Newton for only a few months, and although Avery and Alex had met her a couple of times, they didn't know her well. Walker looked at them all one by one, as if assessing their usefulness, and shook hands as they introduced themselves.

"I have to admit that I think this is pretty irregular bringing you here, but Newton insisted, and he's the boss. However, he's right in suggesting that something odd is going on here. Everyone looks like they're drugged—well, to one degree or another."

"Drugged?" Avery asked, finally feeling like she could speak. Walker hadn't really given them a chance before, anxious to hustle them off the street. "The whole theatre company?"

"Weird, isn't it? But yes. They seem sort of disassociated." She shrugged. "Probably not the greatest word to describe it, but that's the best I can do for now." She nodded up the corridor. "The auditorium is through there, but I'm going to take you to the dressing rooms, for privacy."

"I thought you only investigated murders?" Reuben asked.

"Someone was stabbed!" she said, frowning at him. "We're treating this as attempted murder for now. And besides, the group's state of mind suggests something paranormal, and that means we investigate it."

Walker turned and led them down a warren of tiny passageways, past closed doors, to a musty dressing room crowded with paraphernalia of performing. There was a large mirror and dressing table, a rack of clothes, pots of makeup, and a few chairs. And it was cramped.

Newton was sitting at the dressing table, and his face reflected in the mirror looked grey and tired. He was examining a copy of the play, but noticing their arrival, he turned to look at them, his face grim. Other than a flash of dislike for Hunter, he looked pleased to see them.

"Thanks for coming, guys. I realise it's late."

"That's okay," Briar said, reassuring him. "What can we do to help?"

Newton looked at Walker. "Shut the door please, and go and see how they're doing with the statements."

Walker nodded and disappeared, and as soon as the door was shut, Newton exhaled heavily. "This is a bloody mess. I can't get a coherent statement out of anyone."

"Walker said they seemed drugged," Alex told him, while the rest of them tried to make themselves comfortable in the small space.

Newton nodded. "That's as good a way to describe it as anything. They seem to have lost their identity...well, for a while at least. They kept referring to themselves by their character's names, and when we asked for their real names, a few of them looked utterly confused. One of them even said—" he pulled out his notebook, flicked through it, and then read, "'I am Governal. How dare you accuse me of being someone else!'" He looked up at them. "What the hell! Is there some kind of spell that can make them think they are the characters in the play?"

The witches looked at each other, and several possibilities ran through Avery's head, but it was El who answered first. "It's possible. It sounds a bit like an enchantment."

"But how do you enchant an entire cast?" Briar asked. "And *who* would do that?"

Reuben leaned against the wall, crossing his arms. "The enchantment would have to be powerful, especially for someone to believe they were really that character. Who stabbed who?"

"A woman called Jamie who plays Brangain, stabbed a guy called Lawrence, who plays a character called Frocin. And this is where it gets really weird. In the play, Brangain is Queen Iseult's loyal servant, and Frocin is the guy who leaks Tristan and Iseult's love affair...or something of the sort." Newton shook his head, and threw the script on the table. "I need to read up on it properly."

"I knew it!" Hunter said, looking pleased with himself. He was sitting in a chair in the corner. "Life is imitating art! I wonder whose suggestion it was to do this play for Beltane?"

Despite Newton's obvious antagonism to Hunter, he asked, "You think they're linked?"

Hunter nodded. "I was telling the guys on the way here about the story. Essentially it's a love triangle, set in Cornwall. With Beltane passions rising, it seems a good play to choose, and it's set in Cornwall, so it's a great choice in many respects. It might be just that, a great choice of play. But equally—" he spread his hands wide. "It could be the perfect play to cause trouble!"

Reuben shuffled against the wall and looked sceptical. "Yeah, but most actors don't actually *become* their characters! It wouldn't matter how appropriate this play is to the occasion."

"Which brings it back to an enchantment," El said.

Newton nodded, looking thoughtful. "So potentially the choice of play is a good one for the occasion, and the consequences were unknown and accidental, or, this play was chosen deliberately and the enchantment—if that's what it is—and its consequences were known and planned." He leaned back in the chair. "I prefer the first option to someone deliberately plotting mayhem."

"Can we talk to the cast?" Avery asked, thinking it would be useful.

"Not tonight. Let's keep it official. But I gather the show must go on! They'll be back here tomorrow to do a proper dress rehearsal. I'm hoping you can speak to them then, try to sound this out. In the meantime, I'm giving you free rein of this area. Poke around, see what you can find."

"Where was the guy stabbed?" Alex asked.

"In the kitchen area, which is currently out of bounds."

"Is the victim okay?" Briar asked, concerned.

"He'll live. His attacker is in denial. She says she can't remember doing it, and is down the station as we speak. The rest of the cast is shaken up, but determined to carry on."

"But no longer 'in character?'" Hunter asked, making air quotes.

"Not from the last I heard," Newton admitted, looking hopeful. "However, I want you to be very careful! If this play is enchanted, somehow, I'm really worried there could be more violence, but I can't shut it down. I have no grounds to."

"We'll be careful," Avery told him. "I have no wishes to be stabbed or enchanted, thanks. But," she looked at the others, growing excited, "I am really intrigued to find out what's going on! I can ask Dan more about his friend tomorrow. Maybe get some more insider knowledge."

"Who is Dan's mate?" Newton asked.

"I can't remember," she said, trying to recall the details of their conversation.

"Well, find out," Newton said, rising to his feet and heading to the door. "He's your way in tomorrow." He stepped into the corridor and checked his watch. "You've got an hour before I lock this place up for the night. Long enough?"

"For now," Alex said, and Newton nodded, heading back to the main hall. Then Alex looked at the others. "Wow! I suggest we split up to look around."

Reuben nodded. "This place isn't that big, so shouldn't take very long. But, what exactly are we looking for?"

"Anything that looks odd!"

Reuben grunted. "I was hoping for more specifics from our psychic! Didn't you say you were having funny dreams? Are they related to this?"

Alex stilled for a moment as he stared into space. "Bloody hell. You might be right. I did see people wearing old-fashioned costumes, but they were surrounded by forest. Well," he hesitated, "it was a tangle of branches and vines."

They all stood, ready to investigate behind the stage, and El said, "They're planning to perform at the castle on Saturday afternoon, right by Ravens' Wood. Maybe that's what your dreams are about."

"Maybe," Alex said, nodding. "You know, it could be a haunting that's causing this issue."

"It could," Briar agreed. "But it could also be a cursed object, and we won't know until we start looking."

"Why is the final performance on during the afternoon and not the evening?" Reuben asked, looking confused.

"Because the Beltane parade is in the evening, and they don't want the events to clash," El explained. "The parade has to be at night because of the bonfire, the torchlight procession, and the fire jugglers."

Hunter stripped his jacket and shirt off, ready to turn into his wolf, revealing toned abs and the pale scars he'd sustained in his fight with the previous pack Alpha. "I'll scent more if I change. Some of us should check out the lighting rigs, just in case."

"We'll do that. See you back here," Reuben said, volunteering himself and El, and without another word, they set off down the dimly lit passageway.

"Let's head to the storage rooms," Briar suggested to Hunter, "and you two could check the other dressing rooms."

"Sounds good," Avery started to say, and then pulled Alex out of the room they were in as Hunter went to drop his trousers. "We'll start down here," she called over her shoulder, just in time to see Hunter's roguish smile as he watched her go. "I swear he does that on purpose," Avery grumbled to Alex. "I really don't need to see him naked."

Alex laughed. "I'm pleased to hear you say that. Bloody exhibitionist shifters!"

They headed into the next room, which was as small and cramped as the one they'd left. It was decorated in a similar manner, and again a rack of clothes was in the corner, mainly female. Avery headed straight to them, feeling their fabric. "These seem to be of pretty good quality. I didn't expect that for a local production."

"These Beltane celebrations are a big deal to the town," Alex reminded her. "Lots of visitors are coming, and the council wants the performance to be as good as possible. Stan popped into the pub the other day. They've granted the production some money for costumes and better props." He gestured at the medieval dresses. "They sourced them from a few places. It's the same for the Beltane procession through the town. They've spared no expense for the costumes there, either."

"Really?" Avery asked, stroking the fine embroidery on the dresses. "I suppose that makes sense. Since the Walk of the Spirits at Samhain, there's a huge weight of expectation on this event." The events of previous years had always been good, and the standards high, but Samhain had really put White Haven on the map. However, they weren't the only ones putting on Beltane events. A few towns had their own celebrations planned.

Alex pulled out drawers and rummaged through the makeup. "White Haven is booked solid from this weekend onwards, and so are the surrounding towns. The performance at the castle is sold out!"

"What if it rains?"

"It will be here instead, but I think Stan is making offerings to the Gods." Alex looked over his shoulder at her and laughed.

"He should try the Goddess. Women are far more helpful," she suggested with a smirk. She turned her attention back to the costumes. "You know, I can't feel anything remotely spell-like with these dresses. I'd wondered if these had been bewitched in some way, but of course, they haven't even worn them yet."

"It depends on the strength of the spell. If it's strong enough, just being in their proximity would be sufficient." He started looking though the wigs and hats, and she joined him, until they both admitted that there wasn't anything that felt remotely like magic in the room.

They moved down the corridor methodically, but there were only another couple of small dressing rooms to look through. An additional door housed one big room, which they reasoned most of the cast would use, and again it was full of props and costumes. Once they'd finished there, they poked around in cleaning cupboards, finally bumping into Reuben and El returning from the platforms above them.

El looked invigorated. "This place is amazing! Behind stage is so much fun."

"And hazardous," Reuben added. "Fall from up there, and your brains would be mush."

"What's up there?" Alex asked.

"A couple of gantries to access the lights and the back drops, but nothing too sophisticated. And I didn't see a Phantom of the Opera, either!"

"And no sign of magic, I presume?"

"None."

Avery sighed, frustrated. "None where we've looked, either. From what Dan said to me, they rehearse at peoples' homes, normally. This would only be the first or second time they have been here."

"So whatever is affecting them wouldn't have been here," El reasoned.

"It might have exacerbated it," Reuben suggested. "Anyway, let's head back to the dressing room, see if Briar and lover boy have found anything."

Hunter was pulling his t-shirt on when they entered the room, and Briar was sitting at the table looking at the script that Newton had left there.

"Any luck?" Avery asked, fearing they hadn't found anything. They both looked disappointed and frustrated.

"None," Briar confirmed. "But what's the one thing they would all have had access to for weeks?" She lifted the script and waved it. "This!"

"Of course!" El said. "And? Anything magical?"

"No."

"So, what did you suggest it for, doofus?" Reuben exclaimed.

Briar looked exasperated. "Because there is more than one script, dummy! This is a modern copy—fresh paper, pretty clean. What if there are older scripts lying around that have been enchanted, or cursed, or whatever you want to call it?"

"Briar!" Alex said, grabbing the script from her and scanning it. "That is a stroke of genius!"

She shrugged. "We don't know if I'm right, yet, but it's the most obvious common element."

"And we can't check that out until tomorrow when they resume rehearsals, because they must have their lines with them," Avery pointed out.

While they were talking, Newton returned, and he looked hopeful. "Please tell me you found something."

"Maybe," Briar told him, tentatively. "There's nothing backstage, but I think the common source for whatever's going on here might be the scripts—or some of them." She looked at the others. "Who can come here tomorrow and speak to the cast? I can't, I'm afraid. I can't leave Eli on his own, we're far too busy. I've even roped Hunter in to help me."

Hunter winked. "Spending all day with you is a pleasure, and besides, I feel I should keep an eye on that ladies man, Eli."

"You really don't need to," Briar said, chastising him, but Avery could see she looked pleased.

"I can't make it, either," Alex said. "I'm working tomorrow afternoon, and it's too short notice to get someone to cover."

"I can," El said, eagerly. "We're busy, but nothing that Zoey can't cope with." Zoey was a Wiccan and had worked with El for the last couple of years. Recently, another friend of hers had also started working part-time in the shop on weekends to free El up to make jewellery in her workshop behind the shop.

"So can I," Avery said, nodding. "Dan and Sally will be fine for a few hours. I can check with Dan to see what time they'll be rehearsing. His mate will know."

Reuben grinned. "Count me in." He rubbed his hands together. "Beltane is hotting up guys!"

Ten

"You think the script is *cursed*?"

"Or something like that," Avery speculated, as Dan looked at her in disbelief. "It's just a theory at this stage. I need to get into the rehearsal this afternoon to speak to the cast. Can you arrange it with your mate?"

"Harry? Sure. It shouldn't be a problem." Dan put his coffee cup down and pulled his phone from his back pocket. "I was going to call him anyway after what happened last night. I'm just relieved he wasn't involved."

It was Saturday morning, and Avery and Dan were talking in low voices behind the counter at Happenstance Books. Avery had arrived late to work, as she hadn't gone to bed until nearly three in the morning, and she still felt knackered. This was the first moment she'd had to speak to Dan, as the shop had been so busy. Unfortunately, the customers—locals and tourists—were full of chatter about the stabbing the previous night. A few were worried, but most were intrigued, and if anything, interest in the play had shot up. A couple of locals had informed them that the TV news team had been reporting from outside the theatre, and Avery was relieved there'd been no photographers there the previous night.

Avery looked out the window while Dan called his friend. There was a buzz about White Haven today. The pavement was crowded with people, cars crawled down the streets, and there was a general air of anticipation, helped by the good weather. April was always so changeable, but today there were blue skies with no wind, which meant people strolled rather than hurried between shops. The sea front would look amazing, she just knew it, and she looked forward to heading down there later.

Dan looked bleak when he finished his call. "He sounds terrible!"

"I'm not surprised. One of the cast members went nuts and stabbed another."

"It's more than that," Dan said, worried. "He sounds even more intense than he did the other day!"

"What did he say?" Avery asked, alarmed.

Dan looked around to make sure no one was close enough to hear, but lowered his voice anyway. "Harry said, 'Frocin was asking for it. He should learn not to meddle.'" Dan's eyes were wide. "What the fuck? It sounds like he condones it! And who calls a cast member by their character's name?" Dan rubbed his hands through his hair until it stuck up wildly on his head.

Avery felt a chill run through her. "That sounds bad. Very bad."

"Bad? It sounds nuts!"

"What character does Harry play?"

"Er, Governal, I think."

The name sounded familiar, and Avery struggled to think of why. And then it struck her. "Newton interviewed him last night. He said he struggled to recall his real name, and insisted he was truly called Governal."

Dan's eyes widened further. "You mean he couldn't remember his name was Harry?"

"No." Dan fell silent in shock, and Avery recalled what Hunter had said about the play. "What do you know about this story?" she asked, keeping her voice as low as Dan's.

"A bit," he said, shrugging. "It's a famous Cornish tale that precedes the King Arthur, Guinevere, Lancelot love story. It's thought to have influenced it, and Romeo and Juliet, and it's set in the Arthurian world. In some tales, Tristan is a knight at King Arthur's court. The story is bound up with the myth of Lyonesse, too."

"Lyonesse?" Avery asked, thinking it sounded vaguely familiar. "Why do

I know that name?"

"It's an island that supposedly lay off the Cornish coast, beyond Land's End somewhere, maybe near Scilly, but it sank beneath the waves. Tristan, from the play, was the heir to the Lyonesse throne, but it disappeared while he was at King Mark's court." Seeing Avery's blank expression, he elaborated. "The King Mark that in the play was married to Iseult, who Tristan had fallen in love with."

"Oh!" Avery said, as she remembered. "Of course I've heard of Lyonesse. It's a bit like the Atlantis tale. A mystical isle that was somehow lost beneath the waves. And a legend, right? Not real?"

"Depends on who you ask. Many people believe that Lyonesse once existed. I can read up on it if you like, get some more details." Dan looked pleased to be able to offer help where he could. He had extensive knowledge of many myths and legends, and what he didn't know, he was happy to research.

"Yes please, that would be really useful. Hunter is familiar with the story, but I'm not sure if he knows about the legends behind it."

Dan nodded thoughtfully. "And many of them are legends, Avery. It's tied up with Arthurian myth, and Cornwall is rife with it. It blends so well with our past, it's hard to know where stories end and reality begins."

"Interesting you should say that, when clearly the cast doesn't seem to know the difference, either." She paused, thinking. "How well do you know your mate? I mean, is it years, or more recent?"

"A good ten years, at least. We played on the same football team, and we've all stayed in touch. He's a normal bloke, Avery. He's married too, with a kid. I don't want him to be possessed by his character's spirit, or whatever you call it."

"It's not possession...well, we don't think it is." As she spoke, she saw Dan's face change, his expression harden.

"Avery, you know bugger all right now, so you can't rule it out."

"True," she said, chastened. "Can I go this afternoon? It's really important."

He nodded. "Yes. But I told a little lie, just in case you didn't hear me."

"What little lie?"

"I said you were really interested in acting and were thinking of joining a local company, or getting acting lessons, and would he mind if you and a couple of friends came to see the rehearsal, to really get a feel for things. He said yes."

Shock was her overriding emotion at his admission. "You said we were interested in acting?" Her voice sounded shrill.

"Yes! What did you want me to say? 'My friends are interested in the occult and think you've been enchanted, and they need to come and check you out? Oh, and by the way, they're all witches.' Pull the other one!"

"Sorry, of course," she said, trying to placate Dan. She'd never seen him look so cross, and she knew it was because he was worried. "You're right. Bollocks. Wait until I tell El and Reuben."

White Haven Little Theatre basked in mid-afternoon sunshine, revealing nothing of the unfortunate events of the night before.

It was an ornate structure built of red brick with an impressive entrance, and it seemed to glow in the afternoon light. It was surrounded by other Victorian-era buildings, which had all been converted to restaurants and shops with flats above them.

Avery was loitering across the road, at the start of a small lane that wound between buildings to the seafront where there was also a large car park. She could smell the water, and the faint scent of blossoms. This part of White Haven wasn't as quaint as the centre, and the shops were more mainstream, but it was still charming, and there were the standard hanging baskets and Beltane decorations in the windows. She hadn't been waiting long when El and Reuben arrived together, strolling up the lane from the beach.

El grinned at her. "Are we all set?"

"We are. I'm intrigued as to what we're going to find in there," Avery admitted.

Reuben looked bemused as he gazed across the road at the entrance. "I'm not sure I can really sell myself as the acting type, but I'll try."

El sniggered. "You always ham everything up. You'll do just fine. I've been reading the story of *Tristan and Iseult* this morning, just to get familiar with the tale. It's pretty convoluted!"

"I know," Avery said, nodding. "According to Dan, the legend is very typical of tales of this sort. They can be unbelievable in places, but were designed to highlight loyalty, fealty, and the all-consuming power of love."

"Do we know what role Harry is playing?" Reuben asked.

"Governal, the guy who couldn't remember his own name last night." Avery checked her watch. "It's time. We're to go to the side door where we went in last night, and I have to text him. He'll meet us there."

"Why can't we go through the front?" El asked. "The café is open."

"It's easier, apparently, because the main doors to the auditorium are padlocked for now."

Within minutes of Avery texting, Harry opened the side door and looked suspiciously at them. "Avery?"

This was worrying, he didn't look particularly welcoming, but Avery smiled brightly anyway. "Yes, and you must be Harry?"

Harry was of average height with a stocky build, short, light brown hair, and a thick neck. He was also wearing a medieval costume, rich with colour and embroidery that made him look regal. He nodded, and looked up at Reuben and El, who stood behind her. "These your friends?"

"Yes, Reuben and El. We're all aspiring actors!"

El and Reuben followed suit, greeting him enthusiastically, and Reuben gave him a hearty handshake.

"I should warn you," Harry said as he drew back, allowing them inside, "that we're all a bit shaken up after last night." He ran his hand through his hair, looking distracted and anxious. "To be honest, if it wasn't Dan asking, I'd have said no...but he's a good mate."

"We really appreciate it," Avery said, at her most charming. "I know it's bad timing, but we wanted to see a proper dress rehearsal."

He nodded. "Sure, just be aware that things are a bit tense at the moment. Some of the actors are still dressing, but the rest of us have gathered in the auditorium. Follow me."

Harry led them up the corridor, in the opposite direction they'd gone the previous night, past some steps that led to the side of the stage, and then pushed through a door and into the main hall. For a moment, Avery's attention was completely on the building, and she knew El's was, too.

The ceiling was vaulted high overhead, and the walls were painted a rich red embellished with gold. There was a dress circle that Avery had forgotten about, which extended a third of the way into the space, and there were also a few boxed seats to the left and right. At the back were a series of double doors that led to the entrance and the small café and bar, and turning around, Avery saw the stage, the curtains currently drawn back as a few people scurried around dressing the admittedly simple set.

"Wow," she said, unable to contain her surprise. "It's been years since I've been here. I've forgotten how impressive it is."

Harry nodded. "I know. We're lucky to have such a great place to perform in. It needs a bit of attention though, to be honest. The paint is peeling in a few places, and it needs more heating, but it's still better than a school or community centre."

El was still staring, and she said, "I'm in love! It's fantastic." El loved drama in her decor, so Avery wasn't surprised by her statement, but Harry had already moved on. He led them to the group of actors who were standing by the front row, immediately below the stage.

"Hey everyone, these are the people I was telling you about, my mate's friends. They've come to watch the dress rehearsal."

An overweight man with grey hair who was dressed in everyday clothes nodded at them and said, "Sorry, you're going to find this will be chaotic for a while, dress rehearsals always are. I'm Anthony, the director." He nodded behind him. "Just grab a seat, and we'll be underway soon."

Most people turned and nodded at them in silent greeting, distracted, but quickly went back to the scripts and their own discussions. However, Avery saw Josh and Emma, and they gave them a quick smile and wave before turning their attention to Anthony.

Avery, El, and Reuben did as instructed and settled themselves a few rows back, close enough to hear Anthony talking to two actors who it seemed were replacing the two missing ones: the woman who had stabbed the man, and the victim.

"Are you sure you're okay for tomorrow, Gail?" Anthony asked a blonde woman, wearing a plain medieval dress.

"Yes!" she insisted, her face flushed. "I've been helping Jamie learn her lines, and it's not a big part. I'll be fine!"

"And what about you, Tim?" he said, turning to a short man with grey hair and a red face, also in costume.

"It's a small part, and I'll be fine," he said with a note of impatience. "I've been in this company a long time and I haven't let you down yet!"

"That must be Brangain and Frocin," El said in a hushed voice to Avery. "She's Iseult's maid, and he's the dwarf who betrayed their affair to the King."

Reuben leaned in close, too. "He doesn't look like a dwarf."

"Maybe he'll act like one!" El answered. "He's sometimes played as a hunchback."

While the cast argued and dithered, Avery watched them, noting that many still carried their scripts, some of which looked old and worn. The stage beyond them was set up to look like a ship's deck, the backdrop the ship's rigging and the sea beyond. The company was bigger than Avery had anticipated, and from what she'd gathered from Dan, if you weren't acting, you helped with production. A few of the experienced actors also took turns to direct.

After another ten minutes of robust discussion, and a tearful outburst from some of the cast about the previous night, most actors headed backstage, and Anthony shouted over their heads, "Lower the lights!"

Within seconds the light in the hall darkened, and the stage was lit up.

"They must be practicing the lighting, too," Reuben murmured, looking around to see where the lighting controls were.

"They have to," El said. "It's part of rehearsals—and the first show is tonight! At least they don't need to worry about that at the castle."

The play began, but it became clear there were going to be many interruptions in the action. The prompter was positioned at the side of the stage, and as Anthony corrected where they stood, lines were forgotten, and they restarted the scene.

"Anthony," Josh shouted down, "can we just run through the whole scene, and you correct us after? I just want to get a feel for it, with costumes and the set."

"Sure," Anthony shouted back. "Go from the top."

Avery was concerned less about the performance than the scripts, and she leaned forward, trying to see where the actors had left their copies, because obviously the actors on the stage weren't holding them. After a quick scan of the front seats, she saw a few at the end of the row, and crept out of her seat to grab a copy. Anthony, and a cast member who sat next to him, were so absorbed with the performance they didn't notice, and she was sure wouldn't care.

"This isn't that old," Avery whispered as she turned the pages. There was enough light to see that the pages were grubby, but it looked like modern copy.

"It looks like the one Briar found yesterday," El agreed. "On first impression, no magic here."

"I agree," Reuben said, frowning at the script. He glanced up at the stage. "Those two, however, have got real chemistry. Anthony is letting them get on with it, and the more they act, they more I feel their intensity. Watch."

Avery leaned back, watching Josh and Emma go through the scene, and Reuben was right. It was easy to get caught up in their emotions, and that could be a credit to their acting, or it could be something else. Even as the scene progressed, and other actors came and went, Avery felt as if a spell were stealing over her, and it was only with the greatest effort that she reminded herself that the performance wasn't real.

Then suddenly the hall they sat in disappeared, and there was only the stage. For a moment, Avery heard the sound of the ocean, the calls of the seagulls, and smelt brine. When Brangain brought the potion out to give to Tristan and Iseult, Avery jolted out of her reverie, wanting to cry out for the pair not to take the potion. She jerked upright, her hand gripping El's arm, but that was enough to bring her to her senses, and she glanced at El and Reuben, who were also blinking as if coming out of a trance.

"What the hell happened there?" Reuben whispered, his eyes wide. "I was gone."

"Shh," El hissed, her finger to her lips. "Look at the potion!"

"It's not a bloody potion," he hissed back, "it's coloured water!"

But the water did seem to smoke in the seconds before the actors downed it. Within minutes the scene had ended as they declared their love for each other, and there was a moment's silence until Anthony shouted, "Cut! That was, er, excellent. I'd like to suggest a couple of things."

Anthony sounded as if he was having trouble focussing, and that was doubly true for Emma and Josh. They were locked within each other's gaze, motionless, and it was with the greatest difficulty that they turned and looked down at their director.

"That's just plain freaky," El said, looking at Avery and Reuben. She sat between them, the script in her clenched hands. "That was more than just acting, right?"

Avery nodded, trying to gather her thoughts. "That was definitely an enchantment; I felt it steal over us. It was almost imperceptible, but it was there. So," she nodded at the script, "why can't we feel it in this?"

Reuben leaned in. "Maybe there's another script—a master?" he suggested.

"Harry is playing Governal, Tristan's advisor," Avery whispered back. "He's obviously a support for Tristan, as Brangain is for Iseult. That could explain why she stabbed Frocin, who essentially betrayed her mistress, and why Harry agreed that he deserved it."

"It's nuts!" El said, sounding like Dan. "You can't justify a stabbing because of a bloody play!"

"Unless you're bewitched," Reuben reminded her.

Avery looked to where Anthony was now standing and discussing the scene. "We need to get backstage. Let's sneak around the back. No one will notice, and I'm sure they won't mind. We need to see what the mood is like there."

El pointed to the second row where there were still a few cast members watching. "I'm going to speak to them, get a feel for what they think. You two carry on, and I'll see you when you've finished."

With that they all stood, hoping to find some answers.

Eleven

Backstage at the theatre was buzzing with activity, and the cast members were spread out, absorbed in their preparations, allowing Avery and Reuben to explore.

Some of the cast were grouped in the wings, waiting to go onstage; others were rehearsing lines in the dressing rooms. Additional members who weren't acting were instead liaising between the front and backstage, checking props and costumes. Everyone gripped scripts, and while some people looked nervous, others were laughing and joking. Avery estimated that there were about 20 or 30 company members of a variety of ages and sexes.

However, she definitely detected an air of tension underlying the laughter and general excitement. They received a few inquisitive glances and mumbled greetings, but it was a young woman of Avery's age who finally spoke to them when they reached the large dressing room. It looked as if she was checking the costumes. "You two are Harry's friends, right?"

"A friend of a friend, actually," Avery explained. "He's doing us a favour by letting us look around today."

She shrugged. "That's fine. We're used to people coming to see if it's something they're interested in. I'm Alison, by the way."

"Avery, and Reuben," Avery said, introducing them both. She wondered whether it was too soon to mention the stabbing, but knew she needed to be fairly direct to get the information they needed. "How are your friends? We saw the news about the incident last night."

"Oh, that!" Alison said, looking warily at them. "That was pretty terrible, and quite unusual. We don't normally stab each other! Many of us are good friends. We even all went to Gail's thirtieth birthday party at the pub the other day! Please don't think we're normally like this."

Alarm bells started ringing for Avery, but she tried to sound casual. "A party? That sounds fun. Where was it?"

"The Flying Fish." Alison looked distracted. "Why would we hang out together if we hated each other? This is not right."

The Flying Fish. Avery's thoughts flew back to the woman who had been crying in her shop. She must have been at the same party, and must have been affected by the cast, who no doubt were already bewitched at that point. However, Alison was still talking, as if pleased to unburden herself.

"I think things were a bit tense last night—not that tension excuses it, of course. But Lawrence is fine, fortunately. Jamie stabbed him in the shoulder, so he'll recover, but obviously he won't be performing now."

Reuben nodded encouragingly. "Great news. The possibility of getting stabbed in the name of art did worry me," he joked.

Alison stumbled over her words in her haste to reassure them. "No! That never happens. This performance is a big deal, and I think we're all nervous—you know, we want it to be perfect!"

"Why is it a big deal?" Avery asked.

"Because the council approached us directly to do the play. There are other local theatre groups they could have asked, but chose us, so we feel really privileged. This will give us a real boost."

"And a chance for some of us to actually get noticed!" A voice said from behind them.

They turned around to see a stern-faced, middle-aged man dressed in an elaborate costume. He was sitting in the corner, rehearsing his lines, but he stood and joined them. "Hi, I'm Ian, and I'm playing King Mark." He shook their hands.

"What do you mean, 'get noticed?'" Reuben asked.

"I'd like to act professionally, a few of us do. This play will get a lot of attention." He swelled with pride and expectation as he said it, and Avery wondered if this was something he'd wanted to achieve for years.

"Oh, right," Reuben nodded. "I presume you mean because of the crowds."

"Yes. Normally we only get a couple hundred people watching us, but it will be a lot more this week. More importantly, it also means reviews by the papers, right Alison?"

She nodded enthusiastically. "Yeah, this is really important for some people. I'm not interested in doing this full-time, like Ian. This is just fun for me, so I was happy to be backstage on this one. We all take it in turns to work as crew." She looked at Ian with an almost pleading expression, and Avery noticed her hands were clasped together tightly, the knuckles turning white. "I was telling them that we think it's nerves that is making everyone tense."

Their eyes met for a moment, and it seemed as if something unsaid passed between them. Finally he nodded, almost reluctantly. "Probably. It's been a weird one. This play has got under everyone's skin." He laughed nervously, but the smile didn't meet his eyes.

"Even yours?" Reuben asked, watching him closely.

Ian looked defensive. "I just want to put in a good performance."

An older man stuck his head around the door. "Ian, we need you."

Ian nodded. "Sorry. Must go."

After he'd left the room, Alison said, "I should get on. I need to make sure the costumes are labelled and ready for the next act."

It was clear she didn't want to discuss anything else, but Avery was beyond caring about her sensibilities right now. It was time to use a little magic, something to relax Alison and invite confidences. She used a gentle spell, sending it swirling around Alison, and asked, "What do you think is happening with this play?"

Alison's resistance crumbled. "I think everyone is taking their characters too seriously. There's an undercurrent of fear and suspicion, and the cast is taking sides and whispering about each other. It's insidious, and getting worse. Jamie was so incensed last night with Frocin's—sorry, Lawrence's," she said, correcting herself, "interfering ways that she just lost it. She chased him into the kitchen and grabbed the nearest thing to hand." She buried her face in her hands for a second, and when she looked up again, her eyes were wide with disbelief. "Jamie screamed as soon as it happened, as if she couldn't believe what she'd done, and Lawrence roared and raged. We ran in, and I couldn't believe it. There was blood pouring down Lawrence's back, and the knife was on the floor, and then Jamie just started screaming again. She kept looking at her hands, and then at Lawrence. It was like she couldn't remember doing it!"

Alison staggered to the closest chair and sat down, her hands gripped together, and she stared at the floor.

Reuben pulled a chair up and sat down too, his tone comforting. "But it hasn't affected you. You sound quite rational."

"I haven't been rehearsing. I'm not even a back-up." Alison lowered her voice and leaned closer, and Avery crouched to listen. "Everyone who picks up that script is taking themselves very seriously. Talk about method acting! But—" she shivered and looked around nervously. "I think this theatre has made it worse!"

"In what way?"

"Well, we only arrived here last night, and although things have been tense before, they just got worse, really quickly. I think it's haunted!"

Haunted? Avery groaned inwardly. *This would make everything far more complicated.*

Reuben glanced at Avery and then said to Alison, "What makes you say that?"

"You think I'm stupid, don't you?" she accused, suddenly mutinous.

"No! I believe in those kinds of things," he reassured her, and his glamour rolled around Alison again, soothing her. "Why do you think it's haunted?"

"There are cold spots, icy spots, that I can't explain, and there is a prickling feeling of being watched—a feeling of..." She struggled to find the words, and then said, "Malevolence! And I keep smelling perfume, too, when there's no one else around. And I'm not the only one to notice, either!"

"You've performed here before, right? Notice anything then?"

Alison shook her head. "It's an old theatre, it always feels a bit creepy, but nothing like what I've felt this time around."

Reuben nodded, as if coming to a decision. "Okay, thanks Alison. You'd really like to show us a script now, an old one. Can you get one for us?"

Her eyes clouded for a moment, and then she turned around, scanning the room. "Most of them have gone, but there might be a couple left in the original box."

She walked to a long table crowded with props on the far side of the room, knelt down, and after pushing aside some blankets, picked up a box on the floor. When Alison returned to them, her eyes were still slightly unfocussed. "This is what the council gave us."

Reuben took the box from her, letting Avery look inside. At the bottom were a couple of slim books approximately A5-sized, with *Tristan and Iseult* written on the front. The covers looked worn, grubby, and yellow with age, and as Avery lifted them out she felt a tingle of magic run through her. She looked victoriously at Reuben, and then smiled gratefully at Alison. "I'll borrow both of them, if that's okay?"

"Of course."

Avery tucked the scripts into her bag as Reuben put the box down and flashed Alison his most charming smile and a soothing wave of magic. "Thanks, Alison. I'm sure things will settle down. You're probably right—it's just nerves. And hey, ghosts can't hurt you!"

Alison smiled. "Let's hope so."

Avery stood, eager to leave now, and said, "We'll leave you to it. I can see you're busy. Just one more question first. Who gave you the scripts?"

"Stan, you know, our Druid."

Stan! *Was he behind this? Surely not.* Avery tried to hide her confusion, smiling quickly. "Thanks for your time, and break a leg! That's the saying, right?"

"Right," she confirmed, already turning back to the costumes, and Avery and Reuben headed for a final tour of the backstage before joining El.

The bright sunshine of late afternoon was a shock after the darkness of the old Victorian building, and Avery took a deep breath of fresh sea air and lifted her face to the sun. "I'm so pleased to be out of there!"

"You and me both," Reuben said, raising his pint in salute before taking a long drink.

El, Avery, and Reuben were sitting around a table in the courtyard garden of The Wayward Son, sheltered from the sea breeze by the walls covered in a trellis and climbing plants. The sun would sink behind the walls soon, but while it lasted, Avery enjoyed it.

"What do we think of Stan's involvement in all this?" El asked. She put her pint aside and picked up one of the old scripts, handling it gently. "Wow. There's definitely something here."

Avery sipped her wine and eyed the script as if it might bite. "Stan can't possibly be involved, not malevolently, anyway." She looked at El and Reuben. "I mean, come on, it's Stan!"

"I agree," Reuben said. "Either someone suggested this to him, or he just found the scripts and realised what a good choice of play it would be for Beltane."

El opened the script out on the table, and started to examine it methodically, turning the pages slowly. "But we still have so many questions, the most important being, what spell is on this, and who put it there?"

"And can we break it?" Avery added. "Or at least counteract its effects."

"I want to know where it's been hidden all this time," Reuben said. "We need to speak to Stan, which shouldn't be hard, as he's popping up everywhere at the moment. In fact, he's coming to the nursery tomorrow. He wants to check on the pots we've planted up for along the quay."

"More pots?" Avery asked, surprised.

"Of course! Stan is obsessed with Beltane." Reuben rolled his eyes. "My staff are really good at this, but he can't help adding his suggestions. However, the council is paying us a lot of money, so—" he shrugged. "We put up with it. I'll make sure I'm there when he arrives tomorrow."

"Of course, I forgot you were open seven days a week," Avery said.

He nodded. "We're flat-out now. Spring is our busiest time of year." He sipped his pint thoughtfully. "I'll just praise his brilliance for choosing the play, get him talking—which isn't hard—and see what he says."

"What if someone did suggest it?" Avery asked, already trying to imagine who that could be. "Does that mean they know this script is bewitched?"

Reuben shrugged. "Let's wait and see what he says. We should focus on what we can work with—finding out how the spell works."

"It's odd, isn't it?" El said, looking up at them. "The spell has limits. The cast seem to be able to function normally most of the time, it's just when they're performing the play that it takes hold of them."

"I'm not so sure," Avery replied. "If the lead actors are having an affair, it suggests the enchantment is affecting them outside the play."

They talked through some theories, and within half an hour, Briar, Hunter, and Alex had joined them at the table, eager to hear what they'd found. Once they were settled with drinks and food had been ordered, Avery and Reuben updated them on their conversation in the dressing room, and then El shared what she'd discussed with the cast.

"I realised," El told the group, "that most of the cast had no idea that they were behaving so intensely—if that's the right word? But company members who were acting as crew could see that their behaviour was odd. There was tension among the cast, no doubt about that."

"Who did you speak to?" Alex asked.

"The guys who were playing the three Barons. In the play they are King Mark supporters, and hate Tristan. They were a tight bunch, just as you'd expect. I spoke to some others who had minor parts, and everyone seems to have taken a side."

"What happens to the Barons in the play?" Briar asked. As usual, the arrival of Hunter had given her a glow, and she sat next to him, looking like a flower in the sunshine, while he emanated protection.

Hunter answered. "They died—two at Tristan's hand. I'm not sure about the other."

Avery's eyebrows shot up in shock. "Shit! This is what I'm worrying about. If they meet violent deaths in the play, it could happen in real life!"

"Let's not forget that Tristan and Iseult die at the end, too!" Hunter reminded them.

"Do they?" Reuben asked, looking surprised.

Hunter nodded. "Yep. Just like Romeo and Juliet, remember. This story influenced many writers." While El hurriedly flicked through to the end of the script, Hunter summarised it. "Tristan was wounded in a fight and sends for Iseult to heal him. By this time he's married to another Iseult in Brittany—Iseult of the White Hands. She's obviously a bit cranky that he's sending for his old love to heal him, so lies and tells him that Iseult the Fair hasn't arrived on the ship. He dies from sorrow. However she really is there, and when Iseult the Fair runs to his side and finds him dead, she dies, too."

Reuben snorted with derision. "You can't just die for no reason!"

Hunter smirked at him. "Not even from a broken heart?"

"No! That's bullshit!"

"It's medieval, courtly love!" Hunter reminded him.

"How do people swallow this rubbish?"

"You've clearly never been truly, passionately in love," Briar said, teasing him.

Reuben frowned at El. "Maybe I haven't? I'm not sure I'd die of a broken heart if you left me."

El looked mock offended. "What? Why not?"

"I mean, I'd be upset, of course, but *die*?"

Alex laughed. "It's a play, you tit. It's all about heightened love, and of course written in a time when fealty to your lord was a big deal!"

"Yes, it was," Hunter agreed. "To betray your lord, especially with his wife, was punishable by death. And a huge disgrace, of course."

Alex shook his head. "Well, I think this play is what I'm having dreams about. It has to be! People in medieval dress, in the forest—"

"Oh, yes," Hunter interrupted him. "The lovers ran off to live in the forest together too, forsaking their positions in society for each other—for a while, at least."

"Good grief," Reuben said, rolling his eyes again.

Alex continued, clearly intrigued. "I just assumed it was to do with their performance next to Ravens' Wood."

"And it might be," Hunter said with a shrug.

Avery sighed. "At least the actors playing them haven't run off together yet!"

"I still don't get what my image is of the sea and the thick mist on it," Alex said, still working through his dreams. "I had that one again last night, but this time it was as if something was visible in the mist."

Avery suddenly recalled her conversation with Dan that morning and gasped. "Oh, wow! What if it has something to do with Lyonesse?"

"That sounds familiar," Briar said with a frown.

Avery shared her conversation with Dan that morning, adding, "He's going to find out a bit more, but there must be plenty of stuff online."

"That makes sense, I guess," Alex said thoughtfully. "The isle is related to the story, so that's why it's in my dreams. But does this mean it will actually appear?"

"What if that's what this play and its spell is about?" El suggested, suddenly animated. "Maybe someone wanted to conjure up Lyonesse?"

Reuben groaned. "Why? Who even cares?"

"I have no idea," El answered, "but all of this is for something!"

"That's pretty big magic to conjure up an island from an enchanted script," Hunter pointed out, equally sceptical.

"And potentially there's still someone out there casting love spells," Briar added.

"Oh, no! I don't think there is," Avery said, remembering her conversation with Alison. "Gail, one of the cast members, had a party at The Flying Fish. I'm pretty sure that the woman who was crying in my shop was at that party. I think she was affected by the cast!"

Briar looked relieved. "Well, I guess that's something. Although, essentially that means the play is not only affecting the cast, but is capable of affecting anyone!"

Twelve

On Sunday morning, Avery and Alex slept late, Avery troubled by dreams of love and retribution, and when she finally awoke, it was to feelings of lust she couldn't control, and she rolled over to look at Alex.

Avery was acutely aware of the heat that blazed from him like a furnace. His sculpted muscles called to her fingers, and she traced his tattoos and stroked his shoulders and biceps, sliding around to his flat stomach. She trailed kisses along his neck and he stirred slowly under her touch. He rolled onto his back, catching her in his arms and pulling her on top of him, and desire burned in his eyes too, his hands igniting her skin. Again Avery lost all sense of herself as she indulged her needs, and when they finally got up and went downstairs for breakfast, Avery's cheeks were flushed. She found herself watching Alex surreptitiously over her coffee and toast, still trying to shake off her lustful thoughts.

He looked up from the Sunday newspaper that they had delivered and winked at her. "I'm loving Beltane. Long may these feelings last!"

"I always have these feelings," she protested.

"Not quite like this, you don't. The Goddess is being a wilful tease."

"But it's a bit scary, isn't it? It's like my hormones are out of control. Like I'm a teenage boy somehow."

Alex grimaced. "I'm glad you're not. Besides, you're too clean and don't eat half your bodyweight for breakfast." His eyes darkened. "I know what you mean, though. My hormones are raging too, and yes, it's like I'm a teenager again. Fortunately I'm not, so I'll do the washing up—and then maybe we go for round two." He grinned as he left the table.

Once again, Avery wondered what would happen if these feelings occurred while they were with someone else, and her thoughts returned to Caspian and the kiss at Oswald's. Again she reminded herself that she had been very in control of her feelings then, despite the nudge from the Goddess. But knowing that he had feelings for her was odd, disturbing, and flattering. *What was Beltane doing to him?* She remembered his face that night at the crossroads, his look of utter vulnerability, and she remembered how his arms felt wrapped around her waist, the feel of his breath in her ear, and felt a surge of...what?

Avery blinked away her image of him, thankful that Alex was in the kitchen now. She swallowed her coffee and decided she needed more. This was just Beltane playing tricks with her mind and body. Her phone rang, and thankful for the interruption, she answered, "Hey Newton. How's it going?"

"Bloody awful," he said gruffly. "Mind if I pop in? I'm only ten minutes away."

"Sure." Avery felt flustered, needing to get dressed. *Would she start having lustful thoughts about Newton next?*

"Great. Be there soon."

He rang off, and after letting Alex know that he was on his way, Avery headed upstairs to get changed. While she was in her attic, she lit the fire and lamps, ready to examine the script later that morning. When they left the pub the night before, she and Alex had taken one copy of the play, and El and Reuben had taken the other, promising to share any findings with the others.

The script lay on the table now, unassuming with its worn yellowed pages, dog-eared and covered with scribbled notes. She laid her hand on it, and then jumped as a crackle of magic rippled across the page and slid up her arm.

"Ow!" she exclaimed loudly. "What the hell was *that*?"

That hadn't happened last night.

Before she could think to do anything about it, she heard Newton arrive downstairs and headed to meet him.

Newton looked tired, and although he was wearing his suit, indicating he'd been working, it looked rumpled. He sank onto the sofa as Alex gave him a coffee.

"Bloody hell," Alex exclaimed as he sat on a chair opposite him. "What have you been up to all night?"

"Do I look that bad?" he groaned.

"I'm afraid you do," Avery said, sitting on the sofa, too. "Don't say there's been more weird behaviour?"

"There was another stabbing victim last night—unrelated to the play, you'll be glad to know," he said hurriedly after seeing their questioning expressions. "It was in Truro. A big fight broke out as a few guys were coming out of a pub. They were a bit rowdy, which is nothing unusual on a Saturday night, but things went haywire over a woman."

Avery glanced at Alex. "Uncontrollable jealousy?"

"Sort of. A guy saw red after his girlfriend was chatted up, and his mates waited for the other guy, who also had mates..." He trailed off. "You get the picture. Unfortunately, the man who was stabbed died overnight, so now it's a murder investigation—not that there's much investigating to do. Everyone saw it happen." He looked at them both bleakly. "The question is, why would a normally mild-mannered man stab a guy to death for a cheeky chat up?"

"Holy shit," Avery said, horrified. "No history of violence, I take it?"

"Not according to all his mates, or his girlfriend. We have to consider domestic violence—men hide it well—but his girlfriend swears he's the nicest bloke, normally."

"And what about the man himself?" Alex asked.

"The offender?" Newton said. "Guilt-stricken and horrified. Says he can't remember anything but a blood red mist descending on him."

"Where did he get the knife from?" Alex asked.

"It was a broken bottle." He shook his head and gestured to his neck. "Nasty wound."

Avery sat back, feeling her energy drain from her. "This is odd. Beltane magic shouldn't be this strong, or so violent! Beltane is about love and fertility, the arrival of summer!"

"Some people's definition of love, and what to do in the name of it, is very different from yours, probably," Newton told her. "And everyone responds different to magic, surely."

Alex nodded in agreement. "This is wild magic, Avery, not like spells that we try to craft carefully. And you know love magic can have unexpected consequences."

"True." She thought again of Caspian, and again banished the image from her mind. "How are you, Newton? Any strange feelings or heightened emotions?"

"Yes, actually. I'm finding it hard to stop thinking about Briar. Especially knowing that Hunter is here." He looked at their surprised faces and smiled ruefully. "It is what it is. I had my chance and blew it. I'm an idiot."

Avery glanced at Alex, who looked as surprised at this admission as she felt, and she rushed to answer him, a wave of regret washing through her. "You're not an idiot. You had reservations about magic and being in a relationship with a witch, and you still do." Newton was looking at the floor now, and he nodded, but Avery couldn't see his expression. "I hope you're not thinking of having some kind of fight over her with Hunter, because I'm pretty sure you'd lose against a shifter."

He laughed, a trace of bitterness in his tone, and when he looked up, his face was resigned. "No. I have no uncontrollable jealous urges yet, and I hope it stays that way." He was still cradling his coffee, but he ran his free hand through his hair and sighed. "Ignore me, I'm just tired, and I'm certainly not immune to the Goddess and Green Man's wild magic. Instead, tell me what you've found out about the White Haven Players."

Alex told him about the script that Avery had found, and they led him upstairs to the attic so that he could see it. Newton paused at the threshold to the room, his eyes widening with surprise. "So, this is your spell room?"

Avery was already standing at the large wooden table that she and Alex both now used to prepare their spells, and she looked at him, puzzled. "Haven't you ever been up here before?"

He shook his head, and a smile of genuine pleasure spread across his face, stripping it of his weariness. "No, but I guess if I was going to imagine what a witch's spell room would look like, this would be it!"

Alex laughed. "We don't all have rooms like this. I certainly didn't in my flat, you manage with the space you have, but Avery is lucky enough to have the space."

Avery sat on the stool watching Newton work his way around the attic, pausing as he looked at the dried herbs and roots in bottles on her shelves, the herbs drying from the rafters overhead, the candles, incense, books, gemstones, her worn pack of tarot cards, Alex's scrying implements and other paraphernalia of magic, and then the spell books—all four of them—on the table. Their leather covers were marked with time, soft to the touch, and Avery was unable to pass any of them without stroking them, enjoying the thrill of magic that tingled on her hand.

"Surely you've seen Briar's workshop at the back of her shop," Avery said to him. "It's amazing. She has far more herbs, tinctures, potions, and balms than I'll ever have."

Newton finally tore his gaze away, meeting her eyes. "Yes, I have, but this has a different feel to it. Anyway, is this the script?" he asked, looking at the yellowed pages of the play under Avery's hand.

She handed it to hm. "It is. It looks normal enough, but we can feel the spell on it."

Newton took it from her gingerly, as if it might explode in his hand. "I can't feel a thing."

"Not surprising," Alex said, leaning on the table. "You're not a witch. To be honest though, we can only feel the presence of magic. We've got no idea what spell has been used, or its purpose. We're going to look at it properly today."

Newton slid the book across the table to them. "What will you do?"

Alex glanced at Avery, watching as she opened it tentatively because of the magic shock she'd had earlier. "Good question," he said. The room was already dim due to the sea fog outside, a normal occurrence at this time of year, and he spelled the lamps off, and then spelled a witch-light into the room so that it hovered above the table. "We'll see if this light reveals any unusual marks, runes, or sigils on the pages, for a start."

Curiosity was already eating away at Avery, and she started to turn the first pages, noting the annotations in pencil down the sides of the script with character notes and directions for the actor. It seemed this book had once belonged to the actress who played Iseult, as all the notes referred to her character.

"Nothing yet," she murmured, with Newton and Alex leaning over either shoulder. And then a rumble of excitement spread though her. "Stan said this play was last performed in the sixties. If this book were spelled then, surely there would have been problems with the performance. If we can find out the past performance dates, we might be able to narrow down when the spell was put on it, and by whom?"

Newton nodded with a trace of a smile. "We might find out what the consequences could be."

"You mean as the play continues," Alex said, intrigued. "Of course! That's a great idea! Good thinking, Avery."

"But how do we find out about when the play was performed?" Avery asked.

"Library records with old newspaper clippings?" Newton suggested.

"Or from Stan?" Alex said.

Newton headed to the stairs. "Great. It's a start. I'm going to leave you to it and head home for some sleep. Let me know what you find."

"Will do," Avery said, already turning back to the play as Alex pulled up a stool next to her, ready to begin their search in earnest.

By lunchtime, Avery and Alex had pored over every inch of the play, fuelled by coffee and reviving herbal teas, and they were still frustrated.

They had found several runes revealed only by witch-light, inscribed above key characters such as Tristan, Iseult, King Mark, Brangain, Governal, Frocin, and the three Barons. The sigils varied according to the names.

"Brangain's sigil is one of loyalty...I think," Alex said, consulting several books on symbols and runes that were now spread in front of them.

"And Tristan and Iseult's suggest intense love and obsession," Avery said, as she turned to her own notes. "I wonder if these increase with intensity as the play progresses, or whether just repeating the words helps the power build."

"King Mark's runes also manifest obsessive love and jealousy," Alex noted, "and the Barons' are wilful mischief and jealousy." He exhaled heavily as he looked at Avery. "But they, of course, are open to interpretation."

"Of course. But these are the most likely meanings."

Alex looked at the book, perplexed. "I can't discern a spell though, unless the sigils are it."

Avery nodded absently and checked her watch. "It's late! No wonder I'm hungry—I need lunch. Maybe we'll come back to it with new ideas after we've eaten." She shut the book, and as she did so, had another thought. "You know, when I was alone earlier, I put my hand on the book and it sparked at my touch...right up my arm."

"What were you doing?"

"I'd just lit the fire and the candles."

"You used elemental fire."

Avery nodded. "Yes, but why should that affect the play?"

Alex didn't answer, and instead he held the play lightly within his hands and said a spell. Nothing happened. Then he tried another, and then another. For a few moments, Avery was puzzled, and then she realised he was saying varieties of fire spells combined with revealing spells. He looked at her. "I'm going to try another, but I'm worried it will go up in smoke." Without waiting for a response, he held the book in his left hand and said another spell with a commanding tone, brushing his right hand across the cover. A wave of flame flared from his fingers, enveloping the script, and it rose from Alex's hand and floated in front of their eyes, turning slowly in the air. A faint prick of lines appeared on the cover, becoming more and more complex as they watched, until a complicated network of sigils blazed with light. In seconds it burned down to a glowing script, floating back into Alex's outstretched hands.

"What did you do?" Avery asked, looking at Alex and the book with amazement.

"It was a type of fire reveal spell, a little more intense than the others. I've seen it in my grimoire before but have never used it." Alex turned the play over in his hands, and it was clear the whole cover was a complex image of sigils weaving together that made it difficult to find where one stopped and another began. A single stream of runes ran around the edge of the cover. "It's a type of fire-writing—far more secure than plain old witch-light."

Avery shook her head with amazement. "I've heard of it, but never seen it on books—just stone or metal, perhaps."

"It's an unusual use for it, I'll admit."

Alex was already reaching for his phone. "I'll call El while I get started on lunch. She can do it too, and then we can all work on it. How's a BLT sound?"

"Fantastic!" Avery nodded and stood, stretching. "I'll top the fire up." She looked out of the window, expecting to see the fog that had rolled in that morning to have dissipated, revealing the shops opposite and the street below, but it was still there. "No wonder it's so dark! The sea fog is still here!"

Alex grumbled as he headed downstairs, "Bloody spring!"

Avery dispelled the witch-light, once again lighting candles and lamps, and also burning incense with scents to help concentration. She'd just finished adding logs to the fire when her phone rang, and she saw it was Reuben.

"Hey, Reuben," she said, moving this time to the windows that looked over her back garden, barely discernible through the fog. "Is it foggy by you?"

"Absolute pea soup," he answered. "The whole coastline is covered, from what I can see here. It hasn't deterred Stan, though."

"And?" Avery asked, her free hand gripping the wooden sill.

"The council was in need of office space and decided to clear out one of the rooms in the basement that was normally used for storage. They came across all sorts of interesting things, apparently. Old carnival gear, costumes they'd forgotten they had, advertising signs, and a large box full of these scripts and a few props. Some bright spark thought that Stan should know, and abracadabra..."

"So, it's quite by chance these were found?"

"Seems so."

Avery started to pace the room, a whirl of wind starting to flow around her in agitation. "Did he say what props there were?"

"A glass jar, some jewellery, and he couldn't remember what else."

"Holy cow," Avery said. "They could be spelled, too—or cursed, maybe. What if the glass jar they were using for the potion onstage yesterday was the one Stan found?"

"That's what I thought. I asked if we could see them, but he said he gave everything to the Players. I've asked him to have a real good think about anything else he may have found—with a little push of magic, of course. "

Avery picked up a scrap of paper with the air she was controlling and turned it gently in circles as she spoke, thinking quickly. "Do you think we should raid the theatre tonight to look for the objects?"

"I think we should discuss it over a pint. Let's meet at eight this evening."

Thirteen

The fog hadn't lifted all day, and that was unusual. Normally, it arrived at dawn and cleared by mid-morning as the breeze from the sea moved in, but instead it was still hanging around, seeping into everything.

On Sunday evening, Avery and Alex strolled through the ghostly White Haven streets to The Wayward Son to meet the other witches. The lights from the cafés and restaurants that were still open permeated the gloom, and the shops' window displays looked bright and inviting, though the bunting that hung across the streets was limp in the cold, damp air.

Avery shivered, and tucked herself under Alex's arm. "This is odd for the fog to last for so long," she complained.

"More Beltane weirdness?" Alex asked, squinting into the gloom.

"Maybe."

They paused in the square in the centre of the town, next to the maypole. A fine layer of moisture covered everything, dripping off the spring plants, and beading down the thick wooden maypole. Avery felt it on her cheeks and in her hair, and she shivered again.

"It's unnaturally quiet," Alex observed. "The fog must be muffling everything."

He was right, Avery silently agreed. You could normally hear the chatter of people walking down the street and from the inside of restaurants and pubs. "I can't even hear the sea," Avery said. The sea was the centre of everything in White Haven, and for any coastal town. The tides dominated when the pleasure and fishing boats set out, and how much beach was available to the locals and tourists to enjoy. When it was bright, the sun sparkled off the waves like glinting jewels, and when it was dull, it was like molten metal, absorbing everything. Storms were the most dramatic, when the waves snarled and dashed along the coast, spray flying across the roads, dragging up seaweed and driftwood until it lay thick upon the shore. But right now? She had no idea what it was doing.

As if he'd read her mind, Alex said, "Come on, let's head to the harbour before a pint. It won't matter if we're a few minutes late."

They hurried down to the quayside, and if anything the fog was even thicker on the shore, and Avery shivered again. "I can barely see the boats in the harbour."

"At least we can hear the sea here," Alex said, and then he went silent, listening for the insistent shush of waves on the beach, and the occasional splash of water against the harbour wall. He grabbed her hand. "Let's have a look at the theatre."

They passed the bright lights of the chippie and the seaside tourist shops lining the street, the array of children's fishing gear and seashell decorations in the windows, and headed up the small lane between the shops, lined with cafés, until they stood across the road from the old theatre, looking up at the brightly lit lettering over the entrance, just visible through the fog. "There's a performance tonight," Avery noted. "The café and bar are open."

Alex raised his eyebrows and squeezed her hand. "Indulge me." He pulled her across the road, pushing aside the huge glass doors leading into the foyer. It was then that Avery felt it—the feather-light tickle of magic across her skin and down her neck. Alex looked at her, his dark eyes full of concern. "I'm not entirely sure the fog is natural."

He headed to the counter and addressed the man polishing glasses behind the bar. "Was there a performance this afternoon, as well as tonight?"

It took him a moment to answer, and when he did, his eyes looked vague for a moment. "Yes, the two o'clock matinee. It was a full house, and it is again tonight."

"Great, thanks," Alex said, turning back to Avery and leading her toward the exit. "What time did we have lunch today?"

She frowned. "It was late, after two I think."

"And the fog seemed to get even thicker then—just as the next performance was happening."

"You really think they're related?" she asked in a low voice.

"Unfortunately, yes. Come on. Let's catch up with the others."

The Wayward Son was busy, a mix of locals and tourists filling most of the tables. The TV mounted on the wall was showing the football match from earlier that day, and a rush of warm air and the rich smell of food wrapped around Avery as they headed to the bar.

Simon, Alex's manager, was serving customers, but he nodded in greeting. Avery noticed Zee, the Nephilim, further down the bar polishing glasses with half an eye on the match. He caught Avery's eye and grinned at her, and they both headed to join him.

"Hey boss," he said to Alex. "Avery. How are you two?"

"Cold," Avery complained.

"And worried," Alex said, leaning on the bar. "Any trouble in here tonight?"

"No, but the atmosphere feels a little off," Zee confessed as he started to pour Avery's glass of red wine. He looked at her. "I presume this is what you want?"

"Always," she said gratefully, and immediately took a sip when he placed it in front of her.

"And a pint for you, Alex?"

"Skullduggery Ale, please," he answered. "What do you mean by 'off?'"

He frowned. "It's like there's this air of expectation, like we're all waiting for something to happen." He shrugged and passed Alex his pint, wiping down the counter as he did so. "But there's also this feeling of friskiness and goodwill, too. And the flirt-o-meter is high tonight."

Avery sniggered. "Flirt-o-meter?"

"Good word for it, right? Lots of giggling ladies giving me and Simon the eye, and I've had several *interesting* offers." He winked. "If you know what I mean."

"Well, that's better than jealous boyfriends and husbands threatening each other, I guess," Alex answered as he visibly relaxed. "And, hey, a lucky night for you!"

"It's the women who are getting competitive tonight, not the men. I've heard a few catty comments!" He grimaced. "Ouch! Women are mean!"

Avery glanced around at the patrons, thinking that Zee's word, "flirt-o-meter," was a good way to describe the giggles and overt looks between tables that night. She looked at him, noticing then that the sides of his hair had been shaved, leaving a thick mohawk on top of his head. "What's with the new hairstyle, Zee?"

He groaned. "I made a stupid bet with Shadow this morning while we were sparring in the barn. I said that she should shave her head if she lost the fight. Unfortunately, *I* lost."

Alex threw his head back, laughing loudly. "You really didn't think that through, did you?"

Zee ran his hand along his shaved scalp, grinning ruefully. "Nope. But, I think I like it!"

"I like it, too!" Avery told him, feeling an unexpected rush of desire to want to run her hands along Zee's very well defined muscles and ruffle his mohawk. *Damn Beltane!* She nudged Alex, hoping her illicit thoughts weren't written all over her face. "Come on, we'd better join the others. I presume they're in the back room?" she asked Zee.

"Yep."

"Before we go," Alex said, already pulling away from the bar, "any thoughts on the fog? Do you get anything weird from it?"

"Magically, you mean?" He nodded. "It's feels unnatural. But it's purpose? No idea."

"Bollocks. That's what I thought, too. All right, cheers Zee," Alex said, turning away.

Briar, Hunter, El, and Reuben were in the middle of a discussion when they joined them at the table in the back room, and Reuben explained, "I've just updated them on Stan's news."

Briar was holding El's copy of the play. "I'm so intrigued! Who on Earth did this?"

"It's certainly not an amateur spell caster," Avery reasoned. "The spell is too good."

"And complex," El agreed. "Thanks for the tip, Alex. It took a few attempts until I achieved it. The weaving of the sigils on the cover is very sophisticated. I'm trying to unravel it, but with little success. I'm wondering if the markings on mine are the same as yours. I thought we could compare them later."

Avery patted her bag. "I've brought it with me. We should use your old flat," Avery said to Alex.

"Sounds good." Alex looked around the table at everyone. "What do we think about breaking into the theatre later to check the props?"

"Love it!" Hunter said. "Although, wouldn't we have found something there on Friday night when we first went?"

Reuben shook his head. "A lot of the props would have been onstage, and we couldn't go on there that night—or on Saturday afternoon."

"And on Saturday," El added, "any jewellery would probably have been worn by the actors, because of the dress rehearsal."

"Third time lucky, then," Avery said. "Tonight we need to examine everything! At least we know what we're looking for now."

Briar frowned. "Isn't it too late, though? We have no idea how many affected scripts are out there, but presumably enough for at least the main cast. There's no way we can get them all back—they surely must have taken them home."

"True," Alex said, nodding. "I suspect this fog is unnatural, and that the play has triggered it, and I think it started with the first performance last night."

"It does feel different," Reuben agreed. "But what's its purpose? And will it last all week?"

"I guess we'll find out as the week progresses," El said. "But ultimately, what's our plan? Are we trying to break the spell? That's virtually impossible!"

"Part of me is curious to let it play out and see what happens," Briar said, looking at them speculatively. "It might not be a bad thing, in the end."

"Someone was stabbed," Alex reminded her. "And Newton came by earlier today. There's been more unrest, and another stabbing in Truro last night that was definitely paranormal in nature."

"But that's unlikely to have been caused by this play," Briar argued.

El put her elbow on the table and leaned her chin on her hand. "This is all so confusing. There are too many things going on! Beltane's wild magic is one thing that is completely out of our control. The Goddess is doing her thing with the Green Man, and we are all affected. We can only try to counter the effects, and I don't know about you, but their magic is creeping under my skin. And despite my charms and protections, I'm finding it hard to shake it off." She glanced at Reuben. "I have little flares of jealousy when another woman looks at Reuben, but equally find myself having the odd lustful thought about other men who I would ordinarily have zero interest in!" She looked at their startled faces. "I mean, I'm not going to act on it, but I refuse to believe this is only affecting me!"

There was silence for a moment, as everyone looked nervously at each other, and then Avery confessed, "No, I'm fighting it, too. Just minutes ago I had the strongest urge to run my hands over Zee's muscles." She saw

Alex's face darken. "I'm not going to! It's like El said—Beltane's wild magic is stronger than us!"

Alex looked sheepish. "You're right. I actually found myself watching Kate's arse as she leaned over the bar the other day." He swallowed. "Not my finest moment."

"Oh, but that *is* a fine arse!" Reuben agreed.

With a ripple of sniggers, they all joined in, confessing the odd jealousy and sexual desires they had recently experienced, and Avery felt a wave of relief pass through her. This wasn't just her. But she also realised she couldn't say anything about Caspian. The kiss was too close to home, considering his confession, and Alex would be furious.

"Okay," Alex said finally, once they'd all stopped laughing. "Other than protective charms for ourselves, our homes, and businesses, Beltane magic will have to play itself out. I have no idea if there's someone casting love spells, which could be making things worse, and I also have no idea who enchanted this play!"

Avery carried on. "So, out of the three things we have to focus on, the one thing we can possibly do something about right now is the play. I have more questions. When was it performed before? I mean, I know it was the sixties, but when exactly? Did this happen the last time? Who bewitched the script, and when?"

Reuben drained his pint. "I can answer one of those. Stan thinks the play was last performed in 1964, because the stash of stuff they found with it was from that time. I think he found a poster with the exact dates on it." His face brightened. "I also think it might have been during Beltane then, too."

"I wonder," Hunter speculated, "if someone aimed that spell at the company in particular for some reason, or *someone* in the company?"

"Or was it older, perhaps, and they found it randomly, too?" Reuben countered.

Avery began to feel excited as a way through their confusion presented itself. "At least we have a date now. I'll see if I can find some newspaper clippings on the play and in the news at that time. We can see who the cast was too, hopefully. It may suggest something. I'll do that tomorrow. Dan will know how to search the archives."

"Great," Reuben said, rising to his feet. "Time for another round, and then we can compare those scripts before we go to the theatre after it's closed." He grinned at them. "I'm pleased to see that we're all wearing black. I do enjoy my ninja witch nights!"

Fourteen

It was after midnight when the group made their way to the theatre. The roads still swirled with fog, the street lights barely visible, and it was no exaggeration to say that it was hard to see more than a few feet in front of them.

Their examination of the two scripts side by side confirmed that they were identical, and they could only presume the others were the same. They hoped this knowledge would make it easier to break the spell—if they found a way to. Avery certainly hoped so. Reuben spelled the side door of the theatre open, and they slipped inside the corridor, a tendril of fog finding its way inside too, before Briar shut the door firmly behind them and locked it again. The silence and darkness within was oppressive, prompting them to cast a handful of witch-lights above them that floated down the dark hallway.

"Let's head to the stage first," Alex suggested. "Which way?"

"This way," Avery said, turning to her left, and she led them through the cramped space of the wings and onto the stage, where they fanned out into the echoing space and she shivered. "I feel it, can you?"

"The wisps of an enchantment?" Briar asked. "Yes. I couldn't feel anything on Friday, but I can now."

The stage was still dressed for the final act, which took place in the castle in Brittany, where Tristan was living with Iseult of the White Hands. The set was of a walled garden, and a large bower was in the centre of it containing a bed—on which, Avery presumed, Tristan waited, injured, for his love to come and heal him. The bed instead on which he dies, and Iseult dies in his arms of a broken heart.

Avery stroked the brocade sheets that tumbled over the bed, but felt nothing untoward. The others were engaged in similar activities, touching pieces of the set and poking into the wings, but as far as sets went, it was quite bare.

"We need to find the potion bottle," Avery called out.

"Agreed," Alex said, making his way to her side. "I think the dress rehearsal really started the spell humming, and the first show triggered a new level."

Hunter looked doubtful. "How does a spell in a play know what's a live performance and what isn't?"

"An audience brings its own power," Briar suggested. "A spell—or enchantment, whatever you want to call it—needs energy, and a live audience brings that. It's like when you go to see a band. A live performance is usually amazing. The performers feed off the crowd, and vice versa."

"Interesting idea," Alex said thoughtfully, as he sat on the bed looking up and around the stage. "The fog appeared overnight, either during or after the first show, and the audience must have been the trigger."

"Are you sure the fog isn't related to Beltane?" Hunter asked, still sceptical. "That could answer why it feels unnatural."

Alex wasn't convinced. "I don't think so. It's too much of a coincidence to the play."

El sat next to him, frowning. "Of course, we should consider the fact that whoever spelled the script was present when the play was performed in the sixties. He or she could have been a part of the production, or watching in the audience."

Reuben looked at her in admiration. "Good point, El!"

As they were talking, Avery felt a prickle on the back of her neck, as if someone was watching her, and she wheeled around, staring at the space behind her.

"What's up?" Hunter asked. "Getting spooked?"

Avery shook her head, perplexed. "I don't know. I felt as if someone was watching me. I'm probably just imagining things." She stared for a few moments more at the darkness in the wings, trying to shake off the strange feeling, and then said, "Come on, let's head backstage."

The feeling of being watched subsided as Avery left the stage and led the way to the dressing rooms. Hunter had once again shifted to his wolf form, and Briar and he were now exploring more of the theatre while it was completely empty. Reuben and Alex were in the smaller dressing rooms, leaving El and Avery to investigate the larger one. Once there they switched the lights on, knowing no one could see them since there were no windows.

"This place is really spooky when there's only a few of us," El confessed to Avery as her hands moved deftly through the costumes. "I suppose there have been well over a hundred years' worth of people in here, learning their lines, experiencing the intensity of a performance, and the mix of personalities. It's like they're still here, watching."

Avery laughed while she sorted through some of the props on the long table at the side. "Maybe that's what I felt onstage."

"This place is enough to give anyone the creeps, witch or not." She paused, holding a gown up in front of her. "These are very good quality for a local production. Some are better than others, obviously. When we were watching the other afternoon, though, in the dress rehearsal, they looked even better." She looked up at Avery. "I think the spell cast a bit of glamour on the costumes."

"I guess it's possible." Avery was distracted as she spoke, concentrating on feeling anything remotely magical in the objects under her fingers. There were several glasses and a decanter half-filled with a red liquid, which she sniffed gingerly, but it smelled and looked like coloured water. Then she spied a cut glass bottle about six inches high at the back of the table, half covered with a velvet wrap. It was filled with golden liquid, and as soon as she touched it, she felt the fizz of magic running through it. "Wow! Found it!"

"What?" El said, joining her.

"The potion bottle." Avery held it up to the light. "It looks like a proper potion inside." She took the stopper out of the jar and held it to her nose, taking a tentative sniff. "I can smell roses and lavender, and..." She inhaled again, "Jasmine and rosemary."

"Classic plants used for love magic," El said. "I wonder what else is in it. May I?"

Avery found she was reluctant to hand it over, the scent alone already making her want to hold on to the jar. It was quickly filling her mind with thoughts of golden afternoons of pleasure and nights of passion.

El looked at her face and gently prised it from her. "Wow. This stuff must be good." She took a tentative sniff too, and Avery saw her pupils dilate and a dreamy quality pass across El's face. She put it down on the table quickly, and took deep breaths as if to clear her head. "Well, whoever made that knew what they were doing!"

"How did that get in there?" Avery asked, looking at the bottle as if it might explode. "If Tristan and Iseult are actually drinking that, then it's no wonder things between them are weird."

"They're not called Tristan or Iseult," El reminded her.

Avery nodded, feeling the heady enchantment start to slip away. "Good point. We have to take that with us. It's irresponsible to leave it here." She stared at the jar, and then back at El. "Briar is probably the best with potions. Maybe we should get her to look at it."

"Or Nate?" El suggested. "He's supposedly good with potions, too."

"But how did it get in there?" Avery persisted.

"If the spell's on the jar, then maybe the jar transforms whatever liquid is in it into the potion."

Before Avery could comment, they heard a piercing scream, and they both froze before El cried, "Briar!"

They raced out of the dressing room, immediately running into Reuben and Alex, who shouted, “It came from the auditorium!”

All four raced down the passageway, this time on the other side of the stage, bursting through the door and into the stalls, lit only by half a dozen witch-lights. Briar was standing in the centre aisle halfway down the rows of seats, fire balling in both hands as she stared at the stage. Hunter was next to her, snarling, his fur standing on end. They raced to her side, Avery turning to see what she was staring at. But the curtains were closed, as they’d left them, leaving only the apron of the stage showing, and that was bare.

“What happened?” Reuben asked, energy already crackling from his palms as he looked around the room.

Briar tore her gaze away from the stage to look at them properly. Her eyes were wild with fright. “Sorry. I saw a ghost right *here*.” She held her hand inches from her face. “It scared the shit out of me. And then it disappeared and reappeared there.” She pointed to the stage.

Avery raised a powerful surge of air that lifted her hair and whirled across the seats, disturbing the curtains on the stage, at the same time that El threw another half a dozen witch-lights above them, brightening the room.

“Where has it gone?” Reuben asked, spinning around.

“Vanished into thin air,” Briar answered, taking a deep breath.

Avery felt the uncomfortable prickle of someone watching her again, and she turned slowly, scanning the shadows.

“A ghost?” Alex asked, wide-eyed. “Male or female?”

“Male. He was tall, dark-haired, slim. His eyes were burning with this creepy flame.” She shuddered. “It shouldn’t have made me jump so much, but it was *right here*!” She held her hand in front of her face again.

“You’re allowed to jump,” Avery reassured her. “Ghosts are freaky! I’ve grown used to Helena, but I’m pretty sure I’d scream if I saw another one.
”

Briar looked pale. “It was its closeness. Hunter leapt at it, and that’s why it fled, I think.”

“I could try a spell, try to get it to manifest again,” Alex suggested. “Is it an echo, or did it actually appear to have its own will?"

It was an odd question, but Avery knew what he meant. Ghosts were usually replaying events of past lives, repeated appearances without thought or action—hence, the echo. But some, like Helena, had the ability to think and act, which made them more dangerous.

Briar paused for a moment, looking thoughtful. "It's hard to say at this stage, but I'd say it had intent. It felt malevolent."

"That's unnerving," Reuben said. "That's the word Alison used!"

Avery groaned. "Bollocks! So she wasn't imagining things."

"I wonder if it's related to the spell, or if the theatre's haunted?" El asked.

"Alison said she hadn't experienced this before—and she's performed here a few times," Reuben reminded them. "And if this place had a reputation for being haunted, wouldn't we know about it? It would be common knowledge in White Haven!"

Alex grimaced. "I'd put money on it being related to the play, wouldn't you?"

They all nodded and made their way to the front of the stage, unnerved by the appearance of the spirit and the deep silence of the old theatre, and Avery realised the situation was getting more complicated. "If the ghost is related to the spell, who is it?"

"If someone died because of this spell, maybe it's him and he's stuck to the play," Reuben suggested.

"That's a horrible thought," Avery said.

"Sorry, but it seems logical."

El headed to the side door that led backstage. "Come on, let's get that potion bottle. I want to go home. We have a lot to think about."

Briar dispelled the witch-lights as they filed down the passageway. "You've found the bottle? That's great. We didn't find anything remotely spelled in the rest of the theatre."

But as soon as they entered the large dressing room, Avery's heart sank, and she raced over to the table. "It's gone!" She searched through the props frantically, lifting up the velvet wrap and moving around fake swords, gloves, and hats.

"It can't have gone," El said, joining her in the search. "We left it right here!"

Alex shook his head. "You won't find it now. I have a feeling the spirit appeared as a distraction. He's hidden it. But I'm sure it will be back for tomorrow's performance."

Hunter was already prowling the room, sniffing in corners and under the table where other props were, and where the box containing the script had been.

"Could you summon him?" Reuben asked Alex.

"I could try, but not now. I haven't got the right equipment." Alex stood next to the table, idly picking up props and looking distracted. "We might have to come back another night, but I'd like to learn more about who it could be first. It will give me an advantage."

Avery finally stopped searching, admitting defeat reluctantly, and she straightened and looked at the others. "Well, I can see I'll be in the library for hours tomorrow. Hopefully we can find some information that will help us."

Fifteen

"Of course I can help you in the library," Dan said to Avery. "But it will have to be after the morning rush if we're both going."

They were in the back room at Happenstance Books on Monday morning, drinking their first coffee of the day, and Avery had just updated Sally and Dan on what they had found out over the weekend. The fog was still wrapped around White Haven, but it seemed that the rest of the coastline was unaffected according to the news.

Dan continued thoughtfully, "Actually, I could just look for you. I know what you want, and if you write down a list, I'll make sure I cover it all. It's easy for me—I do it all the time."

Avery sighed with relief. She'd been dreading wading through the old archives, but knew Dan would love it. "Really? That would be amazing! Thank you."

Sally was leaning against the counter, her hands around a coffee cup, looking worried. "Are you sure nothing weird is going to come out of that fog?"

"Like vengeful pirates with a cutlass that will slice your head off?" Dan asked, eyes wide. "Or weird creatures that will eat you like in Stephen King's book?"

Sally just glared at him. "That's exactly what I mean! And it's not funny!"

Avery tried to suppress a snigger, but had to admit she'd had similar worries. "I'm sure that won't happen."

"You don't sound very convinced, Avery."

Avery tried to look more confident. "The fog is unnatural, I'll admit that, but I think it's a manifestation of magic from the script."

"Well, I hope you're right," Sally said, still frowning as she looked out the window onto the lane behind the shop.

Dan finished his coffee and checked his watch. "I'm going to head there now then, if that's okay. You two will be all right on your own, won't you? It might get busy. Rupert is starting his first daytime occult tour this morning, and he'll be coming here."

"Bollocks!" Avery said. "I'd forgotten about that. What time?"

He shrugged. "Mid-morning, that's all I know."

"Let's hope something comes out of the fog and swallows him up," Sally said, her face wrinkling with annoyance.

Dan laughed. "That's the spirit! At least it will be suitably atmospheric for the tour! And don't forget, I'm doing the Beltane talk this afternoon in the shop. We've got posters up already. See you later." He put his jacket on and headed out through the back door, and Sally and Avery walked into the shop. The scent of blossoms filled Avery's senses, and she looked around with pleasure at the flowers behind the counter and on the shelves. Sally immediately steered Avery over to the new display at the front of the shop, right behind the window decorated for Beltane.

"What do you think, Avery? This is what Dan and I finished on Saturday afternoon after you went to the theatre."

Avery gasped with pleasure. "That looks fantastic!"

Sally was already animated, and she pointed to a handful of books. "I put a rush order on a few books about cunning folk and the history of magic, and they arrived on Saturday. There are a few extra boxes in the back, just in case. I'm hoping that we sell quite a few this week."

Avery noticed that they had displayed them with the books about Beltane and the other pagan celebrations, as well as witch related diaries, spell books, and some lovely leather bound notebooks.

Sally continued, "This is just to catch their eye as they come through the main entrance, but we've set up a reading corner in the occult section, and there are more books there." She led the way, clearly excited. "I thought we'd keep the decorations rustic and pagan and tried to steer away from kitsch. We've moved a few chairs here, but seeing as it will be a short talk, most people will stand and browse, and Dan will showcase what we have. Sound good?"

"Sounds fantastic." Avery hugged her. "Thank you for doing this."

Sally smiled at her. "People love witchcraft now. Many want to avoid organised religion, but don't understand the old ways. We'll try to balance Rupert's opinion, if he tries to sensationalise things."

"You know, he may not stir anything up," Avery felt compelled to point out. "It's a subject he's genuinely interested in, too."

Sally sniffed, looking doubtful. "We'll see."

At just after eleven that morning, Avery saw Rupert arrive outside her shop with a group of about a dozen people, and heard his voice filter through the window.

He gestured towards the shop, and Avery heard him mention Helena. She stood behind the counter, half-listening, while she glanced at the flyers that advertised Dan's talks. A couple of people were already reading the poster on the front door and admiring the window display, and looked like they wanted to come in. It was gloomy outside, the thick fog still pooling in the streets. The shops opposite Avery's were barely visible, their bright plants outside their doors and under their windows the only splashes of colour. Avery had made sure her shop looked warm and inviting, and lamps lit up dark corners, aided by displays of candles.

Whatever Rupert was saying, he looked to be entertaining, because the group was nodding and asking questions. Sally came out of the back room with a tray of homemade cookies, and the smell made Avery salivate. She snatched one from the plate before Sally could stop her and took a bite, looking mischievous. "Delicious," she said through a mouthful of crumbs. "And they're warm."

Sally smiled. "The secret is lots of butter. And look, they're coming in!"

The door chimes jangled as Rupert's tour group entered the shop, most sighing with pleasure at the warmth. Rupert immediately threw his arms wide encompassing Avery and her shop. "And here is Avery Hamilton, the direct descendant of Helena Marchmont, who was so cruelly burned at the stake."

Avery froze momentarily, clenching her hands beneath the counter so she didn't throw a fireball at Rupert, and then forced a smile. "Hello and welcome to my shop. Please take your time browsing, and feel free to ask any questions."

She felt Sally bristle next to her, but then she was off with the plate, offering cookies and chatting about their books. Rupert, however, made a beeline for Avery, but not before swiping a cookie, she noticed.

"Avery," he said, greeting her coolly, a malevolent glint to his expression. He looked around the shop, his eyes narrowing in suspicion, as if she'd hidden something. "How are you?"

"I'm fine, thanks Rupert. How's your tour going?"

His hooded gaze finally finished flitting around and settled on her. "Excellent. Although the day is cold, the fog does lend excellent atmosphere, especially at Old Haven Church." He nodded to the flyers on the counter. "I see you're giving a talk."

Avery nodded, falsely bright. "Yes, we thought it was a great opportunity to talk about pagan beliefs and the history of magic, an accompaniment to your tour." She smiled. "Dan is an expert on folklore and local knowledge, and couldn't wait to do it. Your tour has sparked some great ideas for us. And, of course it gives me an opportunity to answer questions about

Helena, and correct any falsehoods."

"What falsehoods could there be?" he asked, challenging her. "She did burn at the stake for being a witch, after all."

"She was accused of witchcraft, like many others at that time. It does not mean she was one."

"And yet here you are with an occult bookshop, stocking witchcraft paraphernalia."

"Just like half the shops in White Haven," she pointed out. "And in case you haven't realised, I'm not Helena."

"Mmm," he mumbled, looking as if he were about to say more. "You do, however, have symbols of protection around the shop...above the door, for example." He pointed to a woven twig pentacle decorated with rosemary and sage. "Are you worried about something?"

Rupert had done his homework, but that wasn't really surprising seeing as they knew he had once attempted to perform necromancy and was mostly likely still trying, as well as having bought the House of Spirits because of his interest in all things occult.

"No," she answered politely. "I think they're lovely for decoration."

Fortunately, before he could ask anything else, a middle-aged women came sidling over to the counter eager to speak to Avery, and with a smile of relief at the interruption, she started to chat to her, turning her back on Rupert.

By the time Dan returned at midday, bringing steaming coffees and hot Cornish pasties for lunch, House of Spirit's Occult Tours had moved on, and Sally was hoping that several of them would return later for the talk. Dan, however, had more pressing topics on his mind, and he raised his eyebrows at Avery. "Well, what a hotbed of salacious gossip and tragedy I've found!"

"Really? You found out about the performance?" Avery looked at him, astonished. She'd half thought it would be a waste of time.

"Of course I have!" He pushed the bag in front of her and Sally. "Come on, eat them while they're hot."

The rich smell of warm pastry and meat filled the shop, and Avery fished hers from the paper bag, breaking off a piece. "Thanks Dan, this is delicious. Don't keep me hanging, now. What have you found out?"

Dan swallowed his mouthful. "Just bear in mind that I've pieced this together from several accounts published over a few days in the local White Haven Gazette, and some articles were really small." When Sally and Avery both nodded, he said, "*Tristan and Iseult* was performed in 1964 at White Haven Little Theatre at Beltane. White Haven has always embraced its witchy past, but it seems that with the arrival of the sixties and a more liberal outlook on life, the pagan celebrations were beginning to grow in popularity."

"Really?" Avery asked. "I thought this town always embraced its magical roots."

"It has, but to a lesser degree. This shop, for example, has always been here, as have a few others. But it was more low-key pre-sixties. There were solstice celebrations too, but nothing like it has become today. Anyway, as you already know, the White Haven Players were performing it then, too."

"Come on, Dan, salacious gossip, please!" Sally prompted him, brushing crumbs from her jumper.

"Patience is a virtue," he said, smirking. "Oh, all right then. The two leads, Tristan and Iseult, had a real-life affair. Tristan was married, but she wasn't. The scandal broke up his marriage. They ended up moving in together, living in a little cottage in West Haven. He had kids, so it was all around quite sad, but I think it's fair to say that the theatre members were a bohemian bunch, anyway—well, for that time. And although the scandal filled the papers for days, it didn't seem to bother them much. But it gets weirder! Iseult also had an affair with the actor playing King Mark, who wasn't married, and went to live with him a few weeks after the end of the play, leaving Tristan heartbroken. And this is where life really imitates art. Tristan killed himself."

"*What*?" Avery said, horrified. "How?"

"There was a summer storm, high seas and winds, and he threw himself off the cliffs somewhere between here and Harecombe—you know, off the coastal walk. Well, that's what they surmised afterwards. His car was found on the car park next to the start of the track. His body was discovered further down the coast."

Avery had stopped eating, her mouth open in shock. "That's terrible. And Iseult?"

"Threw herself under a train a few days later."

Sally's hand flew to her mouth. "Oh, no!"

"And I'm not sure what happened to King Mark—yet. I don't think he killed himself. I have a feeling he moved away." Dan finished his pasty, wiping his fingers on the paper napkin. "I looked at other performances later that year, but his name wasn't on any other bills. I think he either left the company or the area."

Avery leaned back against the wall behind the counter, her mind whirling. "How long was the play on for?"

"One week. Reviews were phenomenal, and the play was packed out." Dan frowned. "The performance really seemed to grab people, although it's hard to get a real flavour from the newspaper reports. Oh, and I should add that there were reports of fights among cast members, too."

"Who?" Avery asked.

"I'm not sure if they said—I'll check."

"That was," Sally paused as she worked out the time frame, "fifty-six years ago. It's possible some of the locals would remember that. I presume you have all of the actor's names?"

"Of course. But there's more," Dan warned them. "I think I know who cast the spell, and you won't like it."

"Please don't say you suspect it was my family," Avery said, her chest tightening with fear.

"No. I think it was Rufus Faversham—Caspian's grandfather."

Avery leapt to her feet, almost upending the stool. "What? How? Why?" Her raised voice drew the attention of a few shoppers, and she sat down quickly and lowered her voice. "Dan?"

All three leaned forward, their heads close together. "The actress who played Iseult was called Yvonne Warner, and I came across a reference to her working for Kernow Industries. She was a secretary there, working for the management team apparently, and she'd left the company only weeks before. Obviously the paper didn't speculate anything, they wouldn't want to be sued for libel, but I wondered what happened with Rufus for her to leave a *very* good job."

"Wow," Sally said. "He would have been as powerful a witch as Caspian, surely. Didn't you say, Avery, that the spell on the script was strong?"

Avery barely heard her speak; her mind was racing with possibilities. "I guess so," she eventually answered. "But it could have been his wife or another family member, too. Perhaps they'd had an affair, or he'd made advances toward her and she had to leave." She straightened, resolute. "I need to speak to Caspian. What was her name, again?"

"Yvonne Warner." Dan pulled a notebook from his backpack. "I noted a few key dates and names, and I'm going to see if I can find out about the other cast members, too. I also have a photo of her, and I copied some of the articles, too." He put down a faded colour image of a very pretty blonde woman on the counter. Everything about it screamed the 1960s—her hair, makeup, and the dress she wore.

"She's so pretty," Sally said, picking the image up. "How tragic."

"And here's one of Tristan." Dan pushed the photocopy of a young man with brown hair across the counter. He was good looking and confident, a smile on his face. "His name was Charles Ball."

"Thanks, Dan. You're a star," Avery said to him. "I'm heading up to my flat so I can phone Caspian."

"He probably won't know anything," Sally said to her, but Avery just nodded and went upstairs.

As soon as she was in the privacy of her home, she stood by the window, composing herself. Calling Caspian may be a bad idea, especially after the last time she saw him at Oswald's. The memory of the kiss flooded back, and she paced across the room, trying to shake it off. The kiss was a mistake—a trick of Beltane. But Caspian could tell them more about the spell. They needed him if they were to avoid the disastrous outcome of the last time the play was performed. She wanted to fly to his office, but decided that would be a terrible idea. He could be in a meeting, or out somewhere. She phoned him, and he picked up in seconds.

"Avery, what a pleasure." He sounded cool and composed. "How can I help you?"

"I need to talk to you about *Tristan and Iseult*—the play, I mean."

"Sure, why?" He sounded amused. "Do you like love triangles?"

Her voice tightened with annoyance. "No, actually. They're messy and horrible. I think your grandfather, Rufus Faversham, may have put a spell on the play."

"What play?"

"The play that's being performed in White Haven right now!"

He laughed. "Are you insane?"

"No! I'm being very reasonable, actually. The White Haven Players are behaving irrationally, the play is bewitched, the theatre now seems to be haunted, and the last time it was performed things ended very badly. We need to stop it, but we were thwarted last night by a ghost at the theatre."

"Wow. You really are sounding a little crazed right now."

Wind whipped around Avery again, and she forced herself to calm down. "It would be helpful if we could talk face to face. You could join us in the pub later, perhaps?"

"Where are you now?"

"At home in my flat."

"Alone?"

"Yes."

He ended the call before Avery could protest, and the familiar swirl of witch-flight appeared before her, solidifying into Caspian.

"You wanted me?" He opened his arms wide, smirking at her. "I'm all yours."

"You can start by behaving," she remonstrated.

"I am!" He looked around her flat, frowning. "Things look different. Oh! Alex has moved in. I suppose that was inevitable. Have you told him we kissed?"

She glared at him. "*No*. And you kissed me!"

He shrugged, still smirking. "So, what's the big deal?"

"There isn't one, and I am not debating our very brief kiss. It won't happen again. Can we discuss the play now?"

"That's okay, Avery, I like that it's our secret." Caspian sat down on one of the chairs around her dining table. "If we must discuss the play, go on."

The word 'secret' needled her, and she didn't like it, but she pushed it to the back of her mind, summarising her conversation with Dan, and explaining about the scripts. "The cover of the play has a very complex series of sigils on it, inscribed with a fire spell, and there are runes above the character's names in the script. It seems that the longer the play goes on, the stronger the magic becomes. We think the first performance has triggered this fog."

For the first time, Caspian looked out of the window. "Bloody hell! We have blue skies in Harecombe."

Avery stood by the French doors that opened out onto her small balcony. "I know. I've seen the news. This fog hasn't shifted since Saturday night. We think that the first performance caused it to manifest."

He stood next to her, peering into the gloom. "An unnatural fog. Interesting. I wonder what it conceals."

"Conceals?" She looked at him, confused. "Why would it conceal anything?"

He shrugged. "Maybe I'm wrong, but normally unnatural fog covers the land or sea, allowing something else to manifest."

Avery remembered the conversation with Sally and Dan earlier and groaned. "I hope it isn't Lyonesse."

"Lyonesse? The mystical isle that vanished beneath the waves?" He looked confused. "That was rumoured to be between Land's End and the Scilly Isles, not here."

"I know that! But Alex has been having dreams about a mist at sea, and this play is associated with Lyonesse—Tristan was its heir. What if that is manifesting out there?"

Caspian stared at her, and Avery became uncomfortably aware of how close he was. She scented his aftershave, something peppery, and stepped back a fraction. "That would be very powerful magic indeed, and ships would be in danger of running aground." He paused, looking out at the fog again, his gaze unfocussed. "Or it could be a powerful illusion, but who knows for what purpose."

Avery folded her arms across her chest. "What do you know about Rufus?"

He turned to look at her again, leaning against the window frame. "My grandfather was a proud man, skilled at magic like all of my family, and a successful businessman who had a happy marriage and three kids—my father, my uncle, and my aunt. He set up Kernow Industries, expanding on Kernow Shipping." Caspian also folded his arms, looking amused. "I'm pretty sure he wouldn't be having an affair with a part-time actress and secretary."

"Your ancestor, Thaddeus, was a successful businessman, and yet he slept with and then abandoned Helena, when she was pregnant, no less! I think it's highly possible."

"Oh! Questioning my family's morals now, are you?"

"Yes! Of course I am considering our chequered history. And I don't think it's a coincidence that Yvonne worked for your grandfather!"

Caspian regarded her silently for a moment, and then said, "All right, I'll look into my grandfather's past, and search our grimoires for spells such as you've mentioned. Although, I still maintain it's ridiculous."

"If you could find a photo of him, that would be helpful," Avery added. "I'd like to know if he looks like the ghost we saw in the theatre."

He nodded. "Show me the play before I go."

Avery led him up to the attic and handed him the script, which had been on her worktable. The sigils' light had faded, but she repeated the spell Alex had taught her and they flared into life again. Avery saw a flash of surprise on Caspian's face, and he stiffened for a moment.

"What?" Avery asked.

He looked up at her, his face growing pale. "I recognise one of those signs. I've seen it in my grimoire, somewhere."

Avery faltered, not sure if this was good or bad. *No, it had to be a good thing*. "Good, that will help decipher it, yes?"

"Maybe. I need to take this with me."

"Okay. But not for long. We need to try to break the enchantment."

"Can't you just get them all back?" he asked, wiggling the script at her. "That would solve everything, surely."

"We're planning on trying a finding spell, but haven't had a chance yet. We also don't want to alarm anyone prematurely."

Caspian nodded absently. "All right, leave it with me. I'll be in touch tomorrow morning." He smiled before he vanished. "Lovely to work with you again."

Sixteen

All afternoon Avery brooded on her conversation with Caspian, and his jibe about their *secret*.

There was a look behind his eyes when he realised that she and Alex were living together. A look of resignation. She suspected his accusation was meant to rile her, and it succeeded. Guilt ate away at her. She loved Alex, and hated to keep secrets from him, but what would he say if he found out? Would he understand that it was the madness of Beltane and that it was all Caspian's doing, or would he be furious? Would he leave her? That was her biggest fear.

She must have looked distracted, because Sally cornered her in the kitchen mid-afternoon, just before Dan was due to give his talk. A few people had already arrived, circling the occult section, and Sally had come in to collect more biscuits.

"What's going on, Avery?"

Avery looked up from the collection of books she'd been sorting through. "What do you mean?"

"You know what I mean. Ever since you saw Caspian, you've looked haunted. What did he say?"

"I told you, he's—"

Sally cut her off. "No! Not that. What else happened?"

Avery froze and then her hands flew to her face, pressing her cheeks. "He kissed me, and I haven't told Alex."

"What?" Sally's voice rose in shock and she put the plate of biscuits down on the table, and put her hands on her hips. "Today? Upstairs?"

"No! Not today. Last week, just before the Witches Council meeting. But it was a moment of madness—Beltane magic! I saw it in his eyes, and he pulled me beneath the trees, and well...it just happened! And it was only for a few seconds before I pushed him away!"

Sally went still for a moment, and then her shoulders dropped. "So, he kissed you?"

"Yes! It all happened so fast that I couldn't react quickly enough. I was horrified." Avery dropped onto a chair and explained in more detail what happened. "What will Alex think? He'll hate me! Oh shit. What if he leaves me?"

Sally rolled her eyes. "Bloody hell, Avery. Alex is not going to leave you over that! But you really shouldn't put yourself in situations where you're going to be alone with Caspian. It just gives him opportunities." She floundered for words. "He's not worthy of you."

"I didn't do it on purpose!" Avery remonstrated. "I used witch-flight to arrive on Oswald's drive, and he appeared only seconds after me! Then the Goddess did her thing and Caspian seized the moment. I could see it in his eyes. He wasn't thinking straight, either."

Sally looked sceptical. "Mmm. Was that Beltane, or was that his feelings for you?" Sally eased into a chair and her voice softened. "Besides, I didn't mean then, I meant today! You should have spoken with him down here."

"He's not some mad rapist, Sally."

"But he likes being alone with you. It makes him feel like he's got one up on Alex. It's sad, really. He knows you love Alex, and that he loves you. Hell, you've moved in together. That must have stung. But Caspian is a grown man, and he'll deal with it. That's why he went away—he's admitted that. Unfortunately, love is not so easily dismissed, is it?"

"Love?" Avery looked at Sally, shocked. "I don't think it's as serious as love."

She looked Avery squarely in the eye, unflinching. "Oh, I think it is.

But regardless, you need to tell Alex, before he finds out in some weird, convoluted way."

"I know. What do you think he'll do?"

"I think he'll be mad as hell, and then because he's reasonable and loves you, he'll calm down, eventually. He might want to punch Caspian, though." Sally shrugged. "But it's also Beltane magic. We're all behaving slightly irrationally right now. Me and Sam are still a bit odd, if I'm honest."

"Oh, no. Are you?" Avery asked, feeling another rush of guilt for not checking in with Sally sooner.

"I'm still getting that jealous itch, and he's still a bit more flirty than normal. I think that protective bundle you gave me is helping." Sally reached for a biscuit, and absently took a bite. "Beltane magic is so unpredictable, have you noticed? I've been thinking about this, a lot! It enhances some people's feelings...sort of brings them to the surface. And for others, it's just random and not real at all! And it's flattering to have someone have such feelings for you. You entertain thoughts you wouldn't normally. You and Caspian are an obvious example. You are now thinking about him in a completely different way, because of what you know about his feelings for you. It's inevitable."

"I suppose it is," Avery confessed. "And, yes, of course it's flattering."

Sally smiled. "You just have to remember your priorities. As do I, in my marriage." She paused again, and then noted, "I've seen it in the customers, too. You've probably been so wrapped up with this play in the last few days you haven't noticed, but everyone is a little edgy, fragile. I think it can only get worse as the day itself approaches."

"It's not only here, either."

"I know. If only this fog would clear, it would be better. It's so oppressive. And tomorrow, they name the May Queen and Green Man. There will be an announcement in the middle of town. Let's hope the fog lifts for that. Anyway," Sally stood and lifted the plate of biscuits. "I'd better go and help Dan. Who, by the way, is having his own Beltane fun!"

"Is he?" Avery asked, intrigued. "How?"

"He has a girlfriend!" she said, with raised eyebrows. And with that, she left Avery to her thoughts.

At about seven o'clock that night, Avery and Alex hosted the witches, Hunter, and Newton at their flat so that they could catch up on each other's news.

Alex had arrived home at just after four when his shift finished. He spent an hour doing accounts in his study off the living room that had been a guest bedroom, and then started to cook a curry. Avery wasn't sure if it was her imagination, because at the moment everything was coloured by her guilt, but Alex also seemed subdued. She had decided to wait until after the meeting to tell him about Caspian, and for a while she shoved the issue to the back of her mind.

When the others arrived, they sat around the table, filling their plates and chatting idly. Avery had spent time cleaning her flat and decorating the table, wanting to make an effort like El had, and for a while felt content with her closest friends gathered around her. It was Alex who jarred her out of it, declaring, "I think we can manage this Beltane script spell without Caspian's help." He frowned at Avery. "You shouldn't have called him."

"I disagree," El said, straight away. "I'm really struggling to decipher those sigils. I've tried various combinations of runes, and none of them work. I'm looking at other things." She shrugged. "I can't work it out, and therefore I can't counteract it."

"Neither can we," Avery said to her. "Besides, we all know it's very hard to break another witch's spell. As for the ghost, if it's not Rufus Faversham, then who is it?"

"I think it's a leap to say it was Rufus," Reuben said, "suspicious though it is. We shouldn't close our mind to other possibilities."

"But we're running out of time!" Briar reminded them. "It's Monday night, and the play ends on Saturday. The last time it also ran for a week, which suggests that this spell will culminate on the final performance, just like last time. We also need to check on the welfare of the actors. They're two days into the performance. Do we know if they're okay?" She looked around the table, and they all shook their heads. "We need to address this, soon!"

"We spoke to Ian, who plays King Mark," El said, "and he seemed okay at the time."

"What's he like now, though?" Alex asked darkly.

"Maybe we need to watch a performance," Hunter suggested. "Or get in there after the performance, maybe tomorrow?"

Reuben reached for a piece of naan bread and topped up his bowl with curry. "I think we need to steal all the scripts, actually." He nodded at Newton. "You could get us the addresses for the actors, and we could break in and grab them. That might work."

Newton glared at Reuben. "I am not about to search for addresses and let you break into peoples' houses!"

"But we're sneaky, and no one would know. Besides, it's for the greater good." He grinned, pleased with himself.

"The likelihood is that there are a few scripts at the theatre now, maybe left overnight," Briar reasoned. "And we found modern copies that weren't spelled. It's not like we'd be leaving them without a script. Crazy though Reuben's idea is, I think it would work."

Reuben beamed at her. "Thanks, Briar."

"But," she added, "if the spell has already taken hold, stealing the scripts might not stop anything."

"I'll think on it," Newton said cautiously, also helping himself to more curry. "But maybe you should go there after the performance and see if you can get some copies. You could go backstage to congratulate them—they know you now."

"Maybe tomorrow, then," Avery suggested. "I'm not sure I can face it tonight. I'm knackered."

Alex nodded. "I agree. I am, too. And Caspian may have some news tomorrow, I guess. What's happened to Jamie, the woman who stabbed Lawrence?"

Newton sighed. "We released her on bail today. She does not have any other criminal charges, and Lawrence does not want to press charges. She's lucky. Obviously she'll go to court, but she may get away without being imprisoned."

"That's good," Avery said, feeling relieved.

"You know, we should involve Ben, Cassie, and Dylan, too," El said, sipping her beer and half watching Reuben put away another bowl of curry, an amused look on her face. "White Haven Little Theatre is obviously haunted! They will be furious if we don't tell them."

"But they're revising for exams and finishing up their experiments," Briar said. "I don't think they'll have time."

El shrugged. "We should tell them anyway."

"All right," Briar said, nodding. "I'll call Cassie. I need to talk to her about work anyway, to see if she wants some hours in the summer."

"And maybe we should contact Eve, too," El added. "She might be able to help shift our supernatural fog."

El was right, Avery mused. Eve was a very skilled weather witch, but Avery knew St Ives had its own problems. "If it's still foggy in the morning, I'll call her." Another thought struck her. "Did Rupert come by your shops today with his occult tour?"

El and Briar both nodded, and Briar said, "I made some decent business from it, too."

"He didn't really linger outside my shop," El told them, "but that's fine. I think I picked up some business from it anyway. How did it go here?"

"Rupert announced that I was Helena's descendant, obviously, but it was fine. Dan did a very popular talk on the origins of witchcraft, and we sold a few books, so I think we successfully capitalised on Rupert's drama-mongering, and righted a few misconceptions."

For a while they chatted idly, agreeing on their plans for the next day. El said she had time to keep trying to identify the sigils, and depending on what Caspian found out, they formalised their idea to go backstage after the next night's performance.

By the time everyone left, Avery was tired, the night before catching up with her, but she knew she couldn't go to bed until she talked to Alex. They started to clear the table, and Avery summoned her courage. "Alex, I need to talk to you."

He paused, his arms full of plates, his face serious. "That sounds ominous."

"It's not really, but I want to be honest with you."

"Is this about Caspian?"

That shouldn't have surprised her; Alex was always suspicious of Caspian, although he controlled it well.

"Yes. Can you sit down, please?"

Alex's face turned to stone, and he put the plates down. "I'll stand, I think."

Avery went to sit, but realised she couldn't talk with Alex standing over her. "I need you to listen until I've finished."

He didn't answer, instead just folding his arms and looking at her.

She swallowed and rushed into the explanation of what had happened before the meeting at Oswald's, and with every word she uttered, Alex became even quieter, if that was possible. Avery could hear her voice rising as she explained about Beltane magic, until eventually he said, very quietly, "You kissed Caspian."

"He kissed me, actually—and I stopped it! I pushed him away!"

"Not quick enough, though. Did you enjoy it?" His dark eyes, normally teasing and lively, were like steel.

"No! Of course I didn't. I was quite annoyed about it, actually. I should have told you at the time, but I've been trying to pretend it didn't happen."

"And this afternoon? Did you kiss him again?"

Alex's complete immobility scared her. "No! And it *never* will. And Caspian knows that, too."

"And yet you didn't think to see him with me around. Interesting. Clearing up unfinished business, obviously."

"No." Avery inwardly cursed herself. "As soon as Dan mentioned Rufus Faversham, I saw red and had to call him. And it *is* important!"

"Yes, and you could have waited for me."

"I'm sorry, I wasn't aware I needed your permission to speak to him," she said, a dangerous edge to her voice. But then, realising that getting angry wasn't going to help, tried to subdue her annoyance. "I love you, and the last thing I want to do is hurt you. I promise it will never happen again."

"Sometimes you are so naïve! You are giving him opportunities, but why? Does it give you a thrill?" Alex shook his head and took a deep breath. "I'm going to sleep at the pub tonight."

He walked down the steps to the entrance hall, pulled his jacket from the hook, and Avery ran after him. "*What*? Why? We need to talk!"

"There's nothing to talk about. It happened, and now I need to decide what to do with it." He shot her a long look, then walked out and slammed the door, leaving the glass shaking and Avery staring after him.

For a second, Avery contemplated whether she should run after Alex, but decided in the end that he was entitled to be furious, even if she thought it was an overreaction. She felt tears start to prick and blinked them away. Tears made her look guilty, and she had nothing to be guilty about! However, she had to admit that she would be annoyed if he'd kissed another woman. She'd been annoyed enough to hear him confess about flirting with Kate in the bar.

Avery sat on the bottom step, thinking through their conversation. He called her naïve. *Was she? Maybe he was right.* He'd virtually said the same as Sally...that she gave Caspian opportunities, and maybe she was guilty of that. It was flattering to have Caspian's attention, but it was also selfish. She wasn't a teenager; she was a grown woman, she really did hate love triangles, and she was damn sure this wasn't going to be one. *If Alex even gave her a second chance...* She groaned at herself. Of course he would. This was an argument, and if their relationship couldn't survive this, they were in trouble anyway.

She felt Medea's warm nose edge under her hand, and she rubbed her thick fur. "I'm such an idiot, pussycat," she murmured softly. "Come on. We need to tidy up."

She walked up the stairs and started to clear the dishes, wishing she had let Briar help when she'd offered earlier, but normally she and Alex would do it together. It was their time to chat about the evening, and wind down. She spelled all the lamps off except for one, and by mostly candlelight she tidied up, filing the dishwasher and wiping down the table, straightening the cushions, and generally trying to work off her nervous energy.

By the time she'd finished, it was clear she wouldn't be able to sleep despite her exhaustion, and Avery looked out the window and shivered. The fog was still so thick. She felt like she was in Victorian London. She drifted from the window back to her sofa, and started to read some of the articles Dan had left with her about the actors in the 1960s and their deaths. She had put them on the coffee table in case anyone had wanted to read them, but in the end no one had, and Avery was planning on reviewing them tomorrow. Now however, with her mind racing, she sat down and started to flick through them, depressing herself further with tales of gloom and lost love before she eventually read something that made her pause. In the final few months before her death, Yvonne Warner had worked at a quayside pub called The Silver Dolphin. There were many pubs in White Haven, but there weren't many by the quay, like Alex's. *Could that mean something?* Her eyes finally started to close, and putting the papers aside, she headed to bed.

Seventeen

When Avery woke the next morning, she was gritty-eyed.

She had slept badly, having dreamt all night about arguing with Alex. She headed straight to the shower and then got dressed, and it was only afterwards that she looked outside and had a shock. The fog had gone. She opened a window in her attic and stuck her head out, taking deep breaths of the fresh, sharp air, pleased to see the higgledy-piggledly tops of houses winding down to the coast, the sea spreading out like blue silk beyond. And then she frowned. There was still a patch of mist leading out to sea. She shook her head and turned her back on it. It was likely only a lingering mist, nothing mysterious.

She headed downstairs to make breakfast, and as soon as the hour felt respectable, she called Briar to check if it would be okay to visit later that morning, hoping that Caspian would call early. Once that was arranged, she toyed with the idea of calling Alex, but decided against it. She didn't want to crowd him, and decided if she hadn't heard from him by lunch, she'd call him then.

Dan had already opened the shop up when she went downstairs, and the front door was open, letting in the fresh spring air. He'd also put some music on, and she heard a blues voice singing, "I've put a spell on you, and now you're mine." Despite her subdued mood, she found herself smiling as she walked across the shop.

"Who sings this, Dan?"

Dan was leaning on the doorframe, coffee in hand as he looked down the street. His dark hair was ruffled, and he appeared to be content. He grinned at her. "Screamin' Jay Hawkins. Like it?"

"Love it!"

"Good. I thought I'd kick off the day with good vibes." He eased away from the door and walked back into the shop. "I'm sick of Beltane woes, and I am determined to make this a good day! Beltane is a celebration! Is it wild and unpredictable and a little bit dangerous? Yes! Is it fun and flirty? Yes! Let's embrace it, Avery!"

"Blimey," she said, following him back into the shop. "I didn't know we'd been so gloomy and doomy!"

"Well, we have, and I'm over it. The sun is out, and the May Queen and her consort will be announced today, so I'm celebrating."

"Is this something to do with your love life?" Avery asked, as he fiddled with the music and the same song started again, but a different version.

"Nina Simone," he explained, before giving her a sly grin. "And maybe, or maybe not. This could be Beltane trickery, but I've decided to enjoy it while it lasts."

Avery leaned on the counter. "Is this Caroline, the lucky lady who got the benefit of the Goddess's little tease the other night?"

Dan looked at her, wide-eyed. "She might be. A gentleman doesn't kiss and tell."

She laughed. "Too late for that, you already did!"

"Damn it! Pretend I didn't."

"Don't worry, your secret's safe with me."

While they were talking, Sally came through the front door, looking flustered. "Sorry I'm late, the kids were playing up. What's going on with you, Dan? You look...different!"

"The joys of spring," Dan said, spreading his arms wide.

Sally just eyed him suspiciously, looking as if she was going to say more, and then decided against it. Instead she asked, "What time is the crowning of the May Queen?"

"Midday," Dan said. "We should close the shop and all go to see it."

Sally nodded as she put her bag on the counter and shrugged out of her jacket. "That's actually a great idea. What do you think, boss?"

"I agree," Avery said brightly. "An hour in the sun will do us all good. When's your next talk, Dan?"

"Tomorrow afternoon. Hopefully we'll have as many come to it as yesterday."

"Any funny questions about Helena?" she asked tentatively.

"Not really, just about the witch trials in general. Most people were horrified."

Sally snorted. "So they should be." She glanced behind her as a couple of customers came through the door. "I'm heading to the back to put in an order, and then I'll be done."

As Sally disappeared, the door chimes rang again, and Caspian came in, frowning, and headed straight to the counter. "Hey Dan," he said, with a nod. "Avery, I've found some photos."

He was carrying a large brown envelope, and he handed it to her. "These are some of my grandfather. I'm not sure if they're exactly from that time, but they're close enough. The script is in there, too."

Avery pulled the photos out and smiled as she looked through them. Caspian's grandfather wasn't as tall as Caspian, and his hair wasn't as dark, but there was still a strong family resemblance. "He's not really the hippie type, is he?"

Caspian laughed. "Did you really think he would be?"

Dan was looking over Avery's shoulder at the images, too. "Your family doesn't strike me as the bohemian type, Caspian."

"Oh, I don't know. My great aunt Rosalind was quite unorthodox, or so I gather, anyway."

Avery slid the photos back into the envelope. "Thanks, Caspian. I'm going to see Briar later this morning. I'll let you know what she says."

"If it is him, I'll obviously help to put this right. Well," he shrugged. "I'll help anyway, if you need me to. Oh, and I was wrong about the sigil. I saw similar ones in the books I consulted, but nothing quite like that. But that's probably because there are several combined."

"That's okay," Avery said, resigned. "Thanks for checking anyway."

Caspian glanced at his watch and turned to go. "I'll collect the photos at some point. Just leave them at the counter when you've finished with them."

Dan watched him go, and then looked at Avery speculatively. "What happened to Caspian?"

"What do you mean?"

"He was civil."

"He's been civil for months—and very helpful."

"Mmm. The things we do for love!" he said with a gleam in his eye.

Avery glared at him. "Dan, don't start."

"Start what?"

"You know very well what."

"All I will say is that you made the right choice. Alex is way cooler."

"There was no choice! It's not like Caspian was ever an option!" she hissed.

"But he wishes he was. Anyway," Dan said, sliding out from behind the counter. "I have some shelf stacking to do." And before Avery could say anything else, he left her stewing with annoyance.

Avery was aiming to head out at about eleven, and kept herself busy until then, trying to distract herself from Alex's absence, but then just as she was planning to leave, he arrived carrying a huge bouquet of flowers. A feeling of utter relief swept over Avery as she looked at him. He paused in the threshold of the shop, just watching her for a moment with an almost unfathomable expression on his face before he walked over, swept her into his arms, and kissed her, earning a round of applause from the surrounding customers.

"Steady on, fella," one of Avery's regular customers said, an older man in his sixties. "This is a public place, you know."

He was clearly joking, but his wife nudged him anyway. "You could learn a few lessons from him." She dropped her voice and winked at Avery. "Lucky you, my dear."

Avery laughed, flustered as she righted herself and accepted the flowers from Alex. "They're beautiful. But you didn't need to do this."

"Yes, I did." He looked around at the curious faces and pulled her towards the back room with a mock bow at the customers. "Excuse us!"

Sally looked up as they entered, and immediately leapt to her feet. "That's my cue. Nice flowers, Alex."

"Thanks, Sally," he said, trying to appear nonchalant. As soon as the door was closed and they were alone, he said, "I'm sorry. I shouldn't have stormed off last night. I was a bit of a drama queen."

Avery was still cradling her flowers, and she smiled at him, the scent enveloping her. "You had every right to be annoyed."

His eyes darkened. "I think I was experiencing a bit of my own guilt, actually."

Avery's bright mood suddenly plummeted. "Why? Who have you kissed?"

"No one. But I found myself flirting a bit too much with Kate at the bar yesterday, and it played on my mind."

"Kate with the nice arse?" Avery asked, struggling to control herself and not be a hypocrite.

"Yes. But yours is better." He hesitated as he looked at her face. "*Much, much* better!"

She laughed at his meek expression. "Yes it is, never forget that. And you always flirt, so I'm not really sure what you're apologising for."

Alex leaned against the wall, his hands in his jeans pockets, looking unbelievably sexy. "Yes, but it felt a bit more serious than it should have, and I have no idea why." He shrugged. "Beltane stupidity. It got under my skin. So, last night when you talked about Caspian, I think it hit a nerve."

"I think we're all feeling edgy," she admitted. "Hence the crazy jazz music playing in the shop. Dan is determined to enjoy the bright side of Beltane, not the dark."

"Good man." Alex stared at her a moment longer, a smile playing across his lips. "Are we okay?"

"We're more than okay."

"Good." He grinned, grabbed her hand, and pulled her to the stairs. "Let's make up in the best possible way!"

"No, I have something to show you," she protested as he pulled her up the stairs into the flat. "Caspian left some photos that we need to show Briar!"

Alex was already starting to peel her clothes off. "Bollocks to Caspian's photos," he said forcefully. "And Briar can wait."

Avery discovered that Briar's shop was a hive of activity, most of it revolving around Eli.

He was working at the counter, grinding and measuring dried herbs, an array of jars and muslin bags next to him, while talking to several young women who were leaning on the counter, watching him and idly chatting. He looked up as they entered and smiled. "Hey guys, can I help you?"

The bevy of females looked around at them, frowning at the interruption, and Avery tried and failed to suppress a grin. "Hey, Eli. You look busy."

Eli was utterly charming. He was as tall and broad-shouldered as the rest of the Nephilim, his voice was deep, his honey-coloured hair curled around his collar, and his smile was lazy and seductive. He joined them at the end of the counter, keeping a wary eye on his harem. "That's one word for it.

You want Briar, don't you?"

"We do—no rest for the wicked," Alex said to him, raising an eyebrow. He looked over at the handful of women who were now chatting amongst themselves, all while watching Eli with surreptitious glances. "I admire your stamina."

Eli leaned forward and lowered his voice. "Supernatural strength has its advantages."

"How do you juggle them all and keep them so happy?" Avery asked, genuinely curious.

"I share my favours equally, and promise nothing. Although, right now," he added with a frown, "Beltane has intensified feelings, which makes my life a little bit harder. I guess it keeps things interesting."

A young woman with glossy blonde hair coughed gently at the other end of the counter, summoning Eli's attention. "Eli, can I buy this, please?"

He turned and beamed at her, and she visibly swooned. "Sure, coming right now." He glanced back at Avery and Alex. "Briar's out the back with Hunter, making more stock."

Leaving Eli with his customers, although Avery wasn't sure that was really the right word for them, they headed to Briar's stockroom, and found her with a row of glass jars in front of her that she was filling with a rose-coloured liquid. Hunter was stirring the contents of a pot on the stove on the far side of the room, and the back door to the small courtyard was open, allowing fresh air to circulate. The room smelt of lilac and lilies, and Avery inhaled with pleasure.

"Hi, guys! Briar, it always smells divine in here."

"Hiya," Briar said, glancing up. "Good to see you. Bear with me a moment while I finish this."

"I can't stop, either," Hunter said, still methodically stirring the pot. "She's got me making potions."

"*Helping* to make potions," Briar corrected him, "and it's a tincture, actually."

He shrugged. "Whatever."

It was odd to see Hunter, dressed all in black and looking completely incongruous in Briar's workshop, engaged in doing something so domestic.

"Good to see Briar has you house trained," Alex said as he joined him.

"There are perks," he answered.

"Aren't you worried about Briar working with Mr Handsome out there?"

Hunter laughed. "Nope. I like to think I can make my woman happy."

Briar snorted. "Did you just say, 'my woman?'"

"Yes I did, and you know you like it," he called back. "Besides, Eli is sort of my God," he admitted in a low voice, making Avery snigger. "Have you watched him at work? That man really knows women. It's a skill, there's no other word for it."

"I hear that," Alex agreed.

Briar finished filling her jars, wiped her hands on a cloth, and headed to Hunter's side. She checked the consistency of the liquid in the pot, checked her watch, and then picked up a bowl of herbs and added it to the mix, uttering a spell under her breath. "You can stop stirring now," she told Hunter, and Avery saw the liquid change colour.

"What's that?"

"It's the base for my skin cream products. I'll give you some to try."

"Thanks, Briar, it smells amazing."

"Anyway," Briar said, satisfied, "have you two got news?"

Alex pulled the photos out of his jacket pocket. "Caspian brought these over this morning—they're of his grandfather. Do you recognise him as the ghost?"

Briar took them off him and shook her head. "I'm afraid not. He wasn't who I saw in the theatre."

"Damn it!" Avery said, not realising she'd put quite so much stock in them. "I really thought it would be him."

"He looks surprisingly like Caspian, doesn't he?" Briar observed as she showed them to Hunter.

Hunter nodded. "But I agree, he's not the ghost."

Alex sighed. "Back to square one, then."

"We need to thoroughly read the articles Dan brought with him from the library," Avery decided. "There must be something in there that we missed. I'll do that this afternoon."

"Will this make it harder for you to summon him?" Hunter asked.

Alex shrugged. "Maybe. Sometimes it helps to know something about the spirit, or to have something personal, but I can still make it work...I hope. I'm still not sure why he's appearing, though. Maybe that's what we should do tonight, after the performance."

"Conduct a séance?" Hunter asked. "I remember the last time you did something like that, and that bloody demon appeared." Hunter shuddered. The appearance of demon in the mirror at the House of Spirits had caused Hunter to turn into his wolf, completely unbidden.

"That won't happen this time," Alex reassured him. "This is a plain old ghost summoning, and maybe a banishing. It all depends how it's bound up with the play." He checked his watch. "I should be working this afternoon, but I could do with searching through my grimoire again. I'll see if I can get some cover."

Avery nodded, pleased they had made some progress. "Come on, we better go." As she spoke, she heard the beating of drums in the distance. "They must have started to celebrate the crowning of the May Queen. Let's see it while we can," she urged Alex. "Are you two going to watch?"

"I've got more stock to make," Briar said. "But you could go, Hunter."

He grimaced. "I'm not really the May Queen type!"

"In that case," Avery said, laughing, "we'll be in touch about tonight."

Once outside, Alex and Avery followed the crowds down to the main street, the drums sounding louder and louder.

As they turned the corner, they saw a parade of school children of a variety of ages marching down the road in spring costumes decorated with flowers and greenery, escorted by proud parents and teachers. Their enthusiasm was infectious, and Avery felt her spirits lift despite her worries as they weaved through the crowd.

In the middle of the procession, and surrounded by some primary school children wearing flower wreaths, was a beautiful young woman in a blue gown covered in tiny flowers—the May Queen. As they reached the square, the parade slowed down, finally congregating together, humming with nervous energy as the young woman waited to be summoned. At the edge of the square on a raised dais were two enormous wooden thrones decorated with spring branches and greenery, and the ribbons of the maypole in the middle were unfurled, lifting lazily in the breeze.

While the May Queen and her maidens waited on the edge of the square, the Morris dancers entertained the watching crowd, and Avery saw Stan waiting at the side in his cloak. It was a struggle to see properly because there were so many people around, but Avery was pleased to see Dan and Sally in the crowd, relieved they'd been able to close the shop. She also saw Rueben and Ash on the far side of the square, and presumed they were there because of the plants they'd provided. A woman stood next to Stan, her shock of her red hair making her stand out from the crowd. It was the Mayor, and she was carrying a beautiful crown of flowers, no doubt for the May Queen.

The Morris dancers completed their performance, but the drums continued to slowly beat, and Stan stepped forward to welcome the onlookers and then urged the crowd to part, allowing a young man dressed in green to enter the square.

It was the Green Man, the consort to the May Queen. Avery estimated that they were both only eighteen or nineteen, but they looked confident, and she knew from what Stan had previously told her that they were drama school students at the local college. *They needed to be*, she reflected. The main procession on Saturday required some maturity, and the ability to act because it was very dramatic. The costumes they would wear then must be far more impressive, and at dusk, with night falling and the fire jugglers lining the streets, they would look spectacular. This was just a warm-up.

Nevertheless, today was an important part of the town's celebrations, and Stan welcomed the Green Man and the May Queen in to the centre of the square, where the Mayor formally congratulated them and placed the crown of flowers upon the May Queen's head. Then they were led to the thrones overlooking the maypole, and the young children who had accompanied the Queen each took a ribbon and started their dance.

The crowd was charmed, and after a few minutes, Alex nudged her arm. "Come on, we'd better get back."

After lunch the two of them settled in the attic, Avery to read the articles that Dan had found, and Alex to search his grimoire and prepare to summon the ghost.

Avery started by reading some of the reviews of the play in the local papers, and Dan was right, they were good. The leads were praised for their acting and the passion they bought to the performance, King Mark was described as regal and stoic in betrayal, and the Barons were suitably Machiavellian. The reviews also described the audience as being enraptured. No wonder, they were under a spell.

Eventually, Avery started to read the reports of the deaths and the background on the main characters, and quickly spotted the reference to Kernow Industries. Then she found the article she'd read the night before that said for the previous few months Yvonne, who had played Iseult, had been working in a pub near the quay called The Silver Dolphin. The regulars spoke of her as friendly and hard working, and said she'd be missed. Avery leaned back on the sofa where she'd curled with the research.

The Silver Dolphin by the quay.

She turned to look at Alex where he sat at the table, head bent over his grimoire as he made notes. "Alex, has your pub always been called The Wayward Son?"

He looked at her for a moment, struggling to focus. "No, it was something else first, but I can't remember what. Something nautical."

"Was it called The Silver Dolphin, perhaps?"

He frowned. "Yes, that's sounds familiar. Why?"

"Yvonne Warner, aka Iseult, worked there in the months before her death, after she worked at Kernow Industries—well, according to this article, anyway."

Alex slumped back in his chair, staring blankly at the pages in front of him. "Did she? My granddad would have owned the place then." His fingers drummed the table, and he finally lifted his gaze and looked at Avery. "Shit. Should I be worried?"

"I don't know. I presume your granddad was a witch?"

"Yes. I have no idea how powerful he was, though, or how he chose to use his magic."

"More importantly, was he tall and dark-haired? Isn't that how Briar described the ghost?"

"I think he was. It's been years since I saw any photos of him, and I never met him, although I've been told I look a bit like him."

"Why didn't you meet him?"

"He was long gone when I arrived in the world."

"Gone where?"

"Dead," he said flatly. "My dad didn't talk about him, and as you know, he's in Scotland now, and I don't hear from him that often."

Avery was trying not to presume too much, and knew Alex would be too, but this was an unfortunate connection. "Alex, have you got some photos of your granddad somewhere?"

He nodded. "Probably in those boxes in the study. They're full of old photos that I've been meaning to scan into the computer." He flicked to the front of the grimoire that had been started in the eighteenth century, and Avery knew he'd be looking for his name. Every witch wrote his or her name on the first pages of the family grimoire, and every witch would have annotated or written new spells. "He's here, Kit Bonneville."

Avery smiled. "Kit! That's a cool name."

"Short for Kitto, I think, very Cornish!" Alex said, smiling briefly. The chair scraped the floor as he rose to his feet and headed to the stairs. "You're wondering if he's the ghost, aren't you? I'm going to look."

"I'm afraid so," she said, untangling herself from the paperwork and rising to her feet. "I'm coming, too."

Alex's study was next to the living room, converted from what had been a spare bedroom. Avery smiled as she looked around. It was obviously his space. The room looked over the road at the front of the house, and he'd placed an old wooden desk there for the view. The computer and printer were lined up on the table, and a sleek leather desk chair sat in front of it. Alex had put shelves on the wall that were mostly filled with his books and other personal items, as well as the old photo albums he'd brought from his flat, accumulated over decades, and encompassing countless family holidays, Christmas mornings, weddings, and birthdays. It was these he headed to now, starting to move them onto the desk and rifle through them.

He pushed a box towards Avery. "Try this one. The ones we want will be really old, from the fifties, maybe sixties."

Avery nodded and picked up a dog-eared envelope with Kodak branding on it, and pulling out the photos, immediately recognised the fashion of the 1980s. She laughed at the clothing. "Wow. Did people really wear these things?"

She put them down, reaching for another packet, and found pictures that were much older. She squinted as she tried to identify buildings, occasionally noting streets she recognised, and stretches of beaches and coves. And then she paused as she came across the photo of a tall, dark-haired man in a smart 1950s-style suit, and what looked to be the bar of a pub behind him.

"Alex, look at this. Is this Kit?"

Alex took the photo from her, and after studying it for a moment, he nodded. "Yes, I think so. Are there any more?"

He leaned over her shoulder as she flicked through the remainder of the pack, eventually finding about half a dozen images, some with two younger men, others with a woman she didn't recognise, and she passed each one back to him.

"Who are the other men?"

"My uncle Treeve, who managed the pub before I took it over, and my dad." He pointed him out. "They look so young."

"You look like them," Avery observed. "Well, apart from the fact that they look so clean cut, and you don't."

Alex laughed. "Neither my uncle or my dad looked that clean cut later in life." His laughter, however, quickly died out. "I suppose we should show these to Briar."

"Take a photo with your phone," she advised. "The quality will be good enough for her to hopefully either recognise him or rule him out."

"Good idea," he said, and quickly snapped the pictures and sent them off.

For several anxious moments they remained silent, and Avery started on another pack while Alex paced the room. But they didn't have to wait long as Alex's phone disturbed the silence and he answered quickly, exchanging a few words with Briar. Avery saw his face change and he sounded resigned as he said, "Thanks Briar, at least we know who it is now. I'll call you later." Alex sank onto his leather chair, his mood sombre. "She's pretty sure it's him, which means my grandfather probably bewitched the play."

"Probably." Avery sat on the edge of the desk. "Any idea why?"

"Nope."

"Are you sure there's nothing in your grimoire that's similar to the sigils on the script?"

"I don't think so, but if I'm honest, there are a lot of sigils, runes, and summoning circles in there. They all sort of blend together after a while. And if I'm really honest, I haven't actually been looking for an exact match—I've been searching for summoning spells."

Avery nodded. "I think you need to have a second look."

Alex looked at the photos again, and then at her. "If my grandfather is responsible for this, I'll be mortified."

"We are not responsible for our ancestors' actions."

"I know. But if he is, he must have met Yvonne at the pub. Was he having an affair with her? Did he fancy her and get rejected? And why did she leave Kernow Industries to work in a pub? It must have been a better job."

"Maybe she was serious about her acting, and the pub offered more flexible hours? Or perhaps she hated the boss and couldn't wait to get out, so she was happy to do anything else?"

"I'm sure being in a small town production wouldn't have been the step to the big time."

"Maybe not, but she might have had dreams. I would imagine this was a very sleepy place back then." Avery reached forward and grabbed his hand, pulling him to his feet. "Come on. Let's get back to it. I'll ring El and Reuben and let them know the plans for tonight have changed, and that we'll be summoning a ghost tonight, and not just stealing scripts."

Eighteen

As they'd agreed, Avery and El arrived at the theatre at the end of that night's performance to talk to the cast, and spelled themselves inside the side door. Reuben hadn't been able to come early, and they had arranged to call him and the others when the theatre was empty.

El looked like an overexcited child. "I love this energy, Avery. Do you think this feeling is normal after every performance, or just because this one has a spell on it?"

The atmosphere backstage was electric, and the energy of the cast was high, if tense. A couple of people had recognised them, giving them vague smiles, but as the play hadn't finished yet, they were still preoccupied. El and Avery had tucked themselves into a small space just beyond the steps to the wings, listening to the muted voices onstage.

Avery shrugged. "I have no idea, but I would imagine this must be pretty normal."

"Maybe I should join up?"

"Are you kidding?" Avery asked, astonished.

"No! I'd love to do all this backstage stuff. I'm more interested in this than acting."

"But what exactly would you do?"

El flattened herself against the wall as King Arthur strode past, a crown on his head, looking imperious. "I don't know—costumes, makeup? I'd love any of it!"

"But would you love it if it was the back of a community centre, and not the awesome setting of the White Haven Little Theatre?"

"Yes, I think I still would."

Both of them retreated again as another cast member scurried past, and Avery said, "This is a stupid place to stand. Let's head to the dressing rooms."

"No, wait." El's hand was on her arm. "Let's check the audience. We can open the door...they won't notice in the dark."

El edged towards the door to the stalls where the end of the corridor was in complete darkness, and pushed it open an inch. Avery crouched down below El, and peered through the gap.

The front rows of the audience were illuminated by the lights from the stage, and they looked mesmerised. A strong wave of magic hit Avery, and El must have felt it too, because she heard her muffle a gasp before she pushed the door open wider so they could get a better look.

Avery squinted at rows that were further back, just about able to see their faces in the dark hall. No one moved. Not a blink, a shuffle, a cough or sneeze, or even a rummage in a bag of sweets. It was eerie. El shut the door and they looked at each other, astounded.

"Wow," El muttered. "That was full-on!"

"They're completely bewitched!"

El grabbed her arm, pulling her quickly back down the corridor. "The cast must be affected, too! Come on, let's head to the dressing rooms."

Avery resisted. "No, wait. If we use the shadow spell, we can squash into the wings."

El nodded and Avery quickly said the spell, sending them shimmering into invisibility, and without waiting to think of the consequences, Avery led the way up the stairs and to the back of the wings.

A cluster of actors and stagehands stood watching the performance, and if anything, the spell felt even more intense from there. Most people watched the performance, and Avery could just see Iseult onstage, kneeling next to Tristan on his bower. She saw Gail, the actress who was playing

Brangain, standing and watching the scene, tears pouring down her face, and Alison who managed the wardrobe was watching her, eyes wide and mouth slightly open in shock. Gail was so utterly absorbed in the play that she didn't even notice.

One of the three Barons stood talking quietly to King Mark—or Ian, Avery reminded herself—and he looked furious. Avery edged close enough to hear him say, "I swear my lord, if he talks to me like that again, I'll kill him."

"And you will have my full support! He has been against me all along—siding with Tristan at every turn. It is traitorous!" Even in the gloomy light of the wings Avery could see the sweat beading Ian's brow, and her blood chilled.

The Baron's hand fell to his sword. "Perhaps we should not wait, then. I will deal with him later."

Ian nodded, his face resolute, and Avery backed away, stumbling into El, who was close behind her, and she felt El's cool fingers grab her arm and pull her back down the stairs to the dim corridor.

As soon as they were away from the wings, she cancelled the spell, and El's pale face emerged from the shadows. "Bloody hell, Avery, the cast is completely bewitched! Come on, dressing rooms, now!"

El strode away, heading for the largest dressing room, and Avery almost ran to keep up. As soon as they were close, they heard raised voices, and by the time they paused at the threshold, it was clear someone was having a full-blown argument.

It seemed that most of the cast members were there, still in full costumes and makeup, clustered around two people in the middle of the room. Avery edged forward and saw that Harry, Dan's friend, was nose to nose with another one of the Barons, and they were yelling at each other about loyalty, friendship, and betrayal, talking over one another so rapidly that Avery could barely understand them. She caught the name Godwin, and realised that was the name of the Baron. Both of them were red faced and sweating profusely, their stage makeup smeared and demonic, but suddenly Harry shoved Godwin hard in the chest, and as he staggered backwards, Harry followed it up with a punch. In seconds Godwin responded, and then the rest of the watching cast joined in, and Avery couldn't work out if they were trying to stop them or were trading punches, too.

Avery looked at El, completely shocked, and they both faltered, wondering what to do. The atmosphere was ugly, and the fight showed no signs of stopping. Someone went flying into a table that upended, sending props scattering, and then a screech made Avery turn to see two women rolling on the floor, tearing at each other's hair and clothes. She ran over, trying to pull them apart, but they ignored her, totally focussed on each other, and almost dragged Avery into the fight.

She staggered back to El's side. "Shit! What are we going to do?"

The clanging of metal made her whirl around again as this time, Harry clashed swords with Godwin, and an ugly welt of blood welled across Godwin's chest.

"Magic. It's the only thing that will stop this, or someone is going to get seriously injured."

"But how? They'll know!"

"I don't think they'll notice a damn thing," El said, stepping back to the doorway to dodge a punch and dragging Avery with her. "And I can see just the thing!" El pointed at the sprinkler on the ceiling. "That!" She sent a stream of flame across the ceiling, engulfing the sprinkler, and in mere seconds water burst from it, drenching everyone below.

Instead of cries of anger, there were shrieks of shock as the ice-cold water brought everyone to their senses. El and Avery retreated to the corridor as the cast rushed out of the dressing room, pushing and shoving in their haste to leave, and with a word, El stopped the sprinkler.

Harry paused next to them, bedraggled and shaking, and utterly confused. "What the hell just happened? Is there a fire?"

Without missing a beat, El said, "We've only just arrived, Harry, so no idea. It probably just malfunctioned. Look around. No other sprinklers are going off, which is a relief!"

The other cast members were standing around shivering, and a young woman next to Avery said, "I don't even remember what I was just doing!"

"Oh my God," another one said, looking down at her dress, and then the pools of water on the floor of the dressing room. "Look at the costumes!"

They were galvanised into action, running inside to salvage what they could, and Avery and El took the opportunity to retreat down the corridor into a store room filled with stage furniture and other props, and shut the door firmly behind them.

"Well," Avery said, her thoughts reeling, "I guess that answers that question. The cast have gone nuts!"

El started to laugh, and then stopped herself with a guilty expression. "Sorry! I shouldn't laugh, but that was funny...well, in places."

"And scary. What if we hadn't arrived?"

"I think someone would have found them and stopped them, maybe the stage crew. I hope. But in the meantime, let's make ourselves comfortable." El rummaged around in the props behind them, and finding a couple of chairs, sat down and patted the seat next to her. "Let's let them settle down out there, and then we'll see what else we can find out."

Avery and El were sitting together on the second row of seats, their feet on the back of the seats in front of them, chatting quietly about the events earlier. It had been spooky with just the two of them waiting in the oppressive silence and near darkness, and Avery was grateful to have El's company. She had been sure that once or twice she had detected Kit's lingering presence, a persistent edge of spite that whispered around them.

"This is becoming a very strange habit," Reuben noted as he and the others entered the deserted auditorium.

"Have you two had fun?" Alex said to Avery and El. He carried a large pack with the items he needed to summon his grandfather's ghost, and he placed it on a chair and slipped his jacket off.

"If I'm honest," Avery said, sitting up and placing her feet on the floor, "it's been a bit weird."

"Everything we do is weird," Hunter told her. He leaned against the stage, his hands in his leather jacket pockets, and his jeans low on his slim hips. Hunter looked dangerous at night, as if he might do anything, and his dark eyes smouldered with a dull yellow fire. "It's why I like you guys. Shifters like weird. Where's the fun in normal?"

"Too true, my friend," Reuben said, slapping his shoulder.

Briar sat next to El, looking concerned. "What happened?"

"Where shall we start?" El said. "With the fight in the dressing room that I had to stop using the water sprinkler? The utterly lovelorn behaviour of Tristan and Iseult, which was no different onstage than off? King Mark's fury at his betrayal, and the second fight that almost started but a stagehand broke up?"

"And don't forget the new potion bottle that also has a spell on it!" Avery added.

A brief silence fell before Alex said, "Wow. You've been busy!"

"I'll give you the details later," Avery said as she stood and stretched, realising she'd gone cold sitting in the dark for the last half an hour. "Are Cassie and the boys coming?"

"They should be behind us," Reuben said, turning to look for them. Right on cue, three familiar figures jostled through the stage doors, carrying bulky bags. "And here they are! Long time no see, guys! Welcome to the Beltane madness."

Cassie, Ben, and Dylan greeted everyone enthusiastically, and Ben said, "It's great to be here! We're sick of finishing up lab studies, and glad to be in the field again."

"Lab studies?" Reuben asked, eyebrows raised.

"Psychometric testing," Cassie explained. "For our finals."

"Not for me," Dylan said, shaking his head. "Just lots of essays. But I've missed this!"

All three of them looked tired, Avery thought, but they must have kept up some of their new exercise regime, because they looked lean and ready for action.

Cassie looked around in wonder. "I can't believe we're in a haunted theatre!" She had barely finished her sentence when the whine of the EMF meter started, and Avery saw Ben already starting to calibrate it.

"This is so cool, guys," he said, his tiredness disappearing as excitement took over. "Thanks for asking us to come."

Avery smiled. "Our pleasure, although you might not thank us later. This place has bad vibes."

"It doesn't seem to be deterring the audience, though," El pointed out. "It was packed tonight, and I saw another stellar review in the paper today!"

"That's because they're bewitched," Avery said, finding it hard to shake off her worry. Bewitching an entire audience was clever and powerful, and Avery was already feeling daunted by the task ahead.

Briar nodded. "It's like I said earlier, the audience brings its own energy. It will fuel whatever's going on here."

"So, what's the plan, Alex?" Reuben asked, already rolling his shoulders as if expecting trouble.

"I'm going to set up in front of the stage," Alex explained. "Seeing as this is where Briar and Hunter saw Kit's spirit, it seems the most charged place."

"You should have been in the dressing room earlier," El said with a half laugh. "It was pretty charged in there!"

Cassie looked at Alex, surprised. "You have a name for the ghost?"

"Sorry! Didn't you know? It's my granddad!"

Cassie's mouth fell open in shock, and while Alex started to prepare his summoning circle, Avery quickly explained what they'd found out that afternoon.

Dylan was setting up his thermal camera as he listened. "Interesting. So the play is bewitched, and the performance seems to have summoned Kit's ghost?"

"That's what we think," she explained with a shrug, "but we're not really sure how. And we're also wondering if it has summoned the ghosts of Yvonne Warner and Charles Ball who played the characters in the sixties. The cast have experienced cold draughts, icy patches in rooms...you know, the usual."

Ben nodded. "I saw that report on the news, but I wasn't sure if it was real or just publicity for the play. Sarah Rutherford again, wasn't it?"

El had been listening, and she said, "Yes, she's covering the Beltane celebrations."

Cassie looked puzzled. "Why couldn't the ghost just be Kit alone? Why do you think there are the other two as well?"

"One of the cast members said they smelt perfume," Avery explained. "I doubt Kit wore perfume!" She went on to explain about the affairs of the leads from the 1960s and how they had committed suicide.

Ben whistled. "Wow. What the hell kind of spell could do that?"

"That's what I'm trying to find out," Alex said, rising to his feet. He had drawn a large salt circle on the floor just in front of the stage, in the centre of which was a curious sign.

Hunter had been sitting on the stage watching and listening, and he now asked, "Aren't you going to banish him?"

"I'd like to," Alex said, "but he'll likely have valuable information I want. I don't think banishing him will stop the spell on the play, and we have to break that. I need to know how he did it."

"You don't know now, I presume?" Dylan asked.

"No. There's a complicated knot of sigils to identify, but we're struggling with it to be honest, and we have no idea how it was activated. All we know is that it's powerful, and that hasn't diminished with time—or my grandfather's death."

Dylan was already starting to film, sweeping the large room with his thermal imaging camera, while Ben paced around with his EMF meter, the static buzz low in the back ground. Cassie had prepared the sheets they used to record any phenomena and was about to start reading temperatures around the hall, but she looked at the witches, worried. "It doesn't sound like we know much at all."

"We know that some of the sigils on the cover mean power, obsession, and revenge, but we think we're missing something," El explained. "It's frustrating. But," she said, her face brightening. "I do have this!" She reached into her backpack that Reuben had brought with him, and pulled out the curved blade of the Empusa's sword.

"Wow!" Avery said, surprised. "I'd forgotten you'd got that!"

"I've been itching to use this ever since Shadow told me what it can do." She gripped it tightly, making loops in the air. "It's just back-up, in case things get dangerous!"

"It better be," Alex warned. "I need him!"

Dylan did a double take when he saw the sword, and he walked over, stopping filming. "Can I?" he asked, holding his hand out.

"Of course," El said, offering him the hilt.

Dylan's eyes ran along the blade. "Bronze? Wow. What a cool sword. Where did you get it from?"

"Shadow defeated the Empusa, and this was our reward. There are two of them."

"What will a sword do against a ghost?" Cassie asked, looking sceptical.

"We recently found out that it has special powers. When you're holding it, you can see ghosts, as if they're flesh and blood," El explained, "and this will cut them as if they're real."

Hearing the discussion, Ben joined them, too. "And how does it do that?"

"Special Underworld properties," Reuben said, "courtesy of Hecate and her servant. Beyond that—no idea!"

Ben shook his head, returning to sweeping the room with the EMF meter. "You guys are full of surprises."

Alex interrupted them. He stood in front of the stage, his hair tied back. "Right, I'm ready. I need you to sit around the salt circle, at your cardinal elements. You don't need to say anything. I'll recite the summoning spell, but I will draw on your strength to help do it." He rubbed his face as he looked at them. "I have a feeling this will be difficult."

Hunter watched the witches take their places around the large circle that was almost two meters in diameter, each sitting behind the glowing light of a candle marking the elemental place on the pentagram Alex had drawn. "Should I hold the Empusa's sword, just in case?"

Alex looked at him for a long moment, considering his suggestion, and he finally sighed. "Yes, okay, but do not use it except as a means to see him! I don't care how hairy it gets!"

"Even if he attacks?" Hunter asked evenly, picking the sword up from the chair where El had left it.

"Yes—although, he shouldn't be able to leave the circle."

Avery immediately argued, "No! If he's trying to kill you, we should use the sword!"

"He won't try to kill me!" Alex said, exasperated. "He's a ghost!"

Avery nodded, reluctantly, wondering how strong the ghost of this particular witch would be. Helena was certainly sentient, and still retained some kind of power, but ghosts generally couldn't touch someone, or possess them. The glow of the candlelight was comforting in the darkness, far more so than the cool white of their witch-lights. She noticed Hunter and the three investigators were keeping their distance from the circle, which was wise. In theory, the spirit would be contained within the circle, but it was best to be safe.

While they had been preparing, Avery hadn't felt anything manifest in the auditorium, but as soon as she was seated around the circle, she felt the room close in. The stage loomed large above her, and the chairs crowded her on the other side. Alex sat confidently on the point of the Spirit to Avery's right, El was to her left, and Briar was opposite her, while Reuben was to Alex's right. They had all sat in these positions many times now, and were comfortable together; strong in their power, and the trust they had in each other.

"Are you all ready?" Alex asked, his grimoire resting on his knees.

They nodded, and Alex began the slow intonation of the spell.

For long moments, nothing happened, and Avery closed her eyes, feeling her energy rise, and a snap as Alex connected to her. It was like flicking on an electric circuit as she felt her fellow witches' energies merge with her own. It was exhilarating, and as Alex's low voice continued the spell, she felt their collective power grow. The air eddied around her slowly, and then a prickle of discomfort spread along her neck and down her spine, and Avery opened her eyes and almost jerked back in shock.

The ghost of Kit Bonneville was standing in the centre of the circle, wearing old-fashioned clothing, with his hair slicked back. His eyes were dark, but a flame seemed to burn within them, and his face was twisted with anger as he glared at Alex. It was uncanny. They were very alike, and if Alex's hair was shorter and he had been clean-shaven, the resemblance would have been obvious.

Kit flickered in and out for a moment, as if a current was breaking, but Alex's voice grew louder as he summoned Kit and commanded him to stay. Kit's mouth moved as if he was trying to speak, and he glared at the witches around the circle. His gaze swept over Avery, and she felt his fury through his icy regard.

Alex stopped reciting the spell and said, "Welcome, Kit."

Kit's mouth moved again, and Avery heard a groan as he tried to speak. It was taking some effort, but finally Kit growled out, "Who are you?"

"I'm your grandson, Alex Bonneville. Finn's son."

Kit crouched down so he was at eye-level with Alex. "Are you now?" He turned his head, glancing at the rest of the witches. "And who are they?"

"My coven—the White Haven witches."

Kit threw his head back and laughed. "There is no coven in White Haven!"

Alex narrowed his eyes at him. "There might not have been in your day, but there is now. The old families are all back."

Kit fell silent for a moment, looking puzzled. "What old families?"

"The families who once lived in White Haven, before the Witchfinder General and the Favershams forced them out. We're members of the Witches Council now."

No wonder Kit was confused. Witchcraft had been firmly pushed into the background in White Haven for years, and the families were never allowed into the council. However, Kit was not impressed. Instead, he sneered. "If you put your faith in them, you'll be sorry."

"I haven't been so far," Alex said evenly. "But that's not why I summoned you, Kit. I want to know about the play, *Tristan and Iseult*, and I need to know about Yvonne Warner."

"Ha! Yvonne!" Kit rose to his feet swiftly and started to pace the circle. He paused at the edge by Briar, and stretched his hand out to where the circle's power vibrated at the salt edge. It flashed a bright blue, and Avery felt the flare of magic vibrate through her. Kit withdrew his hand quickly, whirling around and glaring at Alex. "How dare you seal me in this aberration?"

"It's a summoning circle," Alex said impatiently. "I'm sure you've used one many times. Tell me about Yvonne."

"Why do you care about her? She's been dead a very long time."

"I know. She worked with you, didn't she?"

"What of it?"

"She was in the play, *Tristan and Iseult*, when it was performed in 1964. Strange things happened in that play, Kit, things I think you were responsible for."

"And why would I care about a play?"

"It wasn't the play you cared about, it was Yvonne." Alex waited, but Kit was silent, watching Alex with his arms folded across his chest. Alex continued, "The play is finally being performed again, and the cast are behaving strangely, taking on the emotions and characteristics of the characters in the play. When we examined the scripts they were using—that by the way had been hidden away in the basement of the White Haven Council buildings—we found some very odd sigils and runes on the pages. They have been cursed, and the actors are bewitched. We decided to look at the last time the play was performed, and it led us to Yvonne, Charles, and you."

"I wasn't in the play," Kit pointed out smugly.

"Yvonne worked for you. It's a suspicious coincidence. What happened? Did she reject your advances, and you decided to get your revenge?"

Kit stepped close to the circle's edge again, and crouched so that he was inches from Alex. His eyes were almost black with anger. "I was a married man, Alex, married to your grandmother. You should watch your mouth!"

"A witch bewitched this play—a powerful one. My father and uncle were too young. Who else could it have been?"

Avery had the feeling this could go on for hours; after all, they had no hard proof that Kit had done anything wrong, and he wasn't exactly answering Alex's questions.

Alex continued to hold Kit's stare. "Why are you haunting White Haven Little Theatre at the same time as this play is being performed? It's not a coincidence at all, is it? You cursed the play, and tied yourself to it in some way."

Kit displayed a slow, devious smile that made Avery's skin crawl. From where she sat, close to Alex, she could see Kit's expression clearly, as could Reuben; the other witches would only be able to see his back. He looked up and around him as if seeing where he had been summoned for the first time. "It's a beautiful place, isn't it? There are worse places to be summoned to." He looked insufferably pleased with himself. "I wasn't sure when I cast the spell if it would even work this long, but it seems my power was greater than I hoped."

"So you admit that you put a spell on the play?" Alex asked.

"Yes, I do. And there's nothing you can do about it."

Alex's face hardened. "We'll see about that. It's creating havoc, and I mean to stop it!"

"You'll stop nothing!" Kit spat. "I spelled it, and so it shall remain."

"I'll find all of the scripts and burn them!"

"You can try," Kit said with a sly grin.

Alex had been attempting to remain calm, but now his anger swelled. "Yvonne Warner and Charles Ball killed themselves because of the curse you put on this play! They were bewitched—forced to take on the emotions of the characters in real life! Other cast members fought and almost killed each other! Answer my damn question! Did you have an affair with Yvonne Warner?"

"No!" Kit answered, furious. "The jumped-up bitch had a high opinion of herself, and made it very clear that she would have nothing to do with me—except expect me to pay her damn wages! I'd have sacked her but it would have looked too suspicious, so I did something much better—I cursed the stupid play that she cared so much about!"

Alex's face was pinched with anger. "She killed herself because of you! And so did Charles Ball."

"When did we become so puritanical?" Kit said with a sneer. "The Bonneville witches are powerful—seers, psychics, demon conjurors and spell makers who can take what we want."

"That is not what witchcraft is, and you know it!" Alex answered, forcing himself to be calm after his outburst. "Your curse is now affecting other people. We have to stop it!"

Kit stood up, once again turning to pace around the circle, and again his hard stare passed over Avery. She felt rage still burning within him, the fury of his rejection. "She's here, I know it," Kit said. "I can feel her. She's keeping her distance, but I'd know her anywhere. She's trapped here, and I'll find her eventually."

A chill ran through Avery's blood, and she glanced at Alex, seeing his eyes widen. "What does that mean?"

"It means," Kit said, rounding on him, "that I bound her spirit to this play after death, and now she can't go anywhere." With one final sneer, he raised his hands, and a crackle of energy unleashed, striking the circle with such unexpected force that the circle of protection exploded outwards, and Avery felt her energy leach from her as her body was thrown back several feet. Her head was ringing, and when her vision finally cleared, she saw that Kit had vanished.

Nineteen

The witches staggered to their feet, winded and shaken, and Avery quickly spelled the candles back on.

Hunter was standing in the centre aisle, sword in hand as he spun around looking for Kit, while Cassie, Ben, and Dylan stood close by him, continuing to film and monitor the room.

"Are you guys okay?" Cassie shouted over.

"Fine! If bruised," Reuben shouted back. "Any sign of him?"

"None, he's vanished," Hunter said, still scanning the room. "But this sword is incredible! I don't know how he appeared to you, but he looked as real as you do to me."

"Damn it," Alex said as he rubbed the back of his head where it had struck the stage.

Dylan said, "I can't see him either. There was a sort of flare of energy, and then nothing."

"How the hell did he do that?" Reuben asked, bewildered.

Alex shrugged. "I don't know. He shouldn't be able to summon that much magic as a ghost!"

Briar winced as she untangled herself from the seat she had crashed into. "His magic is bound into the pages of the script, tying his spirit to it in some way, and that's why he's more powerful than he should be. Well, that's my theory anyway."

"It's a good one," El said, nodding in agreement as she dusted herself down. "But it's incredibly vindictive, and well, obsessive really." She looked at Alex. "You said that Kit died before you were born?"

"Yes, in the seventies I think, probably only a few years after these events."

"How?"

"I was told he'd had a heart attack, but that's all." He looked puzzled. "No one really talked about him much. By the time I was born, he'd been dead for years."

"But was that because no one liked him? I mean, did he have a bad reputation in your family?" El asked.

Alex ran his hand through his hair, freeing it from the tie that had been pulling it back. "I always got the feeling that my dad didn't really like him, or my uncle, to be honest, but I didn't really question it. And my gran died when I was young, so I have no idea what she thought of him."

Avery had pulled herself onto the stage, and now sat on its edge, her legs swinging. "I'm intrigued about this binding of his spirit. Did he bind himself to the play at the time he cursed it, or did he do it later? He looked reasonably young as a ghost. Maybe he died earlier than you think, Alex."

Reuben had been quietly listening, but now he nodded in agreement. "Maybe binding himself to the play was what killed him."

Alex fell silent for a while, thinking, and the only sound in the theatre was the low static whine of the EMF meter. Something was playing on Avery's mind, and she couldn't think what it was for a moment, until it struck her. "Kit said he bound Yvonne's spirit to this play too, didn't he?"

"Yes," Briar answered. "I found that particularly terrifying, if I'm honest. He must have been obsessed with her!"

"Or just a vengeful bastard," El said. She was standing by Reuben, both of them watching the progress of the three investigators. "I hope the curse did give him a heart attack!"

"But how did he bind Yvonne's spirit?" Avery asked. "I presume she killed herself, and then he summoned her ghost and did it that way."

Alex started to gather his things together, and then stopped suddenly, looking up at Avery. "Why don't I try to summon *her*? Kit was unwilling to share too much, but Yvonne would likely be more willing."

"Don't you need something personal of hers, though?" Avery asked, sliding off the stage and standing up.

"What about the costume jewels she would have worn during the play?" Briar suggested. "Stan said they found some in the box with the scripts. It might still be backstage."

"Won't the current Iseult be wearing them?" Reuben said. "If she's bewitched, then she might not be taking them off."

"It's worth checking," Alex said, turning as if to head backstage.

But before any of them could do anything else, the EMF meter surged to life, and Ben shouted, "Something's over here! I'm picking up an energy signature—and it's freezing!"

Ben was standing towards the rear of the stalls, under the circle, and everyone raced over, skidding to a halt a short distance away. Alex raised his hands and started to intone a spell, but Hunter thrust the sword into his hand. "It's Yvonne, I can see her."

"Whoa!" Alex said immediately, his eyes wide. He stepped forward carefully, as if approaching a frightened child, gesturing the others back. "Yvonne, can you see me?"

To Avery, it appeared as if the air stirred in front of Alex, a shimmer through which the back of the theatre seemed to waiver. She must have answered because Alex said, "I want to help, Yvonne. Don't be frightened."

Avery shivered. The icy cold air was reaching around them, and Avery's breath appeared as a cloud before her.

Alex said, "I know he's here. He's looking for you. Can you keep hidden from him for a while longer?"

In the silence that followed, Avery stood next to Dylan, watching the thermal image on the screen of the camera. It was eerie. An amorphous figure appeared only a few feet away, the approximation of limbs and a head just visible.

Alex nodded. "I'm going to free your spirit, Yvonne. I don't know how yet, but I will. Can you tell me what happened between you and Kit?"

The thermal image showed Yvonne's arms lifting, and Avery could imagine her despair and anger. If anything the temperature plummeted further, and Avery wrapped her arms around herself and clenched her teeth together to stop them from chattering. Briar's hands were to her lips, her face anguished, and Avery wondered if she was detecting more of Yvonne's emotions.

Alex kept nodding, encouraging her gently, until he finally said, "Thank you, Yvonne. I promise to free your spirit before the play's end, okay? Where is the ring?"

He blanched as she answered, and then within seconds, she'd gone, and the temperature returned to normal.

Reuben was leaning against the back of one of the chairs, and before Alex could speak, he said, "The ring's on her body, isn't it?"

"Yep."

"And where's that?"

"The cemetery on the edge of town." Alex rubbed his face wearily. "We're going to have to dig up her body."

Briar looked horrified. "There must be other options! Surely we can burn the scripts and that will break the spell?"

"Burning grimoires doesn't break spells," Avery pointed out.

"True," Alex agreed. "But the scripts are imbued with power of their own. They are a big part of the spell! However, Yvonne is pretty sure that the ring is what binds her spirit, not the scripts."

El had retrieved the bronze sword from Alex, and continued to scan the auditorium. "What worries me is when you said you'd burn all the scripts, and Kit said you could try. That suggests to me that he's hidden one."

"Fuck it!" Alex exclaimed, starting to pace off his annoyance. "I'd forgotten he said that! You're right, El, that's exactly what he's done. Extra insurance. It could be anywhere!"

"Wrong," Hunter said. "I think it's either here—which is admittedly a very big area to search—or the pub. Didn't you say you're feeling a presence there recently? It's probably him."

Alex looked at Hunter for a long moment, and then nodded. "Yes, you're right. I think these dreams have so affected my sleep that I can't think straight."

"Right," Reuben said, decisively, "Let's head backstage now and collect up as many scripts as we can find and then get out of here. We can meet up again tomorrow night at the cemetery. Maybe we should keep the numbers small. It's gruesome, but I'll do it if no one else wants to."

"I'll come, of course," Alex said.

"So will I," Avery said resolutely. "Who knows what else Kit may have in store? But Reuben's right. We need to get the scripts, find the jewels, and go home. At least we know what we're up against now."

Avery watched as Sally's face grew pale. "He tied her spirit to the play? That's horrific!"

Avery nodded. "Yes it is, and we have to break that connection in the next three days before the play ends."

"Why does the time frame matter?" Dan asked, keeping his voice low as he kept a watchful eye out for approaching customers.

All three were standing behind the counter at Happenstance Books just after they'd opened the shop. So far, it was quiet, with only a few early shoppers browsing the shelves. Once again, the sun was shining, and White Haven looked as if it had been washed clean after the fog of the previous days.

"We're not sure it does," Avery admitted, thinking through their discussions of the previous night. "But Yvonne is convinced that her ring is responsible, so we have to find it and destroy it. She's worried that if the play finishes, she'll disappear with her spirit still bound to it. We can't risk that. Kit strikes me as being a devious bastard, and I don't want to trust any of our assumptions right now."

"Bloody hell, Avery, that sounds complicated!" Dan said, looking bewildered.

"I know! My head hurts just thinking about it."

Sally leaned forward conspiratorially. "Are you really going to dig up her body?"

"Unfortunately, yes. Briar didn't really want to come, but we decided in the end that the more of us that are there, the safer it would be." Avery grimaced. "I don't really want to go either, but we have to do this."

Dan and Sally glanced at each other uneasily, and Dan asked, "How many scripts did you find in the end?"

"Eight, but there'll be more, and we think Kit has hidden one somewhere else."

"How will you find them?" Sally asked.

"We've decided that rather than break into the cast's homes, we'll steal them from backstage tonight. They should be there while they're performing—in theory."

"You'll use glamour, I presume?" Sally asked.

"If we need to. I expect backstage will be as busy and chaotic as it was last night. We might get by without that."

"Any idea how many scripts there were in total?" Dan asked.

Avery shook her head. "No, but Stan may know. I reckon about twenty, and we have ten so far with the two we've already stolen. I'm going to make some copies today, ready to take with us."

"I'll do that for you," Sally said. "You'll be busy enough. What else do you need to do today?"

"I'm going to help Alex search the flat for the script. It was renovated a few years ago, but still could be there somewhere."

"Did you find the other costume jewellery?" Dan asked.

"We found as much as we could, and none of it is cursed, but tonight we'll see what else the cast is wearing."

Dan stroked his chin, his gaze distant before focussing on Avery again. "I've been in touch with Harry a few times this week, and I'm really worried about him. I can't believe he got into a fight last night! I spoke to his wife the other day, and she's concerned, too. We're both worried that something will happen before the play is over. Something violent."

Avery nodded, feeling the weight of responsibility and expectation, and wished Beltane hadn't brought so many problems, but she still smiled. "We'll sort it out, don't worry." She only wished she felt as confident as she sounded.

Avery stood in the middle of the flat above The Wayward Son and looked around, wondering where to start looking for the script.

"From what I remember," Alex said, "the flat was remodelled in the nineties when my uncle took over the pub. He knocked out the old partitions to make one big room—other than the bedroom and bathroom, of course."

"I take it there were lots of little rooms before then?" Avery asked, trying to imagine how it would have looked. It was a big space, covering the whole floor area of the pub below.

Alex nodded as he headed to the fireplace. "Yes. There were two other bedrooms, and the kitchen and living room were split into two separate rooms. The kitchen was tiny. I remember sharing a bedroom with my brother when we were little. About five years ago my uncle completely modernised it again, and then I decorated when I moved in properly about eighteen months ago."

"Where did you live then, once your uncle took over and knocked everything out?"

"We moved into a house on the hill." Alex had started to tap around the fireplace, listening for changes in the sound that might indicate a hollow wall. "My dad didn't want to run the pub anymore."

Avery headed to the kitchen to start tapping at the outside walls. "Surely the renovations would have revealed something."

"Maybe, but we have to check."

For a while they worked in silence, tapping walls, looking inside cupboards, and examining the wall of exposed bricks for any signs of bricks that might move. Then they tried a couple of revealing spells, hoping that something would show, but found nothing. When they finished examining the walls, they started on the floorboards, and it was an hour later when they admitted defeat.

Alex slumped on Avery's old sofa. "This is ridiculous. The script could be anywhere."

Avery sat next to him, snuggling against him. "We haven't looked downstairs yet. That hasn't been renovated as much, I presume?"

"No," Alex admitted, "just superficial decoration. I guess the walls may have been plastered at some point."

Avery checked her watch and saw it was after one o'clock. "Well, we can't search the main pub seeing as it's open, but we could do it early tomorrow morning before opening time."

Alex nodded absently. "If we aim for about eight, that will give us a few hours before the staff arrive, too. There's no point in trying to summon Kit, either. He wouldn't tell us anything."

"There has to be something we can do now," Avery said, frustrated. "Is there a matinee performance today?"

Alex looked at her, surprised. "There might be. You think we should go there now?"

"Why not? We've got enough to do tonight with a bit of grave robbing.

We might find the other scripts and any other pieces of costume jewellery that we haven't found before."

"Great idea," Alex said, regaining his enthusiasm and pulling her to her feet. "We can enter by the front door for a change and check out the foyer. I think we should try and sneak into the performance, too."

Avery feigned disappointment. "You mean we can't break in? Spoil-sport."

"I remember the days when you used to hate breaking into places, and now... You're not the woman you used to be, Avery Hamilton."

She snorted. "That's your fault, you've corrupted me."

Alex grinned and taking her hand, pulled her into the bedroom. "Speaking of corruption, I think we have time for something else before the matinee will be over."

Twenty

White Haven Little Theatre looked far less creepy in bright afternoon sunshine than it had done last night; the light glinted on the brass and glass doors, and bounced off the glasses at the back of the bar.

As agreed, Avery found a seat, and Alex headed to the bar to buy them drinks. Avery chose a seat against the wall where they could watch the comings and goings and get a feel for the atmosphere. The matinee had already started, and a sign indicated it had sold out, but other people were utilising the bar area, enjoying an afternoon drink or snack.

While she waited for Alex, Avery relaxed, stretching out her awareness and trying to feel for any sign of a wayward spirit, but everything was calm, and whatever magic the play might have been weaving in the auditorium, nothing seemed amiss in the bar.

Alex slid a glass of wine in front of her and sat next to her with his beer. "As we thought, it started at two. They've just begun the second act." He sipped his pint and rested it on the table. "I can't feel anything, can you?"

"No," Avery admitted as she reached for her glass. "And everyone seems pretty relaxed. How are the bar staff?"

"A bit cagey, actually. I complimented them on the theatre and asked if it was haunted because it was so old. I laughed as I said it, as if it was a joke, but the girl," he nodded towards where a young woman with short bobbed hair was using the coffee machine, "looked a bit jumpy. She gave the other guy a nervous glance and said, 'No, of course not,' with a nervous laugh." He raised an eyebrow. "I didn't believe her. I'd guess they're feeling that something is happening here."

"It was bound to happen," Avery said, resigned. "With two spirits on the loose and the magic of the spell rising, people who are here a lot are bound to feel things. At least nothing too obvious is happening."

"Yet," Alex said ominously. He gestured towards the double doors that lead to the hallway outside the entrance to the stalls. "There'll be ushers on the other side of that. We'll have to glamour them."

"As soon as we're in, I can use the shadow spell and we can see how the atmosphere feels in there this afternoon. The toilets are through that door too, so we can head through there without raising too much suspicion."

They'd agreed there was no point trying to check the circle. The night before, they'd spent another hour in the theatre, searching upstairs and investigating the old boxes along the side. The seats were no longer used, and the doors were locked. Cassie, Ben, and Dylan had used their equipment everywhere, but neither Yvonne nor Kit reappeared.

They chatted quietly while they finished their drinks, and then casually headed to the toilets while the bar staff were preoccupied with other customers. With luck, they wouldn't notice how long they'd be gone.

As soon as they entered the auditorium, Avery felt the magic of the performance. Once again the audience was spellbound, and the silence was thick and heavy. Alex and Avery paused just inside the door, allowing their eyes to adjust to the darkness, and Avery realised there was no need to glamour the ushers. There were about half a dozen of them spaced across the rear of the stalls, but they were transfixed on the performance.

Avery felt her breath catch as she looked at the stage. Again, it seemed as if the set was all too real. For the second act the stage was dressed as a room in the castle. King Mark was onstage talking to the three Barons, and everything about them suggested wealth and status. Avery took little notice of what they were saying, but looked instead at the usher closest to her.

She was an older woman, dressed in the theatre's uniform of a smart black shirt and skirt. Her eyes were glazed, and her mouth was slack at she looked at the stage. Even though Avery was quite close to her, she didn't stir, and Avery looked over her shoulder at Alex who met her eyes and shook his head. He drew close and whispered in her ear, "Come on. They have no idea that we're here. And look at the stage—there are loads of the cast on there. This is a great chance to get backstage."

Alex was right. The performance was in the middle of a big scene, so they shouldn't waste time. Avery cast the shadow spell over them anyway, and followed Alex as he walked along the rear of the theatre, down the far aisle, and pushed through the stage door. On the other side, it was just as quiet. As they edged forward, looking for the cast, Avery saw movement to her left, and glanced up to the wings to see a few actors huddled together, waiting for their cue. The quiet was to be expected, she guessed. Any noise back here would carry to the stage and the auditorium, although she felt the atmosphere was not as natural as it should have been.

They proceeded down the darkened corridor, lit only by side lights, until they reached the dressing rooms. The first one was empty, and Avery saw a few scripts on the dressing table beneath the mirror. She slipped past Alex and grabbed them, sliding them quickly into her bag and replacing them with the ordinary photocopies.

"How many?" Alex asked, searching through the pots of make up for costume jewellery or other props that may be bewitched.

"Three. Anything there?"

"No. Let's head next door."

The next dressing room, however, was not empty, and instead they found the two leads talking, their heads close together, and for a moment Alex and Avery hung back, watching them. Their arms were wrapped around each other and they gazed into each other's eyes with such a desperate yearning that Avery could feel their despair. Emma lifted her hand to Josh's cheek, and whispered softly to him, but Avery couldn't hear what she said and didn't want to move closer. She pulled Alex away and whispered, "We'll have to search in there later. Let's move on."

He shook his head. "Let's brazen it out. I want to see how they respond. Drop the shadow spell."

Avery was about to argue, but seeing the urgency on his face decided against it and quickly did as he asked. Alex strode forward and knocked on the door loudly, and the actors sprang apart.

"Hi guys, just wanted to say congrats on the performance so far." He grinned. "Hope you don't mind, Harry said we could pop backstage."

Avery immediately added, "It's me, Avery. I was here the other night, remember? I was telling Alex all about it, and couldn't resist bringing him backstage."

Emma nodded, clearly flustered, and then stuttered a surprised welcome. "Er, sure, yes, but isn't the play still going on?"

"It is!" Avery said, grinning sheepishly. "We haven't got tickets, sorry. Just popping in."

"My fault," Alex said, stepping inside the dressing room. "I persuaded her. I've never been backstage before."

"It's a bit irregular during a performance," Josh said, stepping even further away from Emma, as a bright red flush suffused his cheeks. He could barely look at them. "Sorry, we were just going through a scene." He checked his watch. "In fact, I should head to the wings now."

"Yes, me too," Emma said, nodding quickly. She smoothed down her dress and ran her hand across her hair, patting a few loosened strands back into place.

Avery noticed the necklace she wore, resplendent with flashing rubies, and she presumed it was costume jewellery. *But was it also bewitched, like Yvonne's ring?* Avery quickly stepped in front of them before they exited the room, and she pointed at Emma's necklace. "That's so beautiful! Look at those stones. May I?"

She held her hand out as if to touch the necklace, and Emma faltered. "Er, yes, of course."

Avery was aware that Alex was watching intently, and she gently touched the chain, wary for a spark of magic, and then ran her hand across the stones. There was nothing at all magical about them, and she tried to hide her relief. "Lovely. I thought the stones were real, for a moment!"

Emma laughed. "Oh no!"

"Did they come from the council too?" Alex asked.

Josh shook his head. "No, we provided them ourselves. The costume jewellery that came with the scripts was damaged, so we haven't used them. In fact, we threw them away."

"That's a shame," Avery said quickly. "Are they in the rubbish here?"

Emma looked at her, puzzled. "No, we got rid of them weeks ago, why?"

Avery tried to shrug off her interest. "Just that my friend makes jewellery, and she might have been able to repair it, that's all."

"Sorry," Emma said. "I'm afraid it's all gone now."

Alex caught Avery's eye, and gave a slight nod. "We better let you go."

He pulled Avery aside, and without saying another word, Emma and Josh ducked past them, leaving them alone.

Alex looked at Avery. "Well, at least we know there's no cursed jewellery hanging around. But did you notice the size of their pupils? They were huge!"

"The potion!" Avery exclaimed. "Let's try and find the bottle while we're here."

"Grab these too," Alex said, thrusting the scripts at her that had been left on the table.

"Won't they know that we're responsible, though?" Avery asked, putting the new ones on the table. "And they'll notice they're different."

He shrugged. "Who cares, at this stage? We need them. Besides, I'm sure it's nothing that a bit of glamour couldn't soothe."

The next dressing room was the largest, and it was again empty, but there were a few more cursed scripts strewn across the room on chairs and table tops. With a flurry of activity, they gathered them up, replacing them with the copies, and then searched for the potion bottle. With an exultant, "Yes!"

Avery saw it next to the other props, the potion still in it. As soon as she put her hand on it, though, she felt a crackle of energy behind her, and the rasping sound of Kit's voice followed.

"Put that down!"

Avery whirled around to see Kit and Alex almost nose to nose, Kit's ghostly form shimmering. Kit looked furious, his face twisted with anger.

"Back off," Alex said, raising his hands and starting to recite a spell.

But before he could say barely any words, a bolt of light shot from Kit's fingers, hitting Alex squarely in the chest and sending him flying backwards. He hit the table with a crunch and landed, winded, next to Avery. He scrambled to his feet, but Avery stepped in front of him, hoping that he'd know what she was planning to do.

Kit grinned maliciously. "Protecting Alex? My, my, how modern! But with every passing minute of this play, my spirit becomes stronger. You won't stop me now."

He looked as if he was about to strike again, but Avery felt Alex's hands slide around her waist as the wind started to swirl around them. "I wouldn't bet on that, Kit."

Within a split second, air wrapped tightly around them, carrying her, Alex, the scripts, and the potion out of the theatre and safely to her attic. Avery landed steadily, her bag on her shoulder and the potion bottle in her hands, but she felt Alex release her and fall to the floor, retching.

She stepped away, placing the potion bottle on the table next to her bag, and then crouched next to him, her hand on his shoulder. "Can I get you anything?"

Alex shook his head but held his hand out, and she helped pull him to his feet. "I hate that. I don't think I'll ever get used to it."

"Sorry, but—"

"No, that was a brilliant solution!" he said, colour returning to his cheeks. "Very brilliant! He'll be so pissed off right now!"

Avery smiled briefly, and then her face fell. "I wasn't sure if he could follow us, but it seems not. Do you think he'll take revenge on the cast? Or the audience?"

"I doubt it. Although, he might mess the room up a bit!" He shrugged. "We've got the potion bottle. That's a big win for us."

Alex headed to the wooden table, picked the bottle up, and walked to the window, holding it to the light. "I wonder what love spell this is?"

Avery followed him, staring at the remnants of the thick, golden potion that clung to the glass. "You have recipes in your grimoire. It must be one of those."

"There are lots. I may be able to narrow it down, but what would be the point?"

She leaned on the window frame. "We could make an antidote. If we can't counteract the spell on the scripts, or burn them all, it might at least weaken the effects of their bewitching."

He nodded as he thought through her suggestion. "Maybe, but we're pressed for time. However," he said, flashing a broad smile, "at least they won't be drinking any more of it. It should wear off—at least a little."

Avery took the bottle from his hands, and headed back to her table. "We've got a few hours before we're due at the cemetery. Let me see what I can do." She placed it on the shelf, safely out of the way, and gathered all the grimoires. "Besides, if Kit's strength is growing, for all we know he could bewitch whatever bottle they use to replace it."

Avery decided to investigate Alex's grimoire first, as it seemed the most logical place to find the original spell, and while she looked, Alex reached into Avery's bag, pulled the scripts out, and started to count them. "Ten - so with the ones we already have, that's twenty. I wonder how many we might be missing."

"Perhaps Stan counted them," she suggested. "It wouldn't hurt to ask."

"If we use a part of one of the scripts in a finding spell, it might lead us to the others."

Avery paused and looked at him. "It works with blood and personal items, so it should work—in theory. We could use a map of White Haven."

Alex turned decisively and threw a ball of fire into the logs stacked in the fireplace, and with a flash they caught fire. "In the meantime, I'm going to burn all of these, except for a couple. That should weaken the spell, too—and Kit, seeing as he's bound to it."

He separated a couple of scripts from the pile, and leaving them on the table, marched over to the fire with the rest. He was just about to throw them on when Avery yelled, "Stop!"

"What?" he said, frowning at her, the scripts mere inches from the flames.

"What about Yvonne's spirit?"

"What about it?"

"Her spirit is bound to the play, too. What if burning it before we find the ring and release her leaves her in some sort of ghost purgatory—trapped in the theatre forever? With Kit!"

Alex straightened up, scripts still clutched in his hands, and groaned. "I have no idea. Why the hell is this so complicated?"

"It might not be," Avery said apologetically. "I might be overcomplicating it. But we need to make sure." She put her elbow on the table and leaned on her hand. "I'm really confused," she admitted, finally...to him and to herself. "I understand how you can curse a play so that the words take shape and become reality for the actors involved. I understand how that could magnify over time, so that the spell becomes more powerful. I even understand how he can curse the potion bottle to turn anything in it *into* the potion! What I don't understand is how he has bound himself and Yvonne's spirit to the play, too. I think we're missing something, and until we know what it is, we should keep everything safely together." She paused a moment, and then voiced what had been troubling her for the last few days. "I also think we need to find out how Kit died. Maybe he planned this well ahead of time and bound his spirit to the play at the time that he cursed it, but maybe not. We don't know enough yet."

Silence fell, and the only sounds in the room were the chattering of the birds outside and the crackle of the flames in the grate. Alex sat on the sofa, placing the scripts beside him. "I need to phone my dad now, don't I?"

"If that's the best way to find out about Kit, yes."

He fell silent again and Avery watched as a myriad of emotions chased across Alex's face. He looked weary all of a sudden, his stubble thick on his chin and across his cheeks, his hair tangled, and his eyes haunted.

Avery stood up and went to sit next to him, taking his hands in hers. "What's going on?"

He eventually looked at her and squeezed her hands. They were always so warm, Avery noted, even on the coldest days. Everything about him was warm. He was like a giant hot water bottle.

"What are you smiling at?" he asked softly.

"You. I was just thinking how warm you are, and how lucky I am."

"You are very lucky," he said, nodding seriously. "I'm an awesome boyfriend. And I guess you're an okay girlfriend."

She smacked his arm playfully. "I'm very awesome, too! Now stop avoiding the question. What's going on?"

"My dreams have been really bad the past few nights, particularly last night. I think seeing Kit has worsened my visions, but they're also jumbled and confused. I'm still seeing the actors—I presume that's who they are—in the woods, and I see the mist across the sea. But I'm starting to feel real anger in them...anger, frustration, and an edge of violence. And Kit's voice seemed to echo through my dreams all last night. I barely slept, if I'm honest."

"I'm sorry that happened," Avery said, stroking his hands again. "You could try a sleeping potion tonight."

"No. I hate doing that."

"You don't want to phone your dad either, do you?"

He looked guilty and sighed. "Not really. He buggered off to Scotland, and we haven't spoken in years. He pretty much let me fend for myself once

I hit sixteen."

"I remember you telling me," Avery said, thinking back to one of their conversations from when she first began to know him. "I thought you said his visions chased him away."

"Yeah, but it doesn't really excuse him."

"He did send a Christmas card last year," she reminded him.

Alex had just rolled his eyes when it arrived and put it on the shelf. The message was brief, Avery had noted, but he had written a phone number in there.

"If I phone him, I'll have to explain what's going on."

"So? What does that matter?"

"We don't share our lives anymore, and I don't particularly want to now. And," he said, levelling an accusatory glare at her, "you're the same with your mom. You barely talk, and you certainly don't talk about magic."

"That's because she turned her back on it."

"And my dad did the same." Alex gave her hands a final squeeze and then pulled his phone from his pocket as he stood up. "I'll head downstairs to call him and put the kettle on. Want a drink?"

"Tea please," she said, smiling, and watched him go with a heavy heart.

What was it with their families and magic? El and Briar's were the same, as was Reuben's wider family—a result of being shut out of the council for years, and being lost in the magical wilderness. Her friends now had to rely on each other—they were her family. And then she thought of Caspian and his dad. The fact that his family hadn't turned their back on magic hadn't seemed to have improved his relationship with his father, though. Caspian was a changed man since he'd died—well, to a certain degree.

Avery rose to her feet, too. This wasn't getting an antidote to the potion found, so she had better get on with it.

Twenty-One

As agreed with the other witches, Avery and Alex met the group in the back room of The Wayward Son that evening to discuss their plans.

"That's brilliant news!" El said to Alex and Avery after they'd ordered their food and settled around the table with drinks. "How many scripts did you get?"

"Ten," Alex told her. "So, we now have twenty in total. It's difficult to know how many original scripts there were without asking Stan, and he might not have noticed the difference between the new copies and the old." He paused for a moment, thinking. "Anyway, there are twelve main characters, a few minor, a few extras, and the director and the backstage crew." He shrugged. "Maybe twenty-five or thirty in total are needed?"

Reuben was leaning back in his chair, cradling his pint, his long legs stretched out to the side of the table. "Shit. That's not very accurate."

"It also depends," El added, "on how many were in the theatre company at the time, or how many scripts Kit could get hold of. He might have thought twenty was enough to catch all of the main characters and a few extras." She shrugged. "Who cares if the director is bewitched or not, or the lighting crew! What matters are the performance and the main characters. We need to remember Kit's intent, and it sounds as if it was purely to have revenge on Yvonne."

Hunter nodded in agreement. "But in order for that to be as effective as possible, the whole play had to be affected, and consequently the audience was swept up in it, too."

Alex shook his head, and his hair fell over his face for a second before he swept it back out of the way. "I'm pretty horrified by his behaviour right now, to be honest. I would never have thought someone in my family could have done something so horrible."

Briar looked as worried and tired as Alex. Her hair remained slightly wild, resisting all attempts to brush it into tameness, but the green ring around her eyes seemed to give her a twinkle of mischief. She'd been leaning back, listening, with Hunter's arm casually resting on the back of her chair, but now she edged forward. "Alex, don't worry about that. Some of the spells in our grimoires are pretty grim, and we all know magic can be used for lots of horrible things. Most witches choose not to, but some do. That's an unfortunate fact of life."

"And it seems Kit was one of those," Avery said, trying to prompt Alex into sharing the information he'd learned from his dad. The conversation had left him depressed and annoyed.

Alex looked at her and exhaled heavily before turning to the others. "Yeah, my dad confirmed it. It seems Kit wasn't a nice guy. He was a short-tempered, vindictive man for most of his life, and as he got older, he got worse."

"I'm sorry, Alex," Briar said softly. "That's a horrible thing to find out. How was your dad?"

"It's okay. It's like Avery said, we are not responsible for our relatives' actions. And my dad was well." He smiled briefly. "We actually had a half-decent chat. Unfortunately, at the time of these events, my dad was just a kid. He doesn't know anything about the play. However, he does remember Yvonne!"

"Really?" El asked, intrigued. "How come? There must have been quite a few bar staff!"

Alex nodded. "There were, and he and my uncle knew all of them, but of course what made Yvonne memorable was the fact that she was so pretty, and that she died. He said it upset him at the time because she was always so friendly and sweet with them." He laughed. "Apparently, my uncle had a crush on her!" Alex's smile was brief. "My dad said he remembers her death being in the news and the local gossip for weeks, and at the time he struggled to understand how she could have killed herself. He also said it was at the same time that my gran left after a furious argument." He shrugged. "Maybe that prompted it."

Avery squeezed Alex's hand. "It must have been huge for your gran to walk out when your dad was so young."

"I think that was part of the argument. She wanted to take the kids and Kit wouldn't let her."

"Men can be such shits sometimes," Briar said angrily, her face wrinkling with disgust. "Did your dad lose touch with his mom? That's awful!"

"He reconnected when he was older," Alex told her. "But I think he never really forgave her, and neither did my uncle, who apparently went off the rails a bit for a while."

Reuben had been listening quietly, but now he sighed. "Sorry mate, that's crap. Did you find out how Kit died?"

Alex nodded. "He had a massive heart attack in his early sixties and passed away immediately. He was a hard drinker and smoker by that point, so it wasn't a surprise, really. My dad ran the pub for a while, and then my uncle took over." He smiled wryly. "It was his idea to rename it The Wayward Son."

Reuben laughed. "Nice one. So if it was a sudden death, Kit must have linked his spirit to the script at the time he bewitched it."

"Wow," El said, shaking her head in disbelief. "You'd have thought he might have relented over the years and stopped the spell, but obviously not!"

"Unless he forgot," Hunter pointed out.

"You couldn't forget that, surely," El answered.

Reuben drained his pint and thumped his glass back on the table. "Well, at least we have a bit more background now. But it doesn't change the facts, or what we need to do tonight." He looked around the table. "Are we still intent on getting Yvonne's ring?"

"We have to," Alex said. "If we're to save her spirit."

"I've been thinking about tonight," Briar said, "and Yvonne's grave, and I should be able to lift the coffin out with magic, which would make this a lot quicker."

"Good," Reuben said decisively. "I wasn't looking forward to digging for hours."

"What are you going to do with the ring once you find it?" Hunter asked. "I mean, do you know how to break the curse on it?"

"I have a few ideas," Avery told them. "I've been looking through the grimoires and collecting a few spells that might work. At least once we get it we'll have a few days to try some spells out."

"I don't think you'll have to," El said, looking hopeful. "My knife that cuts through metals should destroy the ring."

Avery felt a weight lift from her shoulders. "Of course! Fingers crossed."

"And what will you do about Kit's ghost?" Briar asked Alex.

Alex grimaced and rolled his shoulders. "I'm going to banish his spirit to whatever dark hole I can—or use the Empusa's sword. One way or another, he'll never be able to return again. But unfortunately, that won't be tonight."

Avery parked her van down the lane from the White Haven Cemetery, and looked over her shoulder at the witches and Hunter sitting in the back. "We're here, guys."

White Haven Cemetery was situated on the hills above White Haven and had been in use since the 1920s when the existing graveyards attached to the churches had been too full to accommodate any more burials.

It was clean and well maintained by the council, but it was also large and meandering, the graves spreading across the hillside, overlooking the bay below.

Briar stretched as she jumped out of the van and sighed with pleasure as she looked over the view. "This really is a lovely spot to be buried."

Avery turned and followed Briar's gaze. Below them were the lights of the town and the houses that clustered around it. Beyond, the sea was a lighter patch of grey stretching to the horizon. It was a cloudy night, and a stiff breeze blew off the coast, making Avery shiver in her jacket.

"It is, but I'd rather admire it in the day," she admitted, before turning to Alex. "Have you got the map of the cemetery?"

He patted his pocket. "Right here. Yvonne's grave is on the higher section, to the rear."

"How did you get a map?" Reuben asked, baffled.

"Off the council's website, you twit. The site's so big they keep a list of who's buried where."

Reuben looked mock-offended. "That's a bit harsh. It was a simple question!"

Alex led the way up the lane that was edged by high hedges, bantering with Reuben, until they reached the main entrance where a large and currently empty car park was set before two enormous iron gates. A small brick building was located just beyond them. Alex quickly spelled the gates unlocked, and the hinges creaked as they pushed the gate open and edged inside, shutting it quietly behind them.

It was odd, Avery reflected, that they should keep their voices down and be so quiet. The cemetery was well away from houses, so it wasn't like anyone could hear them. But she guessed it was natural to be quiet in such places. It felt more respectful—which was ironic, considering what they were about to do.

Alex led them onto the main path, and after a short distance turned left, leading them up the hillside. "It's this way."

Hunter was close behind him, and he said, "Kit must be buried here too, Alex."

Alex turned to look at him, his eyes glinting silver under the night sky. "He is, further along to the right. I checked earlier."

"Do you want me to piss on it?"

Briar gave a tiny shriek and smacked his arm. "Hunter!"

Alex laughed unexpectedly. "Thanks for the offer, but not right now. It's his spirit that's worrying me, not his grave."

Hunter shrugged. "If you change your mind, just say the word."

Briar stepped around him and glared. "I cannot believe you just said that."

"I'm being supportive!"

"I expect that of Reuben, but not you!"

"Oh, thanks!" Reuben grumbled from behind Hunter. "It's fine that I'm offensive?"

"No, but you just do it all the time," Briar told him.

El smirked. "Both of you, shut up and move on. And I don't mean you, Briar," she added as Briar looked at her, startled.

Avery sniggered as they continued to toil up the hill towards the plot where Yvonne was buried. She'd rather this banter than stony silence. It was creepy enough with the sound of the wind whistling through the trees, and the faint glow of the headstones in the dark.

Finally Alex slowed down, checking the names as he walked, until he came to a stop in front of a grave marked with a plain, pale headstone. He threw a witch-light over the stone, and silence fell for a moment as they read the simple engraving.

Briar shook her head. "She was only twenty-five! How tragic."

"Avoidably tragic!" Alex added harshly. "Bewitched by my vindictive grandfather."

"Is Charles Ball's grave here somewhere?" El asked.

"A few rows up from here," Alex told her. "I'm presuming his spirit is resting somewhere peacefully, and therefore we don't need to disturb his grave."

"Let's hope so," she said as she pulled her backpack to the ground and extracted the Empusa's sword from it.

"Expecting trouble?" Avery asked.

El gave her a wry smile. "I'm hoping not, but I want to be prepared."

Briar slipped her shoes off and wriggled her feet in the grass. "Let's hope we don't experience what the Nephilim did in Old Haven's churchyard."

"Thanks for reminding us of that, Briar," Reuben said sarcastically. "Hundreds of bodies rising from their graves isn't exactly what I want to think about right now!"

"Nothing like that will happen here," Alex said decisively. "Briar can raise the coffin, then we'll get the ring and go. This will be short and not quite so sweet." He looked at Hunter and Reuben. "Can you two check the approaching paths, just to make sure no one else is here?"

"Sure," Reuben nodded, and after a brief discussion between the two of them, Hunter headed one way and Reuben the other.

"You all need to move back," Briar told El, Avery, and Alex. "I'm going to try to keep this as tightly controlled as possible, but it will still dislodge the ground around the grave for a few feet."

They nodded, and Avery stepped back several paces, watching Alex as he moved his pack and retreated to the next grave. There wasn't a lot of space between the plots, Avery noted, and she hoped they wouldn't disturb them.

When they were out of the way, Briar stood a short distance from the foot of the grave and raised her hands as she started to intone the spell. For a few moments, nothing happened, and then Avery felt a rumble deep beneath her feet. Startled, she stepped back again, catching Alex's eye, and he smiled reassuringly at her before turning his attention to the grave.

The earth churned and the rumble grew in strength until waves of soil thrust the coffin to the surface, and with a loud crack, the headstone tipped back.

Avery gasped, her hand to her mouth, and stepped back with a grimace.

The force of the coffin's expulsion from the ground had caused the already rotten wood to disintegrate, revealing a glimpse of the skeleton within. Alex leapt into action, wasting no time, and Avery gathered herself together and stepped forward to help.

Briar shook her head as she knelt in the earth. "I hate doing this."

Alex glanced up at her. "I'm sorry, Briar. We could have dug it up and saved you the trouble."

"No, it would have taken hours. It's for the best."

Alex gently pulled the coffin lid away, but it virtually collapsed in his hands, and beneath the earth that had seeped into the coffin they saw the pale, skeletal remains of Yvonne. Mummified skin still clung to her bones, and remnants of clothing too, but Avery pushed it to the back of her mind, focussing on clearing the earth gently away from her body. She summoned air beneath her fingers and moved her hands lightly over the remains, blowing the earth away from the bones where she could. Unfortunately, most of the earth was damp and heavy, and they had no choice but to move it with their hands.

"We need more light," El said, pulling a torch from her pack and shining it across the grave. "This will be better than witch-light."

With Alex on one side and Avery on the other they moved quickly, working from the shoulders down the arm to her fingers. But the bones were displaced, and the small hand bones were scattered through the soil.

"Shit!" Alex exclaimed. "This isn't like in the films."

A startling crack made them stop and look around, and in the silence that followed they surveyed the surroundings warily.

"Did I imagine that?" Avery asked.

El panned her torch around, the Empusa's sword clutched tightly in her other hand. "No. It sounded like a pop of energy." She handed the torch to Briar, and summoning a ball of magic into her other hand, said, "I'll keep watch, carry on!"

Avery concentrated on finding the ring, and was vaguely aware that Briar had stood, too. She felt a prickle of discomfort that suggested something else was there with them, but trying to ignore it, she kept filtering through the soil, finally finding some finger bones. "Alex, I've found a hand, but there's no ring!"

He grunted. "Me, too. It must be in the soil somewhere."

"If it's here at all!" she reasoned.

Alex looked up at her sharply. "It has to be. She said it is. Keep looking."

A crackle of magic and a flare of bright white light fizzed around them, and El yelled, "Keep your head down! It's Kit."

Within seconds, flashes of energy were erupting around them, and Avery heard Reuben and Hunter arrive. Avery focussed only on the grave, filtering through debris as quickly as she could, and trying not to gag as she came upon bits of skin and tangles of rotten clothing. Half the time she couldn't even work out what was what. "Why the hell didn't we bring gloves?" she muttered to Alex.

"Because we don't rob graves very often," he grumbled back.

An energy ball whizzed past Avery's ears, and as the rattling report from a shotgun resounded through the night, she flattened herself against the ground. When she finally lifted her head, her mouth fell open in shock.

Kit's spectral form was prowling a few feet away, and his dark eyes glowed with an unearthly light. If anything, his spirit seemed more corporeal than it had only the night before. Energy surrounded him in a nimbus of light and flickered from his fingertips. Reuben and Briar were hurling balls of fire at him, and Hunter pointed Reuben's shotgun loaded with salt shells. Circling as closely as he could, Hunter fired at Kit while El tried to get near enough to attack him with her sword, but he fended them both off.

Avery turned back to the grave, trying to ignore the activity around her. A glint of metal appeared beneath her fingers. "I've found it," she said, relieved, and then had to backtrack. "No, it's a bracelet, sorry."

"It's okay, keep going," Alex muttered.

"Why don't you try to banish him?" Avery suggested as she worked. "I'll do this."

"No. He's too strong now, and it would take too long," Alex said, barely looking at her as he frantically searched through the earth. "And besides, when I finally do it, I want to make sure that everything else is in place."

A shudder ran through the ground beneath them and the earth shifted, and then Avery, Alex, and the coffin began to sink back into the ground. "Briar!" she yelled, trying not to panic.

"Sorry!" Briar shouted back, and with another rumble, they shot back up again.

With a nervous glance at each other, Alex and Avery continued to search with increasing haste until Alex shouted. "Here! I've got it." He held a small ring up to her, crusted with earth and with a bone still in it, and with a grimace he shook the bone free and pocketed the ring.

"Would there be any other rings?" Avery asked.

"No. She said this was it."

They leapt to their feet, and Alex shouted, "I've got it! Briar, sink the coffin again."

His shout attracted Kit's attention, and he rasped, "I can't let you have that, Alex."

They were all spread out now in a loose semicircle around Kit, trying to hold off his attack as best they could. It was obvious he didn't like the salt from the shotgun, because with every blast that hit him, he staggered further back.

"Too late," Alex yelled back, and sent a well-timed burst of searing, jagged energy at Kit's chest, jolting him backwards so far that he flew right through a tree trunk.

Briar, meanwhile, was focussing on burying Yvonne's coffin again, the earth folding around it and drawing it downwards until it completely vanished. The others kept buying her time to smooth the ground over and lift the gravestone back into position. Unfortunately, other graves weren't faring as well. A couple had been hit with magic, pockmarking them with cracks and shards of stone that had dislodged with the fury of their attack.

But Kit kept coming, and Avery knew that unless they could banish him somewhere, he would follow them all the way home—and looking at the worried expression on everyone else's faces, they all knew it.

Alex headed to Avery's side and lowered his voice while the others continued to distract Kit. "There's a bag of salt in my pack—I need your help!"

She nodded, spotting the bag behind the next grave. "What do you want me to do?"

"Find his grave and pour salt around all but a small section. Leave the rest to me—you'll know when to complete the circle."

"Just give me a few minutes!"

Alex nodded and thrust the plan of the graves into her hand, and without saying another word, resumed his attack on Kit, who was proving very resilient.

Avery scrambled to Alex's backpack and pulled the large bag of salt out. Summoning air, she used witch-flight to fly a short distance away and quickly consulted the map. For a few seconds she had trouble placing herself, and then she realised where she was. She ran through the graves, zigzagging along the paths, until she virtually stumbled on it. Like Yvonne's, it was a plain headstone with a simple epitaph. She quickly circled the grave, pouring a thick white line of salt around all but a few inches, and then looked across the cemetery to where the others continued to battle Kit.

White light flashed, illuminating trees and bushes. A scorched smell filled the air, and the silence of the night was disturbed by shouts, thumping, and the regular *boom* of the shotgun. Avery looked towards White Haven, and realised that if anyone were looking up at the hills, they would see the lights. If they weren't quick, the police may arrive.

Avery threw a handful of witch-lights into the air, firing them up like fireworks, in the hope that Alex would see them and know she was ready, but seconds stretched into minutes, and the frenzy of magical energy continued. Just as she was wondering whether to join the others, Kit's spirit streaked past her and plunged into the ground. She leapt forward and completed the salt circle. Summoning her power, she uttered a spell to seal it, and within seconds a bright blue light flashed across the grave.

Silence fell along with the darkness, which seemed more intense than it had been only moments before. But she didn't move. She stood with raised hands watching Kit's grave, until she heard the thundering of footsteps and voices as the others arrived next to her.

Alex sounded breathless as he skidded to a halt at her side. "Is he in there?"

Avery grinned at him as relief swept through her. "Yes, he's there, and I've sealed the circle, too."

"Great," he said with a sigh.

He looked like he'd just battled a hurricane. His hair was wild and dirt was smeared across his face, and when she looked around at the others, she noted they all looked similarly dishevelled. "Wow. Look at you guys. Do I look as shit as you do?"

"Yep—although, you probably smell better than I do," Reuben said, pulling her to him for quick hug. The he grimaced and pushed her away. "Wrong. You stink of dead people."

"Thanks, Reuben. I guess that's what happens when you scrabble about in someone's grave." She looked at the others. "Is Yvonne's grave back to normal?"

Briar shrugged. "I'll smooth it over before we leave. What are we doing with the ring?"

Alex pulled it gingerly out of his pocket, still wrapped in a cloth, and unfolding it gently, he let the others see it.

"It's very pretty," El said, as she pointed the torch on it. Then she shuddered. "I remember the feeling of that cursed necklace, though. That was the worst thing I've ever experienced."

Reuben squeezed her shoulder. "Let's get this over with, Alex."

"Are we sure we want to do this here?" Hunter asked. He still had the shotgun cocked, and he looked as if he was ready to spring into action.

"Yes," Alex answered, looking determined. "I want this ring gone by the time Kit breaks out of this."

El looked at him, puzzled. "What spell did you use?"

"It's a type of binding spell. I've bound Kit's spirit to his bones. It won't last long, because technically his spirit is already free of his body and it was a simple spell, but it will last long enough for us to get this done, at least. Besides," he said, glancing at El, "your knife that can destroy anything should work."

"It didn't work for the Empusa's ring," Briar reminded them.

El pulled the knife free from the scabbard on her waistband. "I'm confident it will for this. Put it on the ground, Alex."

Alex walked away from Kit's grave and placed the ring on the bare earth, and El crouched next to it. She held the knife at arms' length, leaning her head back, too. *It was always wise to be careful with cursed objects*, Avery reflected. El pressed the knife against the ring, and with a puff of black smoke, the ring split into two and then ignited. The flames burned green and black, until only a dirty black reside of metal remained.

Immediately Yvonne's spirit appeared before them, and they all jumped back with surprise. Her ghost was faint, the cemetery clearly visible through her, but Avery's attention was drawn to her face. A broad smile was spread across it, and she saw her lips move soundlessly before she vanished.

"What did she say?" Avery asked Alex, who was grinning and looking very pleased with himself.

"She said 'thank you.' Job done! We freed her spirit!"

"Just like that?" Reuben asked, looking surprised.

Alex nodded. "Just like that. Destroying the ring did it. One spirit down, one to go. Let's get out of here."

Twenty-Two

Avery and Alex stood in the empty lounge area of The Wayward Son and looked around, perplexed.

"Any idea of where we should start?" Avery asked.

"Not really," Alex said, shaking his head. His arms were folded across his chest and he turned slowly. "The walls and floor are the most obvious places, and the fireplace. The structure of the place hasn't changed that much since Kit ran it. I think there may have been a couple of smaller rooms, but they've been knocked out—hence the pillars." He pointed to a couple of large brick columns that supported the ceiling.

"Come on, let's get on with that finding spell we talked about yesterday." Avery headed to the back room where they couldn't be overlooked by anyone who might peer through the windows from the street. "It's worth trying," she said in answer to Alex's sceptical expression as he followed her.

"I wondered what you were running around collecting this morning." Alex nodded. "All right. Did you bring a map so that we can check the locations across White Haven, too?"

She patted her bag. "I'm well prepared."

"You always are."

They sat across from each other at a small table and Avery pulled a script from her bag, gently tearing off a section from the back of the book. She hated damaging books, but she told herself it was for an important purpose. She also pulled a small silver bowl from her pack and placed it in the centre of the table, along with a collection of herbs she'd brought with her.

Alex watched her work. "I'm glad you were with it this morning. I can barely think straight."

She glanced up at him, noting the dark circles beneath his eyes. "I'm running on coffee if I'm honest, and could really do with more sleep." She continued to set up while they talked. "I didn't sleep very well. Running around cemeteries at night is not conducive to decent rest. My mind was racing with ideas about Kit, Yvonne, and the play. And I keep thinking about how tragic this all is."

"And I keep thinking about what a miserable bastard Kit was. I'm ashamed of him. And furious with him, too. More than that, I can't believe that I didn't know anything about this!"

Avery finished laying out her equipment and looked at his stricken face. "It was sixty years ago. Why should you know any of this? It's old news. I don't know any history of my family. It all just disappears in time, doesn't it? All those arguments, petty disagreements, and old jealousies mean nothing now. Even those warm moments—our successes and pleasures. They're momentary, a flash of time!" She clicked her fingers, and sparks flew from the ends of them.

"You're very philosophical," he said, raising an eyebrow.

She rubbed her face. "That's a poor night's sleep for you. And of course being surrounded by dead people last night."

"Which is why we should concentrate on the living. Josh and Emma are swept up in this, as are the rest of the cast. Their lives are at risk—and if we do manage to save them, who knows what will be left of their existing relationships?"

"What if Kit put another spell in the mix that we don't know about?"

"Then we'll deal with that, too. At least he can't threaten us with Yvonne anymore." He gestured at the bowl. "Shall we start?"

Avery nodded. She'd made a bed of the ingredients she needed at the bottom of the bowl and she added the piece of script to it. A detailed map of White Haven was open next to it. She ignited the script with a word and then started to say the spell, a variation on one they had used many times before. The smoke drifted up and across the map, idling over it for a few seconds while Avery continued to cast the spell. She felt the tingle of the magic from the script sitting next to her but ignored it, focussing on following the smoke, but nothing happened. It hung in the air, going nowhere. She met Alex's eyes across the map. "It's not working."

"I can see that."

"What do you suggest?"

"Maybe the sample is too small. Burn the whole script. We have more."

"What if it brings Kit here?"

"Let it. I have another spell up my sleeve for him." He pushed his chair back. "Let's use the fireplace. Have we got enough herbs?"

"No. But I can get some."

Alex checked his watch. "Good. We've got time. I'll prepare the fire in the main room."

Without waiting, Avery used witch-flight to return to her attic and collect more herbs, and then she spotted the stack of scripts on the table. *Maybe they needed them all*, she reflected. *There would be more power with all of them together, even if they only burned one*. She turned to look at the potion bottle sitting innocently on the shelf. Not sure if it was the right thing to do, she picked them both up and returned to the pub. Alex had stacked the wood for the fire, and Avery placed the scripts on the closest table and quickly prepared the herbs. The room was darker than before, and Avery realised he'd closed the blinds.

"Are you worried about spies?"

He laughed. "Yes. I can do without ending up on the front of the White Haven Gazette."

After a few more preparations, they were ready to start again.

"Let's do it together," Avery suggested. "We'll place one script on the fire and the rest in front of us, the bottle on top, join hands, and say the spell as one. Our combined magic may make the difference."

"We can put the map here," he said, pointing to the floor on the other side of them, away from the fire. "And do you know what else we should do?" Alex asked, his eyes widening. "Use my blood!"

"Why?" She hated using blood in spells. It seemed to make the whole affair darker and more sinister.

"Kit is my grandfather," Alex said, already gathering the items. He lowered himself to the floor and sat cross-legged. "His blood is my blood. His magic is my magic. And his power is in that pile of scripts and the bottle."

Avery sat opposite him and made herself comfortable. "I guess you're right," she admitted weakly.

"Of course I am. We need to think of this as one giant spell that's spread across various objects. It's not loads of little spells. I mean, yes, the ring was cursed, but they're all linked." He looked brighter and nodded to himself. "Yes, that's exactly what they are. We haven't been thinking clearly about this. If I wanted to bewitch someone, I'd use as much at my disposal as possible. His primary objective was revenge on Yvonne because she spurned his advances, and he's prepared to do anything to achieve that. Sod the repercussions to anyone else. That's why it's so powerful—and that's why *he's* so powerful right now. I think he's grounded the spell somewhere."

"That's an interesting idea," she told him thoughtfully. "But how? To what?"

He frowned. "I don't know. It's only just occurred to me."

"I thought we'd agreed a script would be hidden here. Is that what you mean by grounded?"

"Not really. I think there's something else."

"Please don't tell me there's something in his grave. I don't want to have to do that again."

"No, I'm sure it's here." He flashed a grin at her. "Well, almost sure."

"He worked and lived here his whole life, so that would make sense."

He nodded at the items between them. "Why did you bring everything we have?"

"It was a feeling."

"Your feelings are good. I trust them. Do you trust me?"

"Of course I do." She reached forward and squeezed his hands. "It's actually really good to be doing this with you. Just us two."

He lifted her hands and kissed the palms softly. "Yes, it is. We better get on with it then."

Alex kept hold of her hands, but rested them either side of the bewitched objects, and Avery started to intone the spell, feeling Alex's magic mix with her own. The more she recited the spell, the stronger she felt his magic mingling with hers, wrapping around her like a cloak. She looked to the fire and ignited it with a word. The flames curled up from the stack of wood, and the layer of herbs caught, filling the air with a pungent smell, far more overwhelming than it had been in the small bowl. Finally, the script they had placed on top ignited, and thick black smoke streamed upwards, very different to the natural wood smoke.

Avery continued to repeat the spell, and after a moment the smoke clotted together, as thick and undulating as a snake, and it nosed between Alex and Avery, causing them to draw back momentarily. Then it completely bypassed the map and started to move around the room. The smoke dipped and rose as it searched the walls, swept along the ceiling, and then oozed under tables and through chair legs.

Alex glanced at Avery. "That's unnerving. It looks like it's alive!"

"I know!" She watched the smoke continue to poke around the room, eventually reaching the bar area.

After several minutes, Avery started to think there was nothing there for the spell to find. Then it streaked up through the ceiling and disappeared.

"Bollocks!" Alex said, leaping to his feet and running to the stairs. "I wasn't expecting *that*."

Avery ran after him, and hard on his heels they burst through the door of the flat, just in time to see the smoke pour up through the ceiling into the attic space. "How do you get up there?" Avery asked him.

But Alex was already running into the bedroom, and she followed him, seeing him point to the square door set into the ceiling. "Through there."

"I didn't even think about attic space," she said, annoyed with herself as she watched Alex stand on the sturdy chest of drawers positioned beneath it, and push the hatch up and away.

He hurled witch-light above him, and then placing his arms either side of the hatch, pulled himself upwards.

"Can you see it?" she shouted.

"Yes," he shouted back. "Bloody hell, there's all sorts of shit up here!"

Avery was itching to go up, but knew she wasn't strong enough or tall enough to pull herself up through the hatch, and she didn't want to risk witch-flight as she had no clear idea of what the layout was, either. *However*, she thought, grinning to herself, *she could use air to propel her there.*

She scrambled onto the chest of drawers and summoned air until it was whirling around her, then she used it to push her upwards through the hatch. She surprised herself at the speed, and with a *whoosh* she floated into the attic, narrowly avoiding braining herself on the heavy beams above her head. She stumbled to her feet and looked around, wide-eyed with pleasure. What was it about attics? They were fascinating places, full of old things that had once been loved and now were no longer needed. And dirt. And cobwebs. *And maybe secrets.*

The attic was large; not quite the full surface area of the ground floor of the pub, Avery estimated, but close. A couple of brick walls intersected the space at the far end, but most of the attic was open, the floor ribbed with beams, and crowded around the chimney was a collection of boxes and old furniture. It was there that Alex was standing, watching the smoke nudge repeatedly up against the chimney's brick wall.

He looked at her over his shoulder. "Your modes of transport are forever fascinating."

"I know." She edged her way over to him, stepping carefully on the beams so she didn't fall through the ceiling. "I like to keep you on your toes."

"Mission accomplished." He nodded at the bricks. "Looks like something is in there." He leaned in closer. "I can see some fine cracks in the bricks, but that could be age." He brushed his fingers across them, dislodging plumes of dust. He coughed and then continued his search, leaving Avery to examine the boxes.

The cardboard was rotten, falling apart beneath her fingers in places, but some of the boxes were wooden and had fared better. Peering into one, she saw stacks of old crockery patterned with old-fashioned designs, and she pulled a plate out, smiling with pleasure. "These are so pretty!"

Alex glanced at her. "They're yours if you want them."

"Even if I don't, we should give them to a second-hand shop. It's a waste to leave them here." She continued to search, finding glasses, stacks of clothing, old Christmas decorations, a couple of lamps, and some other household objects. But a grunt from Alex broke her search, and she whirled around. "What?"

"Bingo," he said softly.

He pulled a Swiss army knife from his pocket, extracted the small blade, and inserted it into the gaps between the stones, wiggling it gently. The cement cracked and fell away, and as he worked, Avery saw other cracks appearing around a section of bricks.

The snake smoke that looked so sentient swirled above them, and as it seemed it had nothing else to show them, Avery dispersed it with a click of her fingers, wondering if it had been too big to be of value with the map. Before she could speculate any further, Alex pulled the bricks out of the wall one after another, revealing a space behind them. He put his hand in and emitted a strangled cry.

"Idiot," Avery said affectionately in answer to his grin. "Wouldn't it be too hot to keep something safe?"

He shook his head. "It's well insulated. There are more layers of brick in there, and the flue will be narrow at this point." His face scrunched with concentration as he felt around, and then he smiled again. "Found something."

He pulled out a rolled-up oilskin packet, and opening it gently found another script. This one, however, had the strange sigils drawn on with ink, and opening it up to look through the pages, they could see the other pages marked the same. "This must be the first one he did," Alex speculated. "The one that links the others. The magic feels strong."

Avery felt relief roll though her. "What do we do with it?"

He looked at her bleakly. "I don't know."

She shook her head, smiling gently. "We're getting closer, though."

When they returned downstairs, they heard a key turning in the lock at the back door and they both froze. The main pub was still full of magical paraphernalia.

"It's only me," a familiar voice called, and Zee rounded the corner into the main room. He looked around and started to laugh, resting his long, lean form against the bar. "What have you two been up to?"

Alex looked visibly relieved. "Thank the Gods it's you. I thought it was Simon."

Zee laughed even more. "I think you'll find that like Sally and Dan, he knows more than he lets on."

Alex rubbed his head ruefully. "You're probably right."

"I know I am!"

"Oh, Sally and Dan don't even pretend anymore," Avery admitted, starting to gather things together in front of the fire.

"True." Zee jerked his head at Alex, a dark lock falling over his forehead. "What you got there?"

"A bewitched script," he said, placing it on the bar for Zee to see. "We think it's the key to the others."

Zee pulled the script towards him, frowning as he examined it. "Interesting. A couple of these are binding sigils, and some magnify emotions, I think." He frowned again as he turned the script around. "And something else. A summoning."

"How do you know that?" Alex asked, surprised. "We're struggling to understand it."

"A sigil is a type of language, and we're good at languages. But not magic or signs so much."

"You can feel it, though?"

"Sure. It's humming with magic." Zee handed it back to Alex. "I assume this is the play that's giving you some bother. Gabe and Shadow told us about it the other night."

"Unfortunately, yes. The actors are bewitched. It's a type of love spell, really, at its heart. The cast is acting out the emotions of the play in real life."

Zee nodded. "Which is some love-crossed triangle of soap opera proportions, I gather."

Avery had finished packing up her magic supplies and opening the blinds, and she joined them at the bar. "What do you know about soap operas?" she asked, intrigued. "You're Nephilim."

Zee sat on a stool, laughing at their surprised faces. "It's in our interests to fit in, so that means we've updated ourselves on anything and everything, mostly. Because I work here, I pick up all sorts, so it's my job to educate the others. We lived a gazillion years ago. Human nature might not change, but everything else has! It's me, Barak, and Ash who educate everyone on films, music, pop culture—you know, all of that stuff." He leaned forward and lowered his voice. "It turns out that Shadow loves disco."

Avery snorted in a very unladylike manner. "*Disco*?"

"I know. It's weird, and quite frankly, disturbing. We often hear the Bee Gees coming from her studio." He rolled his eyes. "Completely my fault. We have to listen to it when she cooks."

Alex looked at Avery wide-eyed and said, "The Bee Gees?"

"Each to their own. To be honest, 'Tragedy' is a classic," she admitted.

"Anyway, boss. I have a question," Zee said, pinning Alex down with an intense stare. "Are you guys responsible for the events at the cemetery last night?"

"Why?" Alex asked, already turning pale.

"The mysterious lights on the hill made the news."

Alex winced. "Yes, that was us. Any pictures?"

"Just some fuzzy images from a long way away of white lights flashing like lightning."

"Shit."

Avery groaned. *Not something else!* "At least there aren't any close-ups. And we left the cemetery in a very tidy state."

"Nope, you didn't," Zee said, shaking his head. "Kit Bonneville's grave was 'heinously disturbed,'" he said, using air quotes. "I think you'll find the press will be here later for a direct quote from you, Alex."

Alex's joking manner disappeared completely. "Disturbed how?"

"Soil everywhere, headstone shattered. 'An outrageous act of vandalism' was what the council said."

Alex sat on a bar stool and rested his head on the counter. "Fuck."

"Want to tell me what happened?" Zee asked brightly, looking more amused than concerned.

"You're enjoying this, aren't you?" Avery said, sitting on a stool and patting Alex on the shoulder.

Zee tried to subdue a grin and failed. "Sort of. We managed to fight a zombie army and didn't get any attention. I feel a bit smug."

"Well, Alex's wayward grandfather's spirit is causing issues. It turns out that he's the one who spelled the play."

"Mmm. Wayward Son, Wayward grandfather! I'm seeing a pattern!"

Alex lifted his head, feigning offence. "Not a wayward grandson!"

"*So* wayward!"

"I like wayward," Avery reassured him.

Zee nudged her arm and pointed to one of the windows that looked out onto the street in front of the pub. "I spot Sarah Rutherford approaching.

And it's nearly opening time."

"Bollocks," Alex said.

"What are you going to say?" Zee asked.

"Well, obviously we don't know anything," Avery said to Alex. "You tell Sarah that the first you knew of it was the news report earlier." She frowned. "You would have thought the council would have phoned you, rather than you find out from the news."

"They might have," he admitted. "I've had my phone on silent."

"Slow down," Zee said, watching them both. "Why is Kit's grave disturbed?"

Alex sighed. "His spirit is very strong right now. As the play progresses, the spell on it magnifies, the cast is more affected, the audience is bewitched, and that in turn has strengthened Kit's ghost. He manifested last night in the cemetery, and I had to send him back to his body—a temporary binding. It seemed that when he broke free it had a physical affect on his grave."

Zee nodded. "You're going to banish him, then?"

"When the time is right. I need to get all my ducks in a row—if you know what I mean." Alex glanced nervously at Avery. "*If* I can banish him. I'm beginning to think this is going to be way more complicated than I thought."

Twenty-Three

It was just after lunch on Thursday when the door chimes rang in Happenstance Books. Avery looked up from where she was restocking the occult section with the new books they had been selling to see Caspian striding inside, looking purposefully around the shop. She called out, "Caspian, I'm here."

He headed to her side, taking one of the books from her hands. "What are you selling?"

"Books on cunning folk, the history of witchcraft, and the witch trials. It's an effort to deflect Rupert's sensationalism. Why?"

He smiled. "Just curious. I didn't know Rupert had started his tours."

"He started this week, unfortunately. But I'm sure you didn't come to chat about books."

His smile disappeared. "No, I saw the news. What happened last night?"

She sighed. "Follow me."

Avery led him to the back room and put the kettle on before explaining their evening, and Caspian listened silently.

"So you identified the ghost as Kit Bonneville?" He laughed. "Nice to know my family aren't the bad guys after all."

Avery felt a rush of guilt. "Sorry. I shouldn't have leapt to conclusions."

Caspian perched on the edge of the table. "That's okay. The circumstances were suspicious. So, what now?"

"Well, that's the million dollar question," Avery said as she gave him a cup of tea. "We need to break the spell on the cast, but we're not entirely sure that burning the scripts will do it."

"I take it you're unwilling to wait and let it run its course?"

"Well, seeing as Josh and Emma, the two leads, might end up killing themselves, and the rest of the cast are at each other's throats, not really!" she said sarcastically.

"Fair point. You should burn the scripts anyway. What would you lose?"

"We're worried that it might make it worse." She held her hand up in a stop sign. "I know! That's probably ridiculous, but we don't want to do anything that might be irreversible."

Caspian nodded. "Tricky, I agree." He sipped his tea. "I must admit that I'm impressed. It's a devious, clever spell."

Avery was sick of worrying about it, and she said, "How are things in Harecombe? Have Beltane passions taken hold there?"

"They're the same as they were last week. Everyone's a little giggly, a little suggestive, and there have been a few jealous spats, but nothing too bad. Nowhere near as bad as Mevagissey," he added with a grin, and Avery laughed, having almost forgotten about Oswald's worries about Ulysses. Caspian continued. "You're sure you won't be coming to the Beltane celebrations tonight at Rasmus's?"

"No. Although with everything happening here, we haven't really planned anything too amazing." Beltane fell on Friday, the day before the official town celebrations, but it was traditional to celebrate on the eve. "We're going to Ravens' Wood, though."

"Be careful. That place is wilder than most, and that will especially be the case at the moment." He finished his tea and placed his mug on the table. "If you need my help breaking the spell, just ask. I'm afraid I haven't been able to find much of use so far, though."

"Thanks Caspian, but I'm sure we'll find a way."

"You'd rather not ask for my help anyway, I assume?" Caspian's gaze was direct, and it made Avery uncomfortable.

"We will if we need to," she assured him. "You've helped us a lot in the past, but I think this is something we can and should do alone."

"Okay," he said finally, although it looked as if he was debating saying more. "I should go; I need to see Gabe."

Avery watched him walk to the door, but before he left, she said, "By the way, I told Alex. We have no secrets."

Caspian paused and flashed her a smile of resignation. "Stay safe, Avery." And without saying another word, he left.

Avery returned to the shop, brooding on their conversation. She hadn't lied to Caspian. The events of the week had completely distracted them from their Beltane plans, and despite their worries about the play, they were meeting on the edge of Ravens' Wood at ten that night. If she was to enjoy it properly, she needed to prepare. After making sure they weren't too busy in the shop, she headed to her garden to pick fresh boughs for their celebrations. Their altar would be decorated with greenery, and she knew Reuben and Briar would bring some, too.

With that done, she headed to her attic, collecting candles and other objects she'd need for the celebrations that night, and then satisfied she was partly prepared, sat at the table and pulled the grimoires to her. She was determined to find something of use, and she needed to be methodical in her search.

Avery referred to the list of spells she had made only the day before, although it felt like a lifetime ago after so much had happened between then and now. She had found spells for bewitching the senses and ensnaring the mind, love spells that promised undying adoration (but more likely meant scary obsession), and spells that caused love to wither and die. She shuddered with revulsion. Most involved spelling food or drink, which should be slipped to the intended victim discretely. She had also found a way of bewitching small objects that would also cause love and obsession, but nothing on such a large scale as a script that could affect so many people.

Frowning, she turned away and looked at Alex's grimoires, noting where he had identified spells that had similar affects. Love spells were one of the most common spells and there were many varied ways to use them. They had talked about anchoring the spell, and it struck Avery that Kit would want to anchor himself to the play and a place. Maybe the theatre was also connected to the spell in a far more concrete way than they'd realised. White Haven Little Theatre was where the play had been performed before. Had Kit tied the play to it, as well as his own spirit? And if he had, how did they find out how he'd done it? Would they need to exorcise the whole building? Was even exorcise the right word? Cleanse it, maybe?

After last night's performance, it was likely that Kit's spirit would be even stronger. He was certainly strong in the cemetery. Would he harm the audience? Perhaps, she mused. Kit would have been unpopular in the town if he really were such a miserable, bitter man. It could be that bewitching the audience was part of the spell after all, rather than an unintended side effect. Perhaps he wanted to punish them, and the play was also feeding the town's behaviour throughout Beltane.

Bollocks!

Avery ran her hands through her hair. She was going around in circles.

Of course!

Circle was surely the right word. The whole spell was circular. Every piece of it fed into the other. The more the play was performed, the stronger the enchantment became; the more obsessive the cast became, the more enraptured the audience was; the odder the town behaved, the stronger Kit became. It was just as Alex had said. It was one big, linked spell. The ring and the potion fed into it.

They needed to break the circle, and the trick was to find the weakest part. And they absolutely needed to get rid of Kit.

It was likely that Kit couldn't manifest in The Wayward Son because of Alex's protection spells, but it was unlikely they could protect the theatre now that Kit was so strong—unless they banished him first, and then they could cleanse it of all the negative energy that was accumulating. It was toxic in there. In fact, White Haven now had an undercurrent of pervasive arguments that were undermining the whole Beltane festival.

She leaned back in her chair, focussing on the candle that burned on the table in front of her. The flame danced in the breeze coming from the open window, and it suddenly struck her. The best way to cleanse was with light or fire. A Beltane fire.

On the eve of Beltane, Ravens' Wood rustled with life. The branches creaked overhead, and the whispering leaves allowed dappled moonlight to shine through to the forest floor.

Avery and the witches met on the outskirts of the wood, and then wandered along small winding paths, letting their instinct guide them, until eventually they came to a secluded grove.

They had heard giggles and murmured conversations as they walked, but they were muffled, as if from some distance away, and Avery couldn't be sure if they were human or something else. The wood felt alive, much as it had when it forced its way through the earth: ancient, wild, and terrifying, and unmistakeably Otherworldly.

Briar had packed a picnic basket, and Hunter placed it at the edge of the clearing, ready for when they'd finished their celebration. He watched them as they started to prepare their circle. "I'll leave you to it for an hour or so."

He was already stripping his clothes off, the moonlight playing across his body, and an unbidden heat rose within Avery. Beltane was quickening her blood.

"Where will you go?" Briar asked him. Her eyes glimmered with an unearthly green fire as her gaze travelled over his naked body.

He met her eyes with his golden ones. "Everywhere. And then I'm coming back for you." He didn't so much speak as growl his words, and then he turned into his wolf and bounded away through the undergrowth.

His words left no room for doubt, and they all knew what Beltane celebrations sometimes entailed. The Great Rite. It was more of a Wiccan concept, but it was essentially a ritual of sexual magic in which the High Priestess embodied the Goddess and the Priest embodied her consort, and their coupling brought about great power. However, it didn't need to be the High Priestess of a coven. Any witch could choose to enact the rite.

Reuben turned to Briar, a smirk spreading across his face. "It's going to be that kind of night, is it?"

Briar shot him a warning look. "Not necessarily, thank you, Reuben!"

"Oh, I think it is!"

El nudged him. "I think we should set up our circle."

While the others prepared their decorations for the altar, El took her sword from her backpack and started to pace out a large circle on the mossy floor of the glade, and their excited chatter from earlier disappeared.

Hunter's promise and Reuben's comment had changed the atmosphere, and the air had thickened with promise and desire. Avery tried to push it away, but Alex caught her eye, and she knew he felt the change within them all, too.

When their preparations were complete, El asked, "Who's going to lead us tonight?"

"I think Briar should," Avery answered straight away. "We're in Ravens' Wood, and it's a part of you, Briar, more than anyone else, and so is the Green Man."

Briar looked surprised. "I think it should be you."

Reuben looked between them both. "No, Avery's right. It should be you."

"Agreed," El and Alex said together.

"All right," she said, and in the candlelight, Avery saw her flush with pleasure.

As soon as their circle was complete they stepped inside, and El sealed it behind them. As usual they had placed candles around and within the circle, but this time they had also built a small fire to one side, and a maypole was inserted in the centre. Briar sank it deep within the earth, and with another few words of command it sprang into life, small shoots and leaves appearing along its length. The ribbons attached to the top swirled in the breeze that Avery created, and she noticed the smell of blossoms fill the space.

Briar lit the fire with a word, and as it blazed, the surrounding wood disappeared into blackness. But it was as if the moonlight was magnified, because as Avery looked up the moon seemed to grow in size, so that it felt very close above them. El placed a crown of flowers on Briar's head, and Reuben picked up the small skin drum, his fingers tapping the beat, and then time seemed to change as Briar led their celebrations, starting with calling upon the elements.

By the time they finished, Avery's blood was singing, and she felt flushed with excitement. They had chanted and danced around the maypole, and any chill from the night air had gone. The fire had burned low, but Alex set it blazing again as El opened the circle once more.

Night sounds returned around them. An owl hooted, and the rush of a stream sounded close by. An excited chatter seemed to whip through the trees as Hunter bounded back into the clearing. Avery wasn't sure if it was a trick of the light, but he seemed bigger than he had before, at least as high as her waist, his paws huge but silent on the forest floor. As soon as he arrived Briar sat on his back, and he loped off thorough the trees.

Avery's blood quickened as she looked at Alex, and he took her hand, a world of promise in his eyes. He pulled her out of the clearing and into the tangle of the wood.

And then all reason disappeared as the Goddess and her consort arrived.

When Avery came to her senses, she was naked on the grass. Alex was sprawled next to her, his limbs wrapped around her own.

For a second she lay there, confused and disorientated, and then her memories flooded back. They were in Ravens' Wood and it was still utterly dark, other than the glint of moonlight slicing through the spring growth above them, illuminating the blossoms so they appeared as stars. There was no sign of the fire they had lit earlier, and Avery wondered how far they had strayed from the clearing.

Alex's breathing was slow and heavy, and she watched his chest rise and fall, his tattoos seeming to writhe across his skin in the half-light. She eased herself out of his arms and sat up to look around, letting her eyes adjust to the dark. The air was cool on her skin, but pleasantly so, like a caress. A rustling sound startled her and she saw a small animal scurry out of sight, but beyond that was something else, and she squinted, trying to work out what she could see. When she did, she shivered, and it had nothing to do with the temperature. She saw the unmistakable shape of a dryad slip by, quickly swallowed by the darkness, and then she heard a throaty laugh from behind her. She twisted around and saw something with hairy legs and cloven feet pass through the undergrowth, just as something else passed out of sight.

What the hell was going on? Had she slipped out of one world and into another?

Avery shook Alex to try to wake him, but other than a grumble and mutter, he didn't stir. But his eyes moved rapidly beneath his flickering eyelids. He was dreaming again. Sweat beaded his brow, and a slick of moisture lay across his arms and chest.

She sat for a moment, undecided as to what to do, but she was alert now with no chance of going back to sleep, so she stood up, feeling strangely comfortable in her nakedness. And that was fortunate, because she couldn't see their clothes at all. If this is Reuben's idea of a joke, I'm going to kill him, she swore to herself.

If she went in search of their clothes, she was scared she might lose Alex. She had no idea where she was, and although her sighting of the Otherworldly creatures was unnerving, she was sure they were still in her world. The Raven King wouldn't be so kind as to give Shadow a way back home.

She heard the murmur of voices, and she made her way towards them, wondering if it was Reuben and El or Briar and Hunter. She had to walk further than she thought, the night and trees distorting sound and distance, but eventually she saw a flame in the darkness. As she drew closer, she became aware that she wasn't alone. Other things seemed to crowd around her, invisible things, but she felt their presence as they progressed together. She now felt that the rustle of the wind through the leaves was actually voices, and the brush of soft vegetation against her skin was the feeling of their bodies.

Together they stumbled to another clearing, this one bigger than the one the witches had found, a circle of flaming torches around its edge. But Avery froze as she saw who was in front of her. It was the Goddess, draped in moonlight and blossoms, and at her feet was the Green Man.

Avery's mouth fell open in shock, and as she stepped onto the edge of the clearing, all of the strange, unseen creatures became visible: the rustling of willowy dryads, the muscled hardness of yellow-eyed satyrs, naiads in diaphanous clothes that appeared like flowing water, and other creatures she didn't recognise.

The Goddess turned to her, her gaze fierce, hard, and timeless. Avery knew instinctively that if she took one more step she would be consumed. Part of her wanted it, but most of her was terrified, and summoning an icy clarity she didn't know she possessed, she stepped back and then turned and ran.

When she eventually stopped running, she was covered in scratches from the branches that whipped at her and the sharp stones beneath her feet. The forest seemed to have turned against her. Her heart was pounding and again she had no idea where she was, but she knew where she wanted to be, if he was still there. Taking a deep breath, she summoned air and flew to Alex's side. With almost a whimper of relief, she saw him lying where she'd left him, and decided she didn't care how deeply asleep he was, he needed to wake up—now.

Twenty-Four

It was well into the night by the time Avery and Alex found the clearing where they celebrated Beltane. They eventually found their clothes strewn atop bushes, and Avery had needed to guide Alex along because he was so disorientated.

It had taken so long that Avery was starting to panic, and when she spotted Reuben and El sitting on logs next to the fire, she almost wept with relief.

"I have never been more pleased to see you two," she said, stumbling to sit next to them on shaking legs.

El and Reuben were sitting close together, El leaning against Reuben. They weren't normally a demonstrative couple, so Avery immediately thought it odd, especially as El looked solemn. "Have you had a really odd few hours?" El asked Avery.

"Yes." Avery rubbed her face as if to clear her mind. "The absolute weirdest night I've ever had, and that's saying something after the night at the crossroads. What about you?"

"Well, best sex I've had in years," Reuben said, "but I could have done without seeing the satyrs."

"You saw them, too?"

"What?" Alex asked, looking between them, clearly confused. "Do you mean in your dreams?"

"Nope. I mean right here," Reuben answered, gesturing around him.

"Did you dream about them, Alex?" Avery asked. She hadn't stopped to talk to Alex once she had woken him, feeling it was more important to return to the safety of their friends.

"I dreamt about satyrs, dryads, blood, passion, revenge, Tristan, Iseult, and King Mark, and all sorts of other weird as shit things."

Reuben nodded, as he watched his friend with concern. "Please tell me you at least had great sex before that happened."

Avery couldn't help but laugh as Alex said, "Yes, don't worry. We did."

"Do you have any idea of the time?" Avery asked them. "Or where Briar and Hunter are?"

El checked her watch. "It's close to three in the morning. And I have no idea where they are, but I'm hoping they'll be here soon."

Reuben stood, picked up the picnic basket, and carried it back to the fire. "I was going to wait for everyone, but I'm starving, and I'm sure Briar won't mind." He lifted the lid and started laying out the cold cuts of meat and cheese that Briar had packed.

El was watching Avery. "You're covered in scratches, and if I'm honest, you look shell-shocked. What happened?"

Avery didn't speak for a moment, wondering how to explain what she'd experienced. "I'm not entirely sure it was real. It felt like I was hallucinating." She took a deep breath and then explained about the clearing in the forest.

For a second, no one said anything, and then El sighed. "An hour ago, I'd have said you were dreaming, but not now. I don't know quite what's happening here, but I believe you. Reuben wasn't joking—we really did see a satyr striding through the forest, and well, I don't know what the other things were—shadows that seemed alive."

"Have we crossed a boundary somehow?" Alex asked. He was looking better now that he was eating and drinking. He was sitting close to the fire, wrapped in a blanket, and his eyes were once again bright and focussed.

"I wondered that," Avery told them. "But I don't think we have, I think they have—those Otherworldly creatures. Maybe the Goddess brought them here."

Reuben frowned. "What do you think would have happened if you had stepped inside that clearing?"

"Honestly? I think I'd have gone mad. I could feel her power—her Otherness. And her utter disregard for me. Seeing Hecate at the crossroads was a powerful moment, but this felt completely different." Avery paused as she thought through her feelings. "With Hecate I felt acknowledged as a person, and a witch. But back there...I felt I was nothing to her."

"I guess you had stumbled upon something you weren't meant to see," Reuben reasoned.

"In that case, why be here at all?" Avery asked. She looked around at the safe space of the circle they were sitting in. Even though they had opened it, it still felt a haven. Beyond seemed wild and unpredictable. "I don't think I want to leave here until dawn."

"I'm with you there, sister," El said softly. "I just hope Briar is okay."

It was close to five in the morning when Briar finally returned with Hunter. He loped into the clearing, Briar walking next to him, and both of them had twigs and leaves caught in hair and fur, and Briar was smeared with dirt. Hunter changed back to his human form straight away, and for a moment it looked as if he'd forgotten he was naked as he went to sit next to the fire, but then he shook his head as if to clear it and pulled his jeans on. Both of them looked dazed.

"We've been very worried about you two," El said, rising swiftly to hug Briar. "Where have you been?"

Briar sat down, warming her hands over the flames. "I honestly have no idea. I feel like we travelled for miles, and yet we couldn't possibly have! This forest isn't that big!"

Hunter helped himself to some food and then sat next to her. "I scented things in here I have never smelt before. I also lost my way—and I never do that! It was exhilarating and terrifying, all at the same time."

"We saw the Goddess, too," Briar said, staring into the fire.

"So did I!" Avery told her, thankful to find she hadn't lost her mind. "In the clearing?"

Briar looked at her, and Avery could see that her pupils were huge, as if she'd been drugged. "We saw the Great Wedding."

"Of the Goddess and the Green Man?" Reuben asked, almost spitting his drink out.

"Yes. Can you believe that? It was an accident—we just stumbled on it, almost into it, before Hunter realised what was happening." She bit her bottom lip and then grinned. "It was amazing. We hid in the trees at the edge of the clearing, but the Green Man saw me. He just looked straight at me, as if he recognised me, and I felt him—in here." Briar clutched her hand to her chest. "And he told me to run—so we did. And then we got lost again. I'm pretty pleased to be back here, to be honest."

"I think we all are," Avery said softly. "We thought we'd wait until dawn to leave. I'm not walking through there in the dark again!"

Alex nodded. "Not long now—I can feel it coming, and the birds do, too."

He was right. Avery felt the change in the air and detected the almost imperceptible rising of the daylight. "I can honestly say this has felt like the longest night of my life."

"No time for sleep though, Ave," Reuben said. "We have to stop Kit's spell. Have we got any ideas?"

"Yes and no," Avery said, thinking about her research from the day before. "Yesterday afternoon I searched through the grimoires again, and something Alex said stuck in my head."

"It did?" Alex asked, looking hopeful.

"Yes. We were talking about how everything feeds into each other—how the spell continually reinforces itself. It's circular. Those are the spells I looked for, and I found some. They're called Hring spells in my grimoire."

"I don't think I've heard of those," El said, puzzled.

"From what I can gather, they're not common because they're so complex, and that makes them very effective. Each part strengthens the next, so in theory we need to break one part to weaken the rest. That's why the sigils are so complex on the front cover."

"Like toppling a house of cards," Alex said, nodding. "But that's going to be impossible. Breaking another witch's spell is hard, and I don't think there are any weak spots."

"I know." Avery grimaced as she finally admitted to herself what had been niggling her all day. "We can't break it. It is impossible. That's why Kit is so damn pleased with himself, too."

"Why didn't you mention this last night?" Alex asked. He looked slightly resentful, which was reasonable. Normally, she would share something like this immediately.

"I've been mulling it over, and of course I wanted to celebrate Beltane and get it out of my mind for a while." Avery laughed shakily. "That certainly happened—and not in the way I expected."

"I know what you mean," Briar said, shivering, and she whispered a spell, sending the fire blazing again. Avery wasn't sure if Briar was cold or if it was the dark eyes of the forest around them that made her nervous, but looking satisfied with her handiwork, Briar turned to Avery. "Where does this leave us? There must be something we can do!"

"I have had an idea," Avery said tentatively. "This spell breeds negativity, obsession, and revenge, and it has spread through the cast and into the town. We need to cleanse it."

"By 'it' do you mean the town or the cast?" El asked.

They were all watching her intently, and Avery swallowed nervously. "I mean everything—and we can do that with fire. Tomorrow night a huge Beltane fire will be burning on Spriggan Beach. And there'll be fire jugglers and dancers—"

"And they've got iron braziers lining the streets, so there'll be small fires all down the high street, too," Reuben said, nodding as he realised what she intended. "We can use the fires to cleanse the town."

"Yes."

"Holy crap, Avery," Briar said, reaching forward to fill a plate with food, "that's a big ask!"

"I know." Avery looked around at her coven's anxious expressions. "But if we can't break the spell, and the hold it has on the leads in particular, then cleansing the town and them will burn away the enchantment...I hope."

Alex nodded, a smile of appreciation starting to spread across his face. "So we burn the scripts as we discussed, but tie it to something bigger."

She grinned. "Much bigger!"

"What about Kit?" Reuben asked.

"Good question," Alex said. "If we cleanse the town of the spell's negative energy and burn the scripts, I doubt it will banish Kit. He's too strong. I'll tackle him separately." Alex paused for moment to chew some cheese thoughtfully, his gaze distant. "I think the only way to be sure is to do everything simultaneously. While the bewitched copies of the play burn and the cleansing spell sweeps across White Haven, I will summon his spirit and banish him."

Briar looked worried. "But by tomorrow night, the production will be over—the final performance is Saturday afternoon. That means the spell will be at its strongest already. We could be putting the cast in grave danger by letting it run its course. And it will be here, on the edge of the Ravens' Wood. I know it will be daytime, but what if the wood's magic exacerbates things? That could be disastrous!"

Avery felt lightheaded with tiredness, and she could feel a headache starting to buzz insistently, but she ignored it. "We need to be here for the final performance. We need to keep them safe. Alex's dream visions keep showing a wood and people in costume—"

"And blood," Alex reminded them. "Anger and betrayal are the overriding emotions. And tonight they were even more vivid. Something will happen here tomorrow afternoon, I'm sure."

Reuben nodded. "That sounds like a good plan. And didn't you find the potion bottle and steal it? Surely that will help."

"We did," Alex confirmed. "But we weren't sure if Kit could curse another one. He's strong enough to."

"Then we need to find out. If he hasn't, we might have an advantage. And if he has, we need to destroy it before they can use it in the final performance. That's one thing we can influence, surely, and it should help reduce the risk."

Hunter stirred from where he had been lying next to the fire. "So we have to be here tomorrow afternoon, then. Someone needs to be close enough to the stage to stop Emma and Josh seconds before they drink it. That's the only way to be sure."

"We also need to be spread out through the town tomorrow night," El said. "I'm the most skilled with elemental fire. I should be by the bonfire."

"And I need to be in the theatre," Alex reminded them. "That's where Kit's spirit will be strongest, and therefore it's the best place to banish him."

Reuben shuffled on the log, trying to make himself more comfortable. "That's going to spread us very thin."

"It is, but we're strong enough," Alex reasoned. He looked up and his grim expression lifted. "And look, it's dawn now. Light enough to leave."

Avery had been so focussed on their discussion that she hadn't really looked around, but she did so now, and realised she could see the pale dawn light filtering through the thick leafy branches, and spotted the path through the trees.

"Let's go and get some sleep," Alex continued. "We can meet again later today. I don't see any point in going to the play tonight, but we can plan for tomorrow."

"Leave the fire spell to me," El said, rising to her feet and stretching. "I think I might have just the thing."

Avery stood up too and started to collect their things together, feeling almost giddy with tiredness, and also drained from the strange emotions and experiences that Ravens' Wood had brought. "Guys, I just want to say thank you for an awesome Beltane celebration, but next year, maybe we should go somewhere else."

Twenty-Five

Happenstance Books was very busy. Customers trailed in and out with a chatter of questions about Beltane and witches, and there was an air of general excitement about the celebrations. A few people had gathered in the square at dawn to watch the Morris dancers welcome May Day, and the dancers were still in the town. Avery could hear the jingle of their bells as they walked the streets.

Avery, however, was finding it hard to share their enthusiasm. As soon as she and Alex returned home, she tried to sleep, and for a few hours she did. But it was only a light sleep, full of strange dreams, and she woke in the late morning feeling terrible. She was trying her best to be bright and breezy, but it was taking its toll.

Dan pushed her onto the stool behind the counter and gave her a coffee and biscuits. "Bloody hell, Avery, sit down for a minute and take a breather. You'll scare off the customers."

Avery grimaced, and tried to look at her reflection in the window. "Do I look that bad?"

"Worse. What on Earth did you get up to last night?"

She lowered her voice. "We celebrated Beltane in Ravens' Wood, but it all got very weird." She sipped her coffee, and then thinking it tasted like the best coffee she'd ever had, drank another few sips, trying not to scald her tongue.

"Aha! I thought so. Sally and I were talking about it earlier. You haven't seen the news again, have you?"

"No. Why?"

He took a bite of biscuit, and through a mouthful of crumbs, said, "You didn't really think you'd be the only ones in the wood last night, did you?"

"Well, no, of course not," she said, fearing Dan was about to tell her something bad. "We did see a few people when we arrived, but then no one—well, no one normal at least."

He raised an eyebrow. "Normal? So what did you see?"

Avery looked at him suspiciously. "You first. What have you heard?"

"Well, there were a few wild moments last night in the wood—some people even got lost and called the police in a panic. And," he smirked, "quite a few couples headed there for their own private celebrations, if you know what I mean."

Avery met his eyes and felt her cheeks flush. She knew exactly what that meant, and she thought of the absolute abandonment that came over her and Alex once they left the circle.

Dan smirked again. "Oh! So you, too! Apparently, the police turned a blind eye on 'lewd behaviour' because there was so much of it happening. And besides, they were too busy calming down the people who were freaking out."

Had the magic been so strong last night that anyone could see the Otherness in the wood? "Freaking out how?"

"One woman swore she saw the devil." Dan watched her carefully. "She said she saw a cloven-hoofed creature with yellow eyes and thought she was going to die."

"Oh, shit!"

Dan narrowed his eyes. "I presume it wasn't the devil?"

"Of course it wasn't the bloody devil," Avery said, exasperated.

"Good old Sarah Rutherford suggested hi-jinks and pranks on Beltane—like at Samhain up at Old Haven Church, but we both know that wasn't a joke, so—"

A young woman bustled up to the counter with half a dozen books, and

Dan scooted behind the till to ring up the order. As soon as she'd paid, he turned again to Avery, looking expectant.

Avery rubbed her face, feeling a headache starting again, and wished she'd made herself a detox tea instead.

"So?" Dan repeated, clearly not about to let her off the hook.

"Ravens' Wood seemed to have let the Otherworld in last night. I saw things that shouldn't exist here—satyrs, for example."

Dan almost inhaled his biscuit in shock and Avery slapped him on the back. When he eventually finished coughing, he wheezed out a stunned, "Wow! Hence why that woman thought she'd seen the devil, I presume?"

"I guess. They were huge and very odd looking." She shook her head at the memory. "It was surreal. I'd love to know what Shadow made of it—if she was even there." She filled him in on what they had experienced, and what they decided to do about the play. "How's Harry, by the way?"

"I called him yesterday—I've been making a point of it, actually. He still sounds intense...and cranky. He's got a real thing about one of the guys who plays a Baron. It's so unlike him." He brushed a few crumbs off his shirt, and then said, "I think I should be there tomorrow afternoon. I know Harry. If things get really weird, I can help!"

"I don't think that's a good idea, Dan."

"It might not be, but Harry's my mate, and I don't want him hurt. He has a family, Avery!"

"But we can't leave Sally on her own—and I have to be there, too!"

He threw back his shoulders and looked her resolutely in the eye. "I'll be there, and you won't talk me out of it."

She had to admire his resolve; that was the great thing about Dan. He didn't shy away from anything. "All right, you win. We'll close the shop at lunch tomorrow."

Avery glared at Reuben as he glanced around the table at her, Alex, El, Briar, and Hunter, an amused look on his face. "How's everyone feeling?"

It was Friday evening, and they were at The Wayward Son discussing their progress. Reuben looked annoyingly refreshed and energetic, while she still felt awful. "Crap," she admitted grumpily. "You, however, look fine!"

"You should have come surfing. That would have washed those cobwebs away!" He nodded at Hunter, who also looked alert. "It worked for Hunter."

Hunter smiled back. "It certainly helped, although I was feeling fine anyway. My wolf half is stronger than I am, and I'm used to hunting all night."

"When did you learn to surf?" Alex asked, puzzled.

"Years ago, but I'm terrible at it." He laughed. "It doesn't stop me trying though, and Reuben is a good teacher."

"Oh, well, bully for you!" Avery said, uncharacteristically annoyed. She reached for her wine and took a healthy slug, knowing it was probably the wrong thing to drink to feel better, but deciding her liver could get stuffed.

Briar looked at her sympathetically. "I know how you feel. I didn't sleep well either, and the shop was so busy. And those bloody women who throw themselves at Eli annoyed the crap out of me all day. I eventually sent them off with a spell so we could both get some peace."

"You actually put a spell on Eli's harem?" El's eyes lit up with glee. "That is not like you!"

"What about all this 'harm none' thing we bang on about?" Alex asked, teasing her.

Briar bridled. "I did not harm anyone! I merely made them feel very uncomfortable for a while."

Avery felt her spirits start to rise at Briar's mischief. "How uncomfortable?"

"I may have glamoured the mirror to make them all look a little uglier. I also gave one spots, another a rash, and a third one had a sudden attack of wind." She was trying to look sheepish, but she couldn't disguise her amusement. "It was all very temporary. I'm sure they are feeling better now."

Avery's mouth fell open in shock, and sniggers sounded around the table.

"That is bloody brilliant," Reuben said admiringly. "I bet Eli was a bit miffed, though."

"No, actually. He couldn't thank me quick enough. If I'm honest, he looks tired too, and I didn't expect that of a Nephilim." She giggled. "I have a feeling I could be doing it a little more often. We both got peace and quiet, and my other regulars seemed to love it, too. It made me realise how patient I've been with these obsessed women."

Alex laughed. "You can't give them a weekly rash. It would be too suspicious, and they'd blame Eli!"

"Oh, please," Briar teased. "I can be inventive."

"Well," El said, pushing her empty plate away, "I've also been inventive today." She smiled at their surprised faces. "I found a spell that will work tomorrow night."

"So clever!" Reuben praised her.

She patted his hand. "I know. But I'll need all of those scripts tonight so I can plant them under the bonfire."

"But that bonfire is huge," Briar said. "How will you manage it?"

"I was looking at it this afternoon," El told her. "There's a crawlspace through to the middle. That's the best way to light it. I can crawl through tonight and push the scripts up and into the wood at the bottom."

Alex ran his finger across his bottom lip. "Just the scripts?"

"No. I have a very large bundle of herbs, a few crushed gemstones, certain special feathers, and a few other things. They'll be wrapped around the scripts. And," she added, taking a deep breath, "I have made a very large herb bundle that needs to be burned and carried around the centre of town." She looked at Avery and Briar. "I'll need some more supplies, so I'll get them from you in the morning, if that's okay. I'm going to make another couple of bundles."

Briar nodded with understanding. "You're making giant smudge sticks!"

"Yes. With all the torches that will be burning alongside the procession tomorrow, no one will notice. I'll make smaller bundles too to drop into the fires as you pass them."

Avery's tiredness began to disappear as she became caught up in El's plans. "We could do the same to our fires at home—or even here at the pub!"

"Exactly," El said, looking pleased. "And all of the other elements will be present, too—Fire, Water, Air, Earth."

Hunter leaned forward, excited. "I can carry one—I won't need magic, will I?"

"No. Just make sure you waft your bundle everywhere." El looked at Reuben. "You can do that, too. I'll wait by the bonfire. As soon as the Goddess and the Green Man draw close, the fire will be lit, or so I gathered from Stan. A couple of people at the front of the procession will light it—the fire jugglers, I think. As soon as it catches, I'll start the spell. I'll be on the dunes overlooking it, like last time," she said, reminding them of when they were trying to fight off the mermaids the year before.

Briar picked up a chip off Avery's plate and absently took a bite. "We should bless the smudge bundles, too. Why don't you two," she said to El and Avery, "come to my shop in the morning with all the supplies and the bundles you've already made, El, and we'll do it in my back room? It won't take long."

El and Avery nodded in agreement, and Avery said, "I think I should be with Alex tomorrow evening. I'll wait by the beach to see the procession arrive, along with my smudge bundle, and then when the fire starts, I'll join Alex."

Briar smiled. "And I'll support El, while Hunter and Reuben continue to walk around the town."

Reuben scratched his chin, perplexed. "You know, we probably haven't got all of the copies of the play."

"But we have the key copy—the one that binds them," El said confidently. "Once that's gone, I think the rest will be impotent. And besides, it's the best we can do under the circumstances. We're pretty sure there are no more bewitched costumes or jewellery, so we've covered all our bases!"

Avery felt the mood around the table lift as they discussed their plans, and she started to feel better than she had in days.

And then El suddenly frowned. "Actually, Alex, won't you need the key script to deal with Kit?"

"No. I have something else in mind." He smiled, looking pleased with himself.

"Care to share?"

He shook his head. "Not right now."

They all looked at him, intrigued, and Avery said, "But we were concerned he'd grounded himself or the spell in some way. Will that be an issue?"

"Not with what I have planned!" He winked. "Trust me."

"Okay," El said, clearly resisting the urge to ask more. "Do you need the Empusa's sword?"

"Nope. Besides, I'm not the one who is good at sword fighting. I confess that it's tomorrow afternoon that is worrying me more," Alex admitted, his dark eyes haunted. "There's so much bloodshed and anger in my dreams. I can't shake it off. Anything could happen!"

"We should tell Newton," Avery said, realising they hadn't kept him up to date with recent events. "He might be able to get a few policemen at the event—you know, community policing. It might be handy!"

"That's actually a good idea," El agreed.

"Good, I'll call him tonight. The more notice he has, the better."

At ten the next morning, Avery, El, and Briar were gathered in the back of Briar's shop, assembling more smudge sticks. By the time they'd finished, they had a dozen small ones, and half a dozen large ones.

El looked at their efforts and gave a satisfied smile. "Excellent. The mix of herbs in here will work really well."

"They're for more than just cleansing though, aren't they?" Avery asked, as she considered the different plants they'd used. "There are some that are useful for protection, too."

El nodded. "Sage, rosemary, cedar, angelica, and juniper will cleanse and protect. Lemon balm will aid in clarity, and I thought frankincense and sandalwood would enhance the power and intent of our spell, too. And of course a few other herbs are in there as well."

Briar finished securing the last large bundle of herbs to a slender wooden branch she'd taken from her allotment. She tied it with a long piece of string and wove a spell into it as she tied the knot. "They look like besom brooms—well, sort of."

"Very apt," El said, laughing. "But they'll look good being carried down the high street with the procession. No one will take any notice."

"I think many people watching will be dressed up too, don't you think?" Briar asked. "And lots will wear masks."

El gathered the bundles together in the centre of the floor and lit the candles that were placed around them. "

Reuben's thinking of wearing one. You know what he's like—he loves to throw himself into these things! Anyway, let's spell these with some calming and positive intentions, as well as cleansing. By the time we've finished, the town will be renewed."

Avery prepared herself as the three witches formed a triangle around the bundles. "What I'm wondering is, how will we know if it's worked? I mean, will we have to follow the cast for days to find out? And what if the power of the Goddess and the Green Man throw all our plans out? It's possible."

"We can feel the undercurrent of tension in the town now," Briar said, frowning at both of them, "so surely we'll feel it lift!"

"I'll ask Dan to stick with Harry. If his behaviour improves, then we know it's okay," Avery said decisively. "And I think once Kit has gone, we'll know for sure."

They began the spell to empower the bundles, and Avery pushed her worries to the back of her mind, trying to subdue her fear that nothing would be simple that day.

Twenty-Six

White Haven Castle looked resplendent in the sunshine on Saturday afternoon, and drew many admiring glances from the crowds that wandered up from the car park as they headed to the field next door where the stage had been set up.

They were lucky with the weather, Avery reflected. Clouds were scudding overhead, but it was warm and dry enough for the outdoor performance. The audience was walking in carrying blankets and camping chairs, and the atmosphere was generally relaxed, but even so, Avery could feel an undercurrent of tension and heightened emotions. The council had also consented to people bringing in picnic baskets, but no alcohol. A marquee had been set up to provide drinks, and Avery was impressed with the organisation. It wasn't all Stan's doing. He had told them that quite a few councillors had been involved, and she spotted him by the bar, consulting with the events manager. He hadn't yet donned his Druid's clothes, but she knew he'd be wearing them later.

The stage was at the rear of the field, the ancient trees of Ravens' Wood curving around it, full-leaved and gnarly, while beneath, shielded from sunlight, it was dark and mysterious. A row of ravens was already watching from atop the castle wall, which marked the boundary to the left. It was as if they knew something was going to happen.

Avery hadn't got a ticket, but she had glamoured her way in, and she now worked her way through the crowd to the stage with its simple backdrop. She saw Briar and Hunter to the right of the stage and waved. They had both wanted to see the performance, and it was a good way of monitoring the crowd. They were all wearing protective amulets, so they would be shielded from the effects of the spell. On the edge of the field, watching the crowd arrive with suspicion and a scowl was Newton, standing with Moore and a couple of policemen. Avery threaded her way towards them, and seeing her, Newton strode to meet her so they could talk privately.

He looked at her sceptically. "Are you sure we need to be at this teddy bear's picnic?"

"Yes! It's like I said on the phone. We're not sure what will happen, but we're pretty sure there'll be trouble with the cast. Isn't it better to be safe than sorry?"

He rolled his eyes. "I suppose so. I'll be glad when this Beltane bollocks is over."

"It's not bollocks, but I know what you mean." Avery pulled a protective amulet from her pocket and handed it to him. "Wear this—just in case."

He nodded and without argument, slipped it into his pocket. "Thanks. Where will you be?"

"In the woods just behind the tree line. I suggest you keep close to the stage as the play ends—if anything happens, it will be then. Otherwise, it will just be a nice afternoon at the theatre."

She grinned at his grumpy expression, and leaving him to it, headed around the stage, passing the rudimentary dressing area behind it, screened off with fencing, until she reached the dappled forest where Alex, Reuben, and El were waiting.

Alex was seated on the forest floor, leaning against a large oak tree, and he looked up as she arrived. "How is it out there?"

Avery sat on the cool earth next to him. "Fine, so far. Just a bit of an undercurrent of tension—what we've been used to. Have you spoken to the cast?"

He shook his head. "No. They look busy, but we've kept an eye on them."

"They look busy and tetchy!" Reuben said, adjusting his position. He was also leaning against a tree trunk, and he stretched out, yawning. "How long is this play?"

"Just a couple of hours," Avery answered. "I hope Dan is backstage. He said he'd be here."

"I'm sure he will be," Alex said. "Does he know where we are?"

"Yep."

El laughed. "This is weird. We are actually waiting for disaster to happen. Did you see Briar and Hunter?"

Avery nodded. "Yes, they should be able to get here quickly afterwards."

"Good," Reuben said, settling himself on the ground and closing his eyes. "Wake me up when you need me."

As soon as the play was underway, Avery and Alex positioned themselves to the side of the stage, hidden at the edge of the trees. They had a good view of the performance, and watched intently as they came to the part where Brangain, Iseult's maid, offered Tristan and Iseult the potion bottle.

"How are we going to do this?" Alex asked, watching Brangain make her speech.

"I could make the glass shatter, but that would be a bit dramatic. How about if we make the potion spill out?" They had discussed this earlier, but still hadn't come to a decision about how best to tackle this moment, hoping that inspiration would strike at some point.

"By jerking the bottle?" Alex asked, still watching Brangain closely.

Avery nodded, half an eye on the watching crowd. They were silent, eyes fixed firmly on the stage, and once again, Avery felt the magic of the performance steel over her—a potent heaviness that spoke of obsession. "I think they are so caught up in this performance, they won't really notice a fumble."

Alex touched her arm, drawing her attention. "She's handing it over now."

Avery watched as Brangain poured the potion into a glass. Although the bottle looked different, once again the liquid inside looked golden, glinting in the sunlight. Avery sent a push of air towards it as Iseult lifted it to her lips, and then she fumbled momentarily, the liquid splashing on her chin. Iseult looked startled, but she continued to act, brushing the liquid away with one hand as she handed the potion to Tristan. Avery glanced at the crowd, and then back to Tristan, relieved to see that no one sniggered. She took a deep breath and focussed again on jolting the bottle. A screech of a raven above her disturbed her concentration and she jerked in shock, Tristan doing the same, and this time the liquid splashed down his shirt.

Avery and Alex both held their breath, but Josh, although shocked, recovered quickly, and again the audience was unmoving. "At least the enchantment has some advantages," Avery whispered to Alex. "Although, I could do without those!" She looked up above her and glared at the raven. It fixed her with a beady eye, and then flew into the depths of the forest.

Alex exhaled heavily. "Maybe the Green Man is not on our side. We're interfering with passion and love to die for."

"A bewitched love to die for!" Avery huffed, annoyed. "If he thinks he's got an easy ride coming tonight, he's very much mistaken."

Within minutes the scene had ended and Alex looked at Avery, a half smile on his lips. "Well done! Strike one for us."

By the middle of the third act, Avery could feel the tension rolling off the audience, seeping around them where they sheltered beneath the trees.

The heat had increased as the afternoon progressed, and it lay across them like a blanket. Avery swatted at the flies that buzzed around them, until El eventually sent them off with a jet of flame, blown from a ball of fire that she conjured on her palm. They were just debating whether they should head backstage when the audience started to clap and cheer, and Avery felt a shudder reverberate through the air and the earth below. A sound like a distant bell echoed around them, and they all jumped to their feet, hands raised.

"You all felt that, right?" Reuben asked.

Avery nodded, staring towards the stage. "The end of the play must have triggered another level of the spell."

They ran to the edge of the wood, just in time to watch the cast take their bows. The audience was on its feet, still clapping, and if anyone had felt the wave of magic, it seemed they were taking no notice of it. Mixed emotions were emanating from the audience—jealousy, pleasure, suspicion, and passion, all mingling together and feeding into one another.

As they had planned, the witches linked hands and uttered the spell they had agreed on. Avery felt Briar's magic reaching theirs as they pushed positivity through the crowds, easing tension, and as the cast left the stage after their final bows, it was clear their magic was working as everyone started to collect their belongings, chattering excitedly to each other.

They continued their spell for a few more minutes, and eventually satisfied the crowd was at least calmer, they stopped, still feeling its effects filtering across the field.

Alex looked pleased. "That seemed to work. Now, let's head to the dressing rooms."

But the words were barely out of his mouth when they heard muffled shouts and screams from behind the stage.

Without another word they ran, and just as they approached the fence, Dan darted through the gap, looking flushed. "Come quickly! They're already starting to fight, and they won't listen to me!"

Dan headed back inside and they raced after him, skidding to a halt as they arrived in the dressing area and saw the scene in front of them. Harry and the actor who played King Arthur were still in full costume, and they had drawn their weapons on the three Barons and King Mark. They were surrounded by an angry cast, who it seemed had all taken sides, egging each other on.

One of the Barons was covered in blood, and for a second Avery thought it was fake, until she saw him stagger and fall, his hand clutched to his side. Harry raised his sword, and blood dripped along its gleaming edge.

"Bollocks!" Reuben said. "The spell has made the weapons real!"

The sight of blood did nothing to deter them; if anything, it spurred them on, and they clashed again, angry accusations filling the air, which now simmered with rage. Immediately the surrounding cast reacted too, some shouting, others fighting, fists flying, and within seconds, the atmosphere was ugly and dangerous.

The witches leapt into action, using magic to try to subdue the raging emotions, but they barely dented the surface, and then they resorted to other magic to stop the fighting.

Avery sent air whipping through them, trying to separate them, and Reuben and Alex waded in with Dan, pulling the actors apart and spelling the swords and daggers out of hands and safely out of harm's way. Avery ran through the fighting, constantly using spells to try and return reason, and when that seemed to fail, she used blasts of magic to pull them apart. She saw Briar and Hunter arrive, and they joined in the fray to help.

For a few minutes, it seemed as if nothing was working, and then the cast slowed down as reason inched its way back in. That is, until Emma screamed so loudly that everyone stopped and turned. Emma, Josh, and Ian were well away from the others at the far end of the dressing room. Time slowed as Avery watched Ian straddle Josh, who was prostrate on the floor, punching him repeatedly, and before anyone could do anything, Emma raised a heavy piece of wood and smacked Ian on the head, sending him crashing to the side, unconscious. She grabbed Josh, pulled him to his feet, and they fled into the forest.

The fighting started again, but this time Newton arrived, the policemen in tow. Behind them were Stan, the event manager, a few other officials, the bar staff and a couple of security staff. It was too hard to use obvious magic now.

The witches clustered together, and Alex said, "We have to go after Emma and Josh."

"You go," Briar said. "I'll help the wounded."

"I'll stay," Reuben said, glancing at the fighting cast. "I'll help stop this." And without another word, he headed back into the melee, and Hunter followed.

El jerked her head, gesturing beyond them. "Go! And good luck!"

The wood was quiet after the chaos backstage, and Avery and Alex ran in the direction Emma and Josh had taken, but within minutes it was clear they had no idea where they had gone.

They paused and listened, but other than the creak of branches, the wildwood was utterly silent.

"It's too quiet," Alex said, looking around. "I can't even hear the ravens!"

He was right. Normally, the ravens squawked and cackled endlessly, but not now. A soporific silence lapped around them.

"The forest is hiding them," Avery whispered.

"Don't say that—we might never find them. Remember how it felt the other night? Who knows where they are!"

Avery looked at him in disbelief. "I will never forget the other night! Come on, think! How do we find them?" She didn't speak for a moment as she raced through ideas.

"We fucked up, Avery. *I* fucked up." Alex leaned against the closest tree, looking around despondently. "We should have burnt the copies of the play as soon as we had them, but I was so obsessed with getting rid of Kit that I waited. We might have prevented this!"

Avery tried to keep the impatience from her voice. That wouldn't help anything. "We all agreed, and for good reason. Kit needs to go or his ghost will haunt that theatre forever, and who knows what havoc he may cause with other plays. The spell was already in motion, and we couldn't have stopped it!"

"But burning them might have weakened it. Kit's spirit is tied to it, and we might have lessened the effects."

"Burning grimoires doesn't stop spells from working!" she said forcefully. "The cast is bewitched! And as we discussed before, it might have achieved nothing but weakened our chance of getting rid of him." Avery was aware that with every passing second Emma and Josh were getting harder to find, but she had to snap Alex out of it. "Don't let this get to you. We knew this would happen—your dreams told you so. The cast will be okay now that other people are there. We need to find Josh and Emma!"

Alex took a deep breath and pushed his hair away from his face. "Yes, you're right. My thoughts are all over the place."

"Then lend your power to me, because I've just had a good idea. We follow the magic!"

"What?" Alex asked, confused.

"They're bewitched—we know how that spell feels. The passion and obsession, and the underlying feeling of loss. We find it and follow it." She grabbed his hand and squeezed it. "Come on, let's combine our magic, and I'll find them."

As Alex's magic joined with hers, Avery felt her strength grow, and she turned slowly, sending out her senses and feeling for the play's magic that was very different to the wild magic of the wood. For what seemed like endless minutes, she felt nothing, and then she found it; a tendril of longing, so desolate that it almost broke her heart.

"I've found it."

Still clasping Alex's hand tightly, she pulled him along the leafy, shadow-soaked paths, feeling the afternoon heat thicken around them like amber. The path was winding and barely there in places, and she pushed through undergrowth, stray branches catching her clothes like grasping fingers. All the while the feeling of love and longing grew stronger, until she felt it affecting her own mood, despite her protective amulet. She drew on Alex's strength even more, trying to flush the negative emotions from her body, and she felt him do the same.

Then suddenly, as if they'd broken through a barrier, a wave of utter despair hit them, and ahead, under a huge oak tree, they saw Tristan and Iseult together, arms around each other as they gazed into each other's eyes. Avery shook her head with disbelief. *Not Tristan or Iseult, it was Josh and Emma!* The spell was getting to her, too.

She loosed Alex's hand as they stepped closer, and Avery called out, "Emma, Josh! We've been looking for you. Are you okay?"

They looked up, alarmed. Josh's face was bloodied and bruised, and blood had stained his fine shirt, but he straightened his shoulders and pushed Emma behind him. "Leave us alone. You don't belong here."

"Neither do you," Alex said. He walked forward a few paces, very slowly, as if approaching a frightened child. "You're injured. Let us help."

"No!" He backed away, Emma retreating with him, and Avery could see her frightened face behind his shoulder, tear-stained and red from crying.

"Emma," she called. "You look scared. Let us help."

"My name is Iseult, and you can't help us. My husband will kill him, and I may as well die, too!"

Shit.

Avery kept her gaze fixed on Emma and slowly advanced, aware of Alex keeping pace with her. "You are not Iseult! Your names are Emma and Josh!" As Avery said their names, she uttered a spell for clarity, sending it across the clearing with a gentle breeze.

"No!" Josh said again, more forcefully this time. "We have had enough lies! Leave us be!" And then he pulled a short dagger from his belt. "I will not return to the court to be sentenced to death. We will end it here and now!"

Emma stepped around him, her face impassive. "You heard him. Go!"

Avery faltered, and then said her spell again, but Alex had a different idea, and he said, "I will intervene on your behalf. Plea for mercy."

Josh shook his head. "I have had my chance, but I betrayed my lord. Only death will suffice."

Emma turned to Josh. "Kill me first!"

Horror filled Avery as she watched Josh plunge the knife towards her and without hesitation, she flicked it away with a powerful blast of magic, satisfied to see the knife jerk out of his grip and hit the ground behind them. As soon as it left his hand, Alex lunged and tackled Josh to the ground, and Avery used a blast of air to lift Emma and pin her against the tree. Neither of them had earth magic as strong as Briar's, but Alex manipulated tree roots out of the ground, using them to bind Josh, and Avery did the same using the ivy that trailed out of the tree's branches, until both were immobile.

They both looked terrified, but still writhed within their bonds.

"What now?" Avery asked, exasperated. "They are far too bewitched to break through! So much for spilling that potion—it achieved nothing!"

"We need Newton to arrest them!"

"What for? Madness?"

"Affray! Assault! He'll be in there now, arresting the whole cast. They need locking up until we end this tonight! It's the only way to keep them safe."

Avery nodded as she realised it was the best way. "Okay. I'll run back. Will you be okay here?"

He nodded, and then as she turned away he ran to catch up with her, pulling her into his arms, and he kissed her as if he'd never see her again. "I'm sorry if I've been an idiot all week."

"You haven't been! What's this about?"

"Beltane jealousies. I love you, just remember that." He kissed her again, but gently this time.

Avery placed her hands on his face, her thumbs running over his stubble.

"Of course I remember, and you need to remember that I love you—and only you. I'll be back soon."

It was close to six o'clock when Avery and the rest of the witches, Hunter, and Dan stood together on the rise of the hill above the castle car park, watching the police put the entire White Haven Players cast and crew into the big black police vans below. As the last van left the car park, Newton strolled up the path to join them, leaving Moore leaning against his BMW, smoking.

"Bloody hell," Reuben said, nursing his jaw where a ripe bruise was blossoming. "That was a bit hairier than I expected."

El raised her hand to his cheek, cradling it gently. "More than any of us expected."

Hunter's hands were jammed in his jean pockets, and he sat down on a low castle wall. He was also covered in minor cuts and bruises, but he looked invigorated. "I enjoyed it!"

"That's your wolf talking!" Briar said, looking at him with amusement.

He grinned. "I like it when you rub your salves all over me."

"I'll make sure these ones sting!"

"Even better."

Avery laughed, despite her mood, and tried to cheer Alex up. "That's a damn strong spell, Alex. Your granddad was good."

"I wish I could be proud of that," Alex grumbled. "Now I'm beginning to doubt our plan for tonight."

"I was going to watch the procession," Dan said ruefully. "Now I'm not so sure."

"How was Harry?" Avery asked, watching him pull his car keys from his pocket.

He looked at her bleakly. "Bloody awful. He barely recognised me, and I couldn't get through to him! I can't believe how bad that became! I think I should go to the station to support him."

Avery reached up and hugged him. Dan had never been with them when they dealt with things like this—except for the mermaids, and he was drugged by Siren magic then. He only heard the good results after the madness had passed. "Sorry. I should have prepared you better...but it took us by surprise."

"And tonight?"

"Tonight will be fine," she said, trying to sound more confident than she felt.

"Remind me what you're doing, again?" Newton said, reaching their side.

"The giant cleansing spell," Briar explained. "The one Avery told you about."

"Will it be as giant a disaster as this?"

They all glared at him, but Briar answered him with a tightly controlled voice. "Do you think you could have done better?"

"I'd have brought more police with me if I had realised it would be this bad!" He sat heavily on the wall next to Hunter. "At least the crowd left without any trouble. Stan was pretty good, too. The council cleared the last of the audience who were trying to hang around. It's bound to hit the news—even though the press had left before the end."

"Sarah Rutherford?" Alex asked.

"Yep. She's like a bad penny."

"It is her job," Avery reminded him. "And you will be nice to the cast, won't you? It's not their fault they behaved this way. They're bewitched."

Newton nodded. "I'll try, but half of them did try to kill the other half. And don't forget, one of them was stabbed. He's on his way to the hospital right now." He stood up and straightened his tie, and then smoothed his hair. "I better get to the station to start processing this mess."

"We'd better go, too," Reuben said. "We need to get in place for tonight. We'll let you know when it's done, Newton. With luck, you'll see a change in the cast."

"Where are you taking them?" Avery asked, having a horrible thought. "They need to be here to get the benefit of the cleansing spell."

Newton looked incredulous. "We were taking them to Truro!"

"You have to keep them here, in White Haven!"

"It's a very small police station!"

"But you have to, or it won't work!"

"Fuck!" he yelled into the air, disturbing the ravens that scattered with raucous calls. Without another word he pulled out his phone and stalked down the path, leaving them dumbfounded.

It was only when Newton was out of earshot that Reuben said, "Oops."

Twenty-Seven

The drums resounded through the streets of White Haven, announcing the arrival of the Goddess and the Green Man. Firelight flared at intermittent points along the high street, and the murmur of the crowd was thick with excitement.

Avery could feel a remnant of their earlier magic carried by those who had been at the play. Mixing with that was the magic from their smudge bundles. As agreed, Avery had worked her way down the lower half of the town, dropping the small bundles into the braziers that were protected by costumed members of the event, and she whispered spells to enhance them as she went. Her giant smudge bundle besom broom was already smoking, the rich scent of the herbs filling the air. Somewhere further along the street was Briar, Hunter, and Reuben, also delivering the cleansing herbs. So far she could feel only positive emotions from the crowd, and she hoped it stayed that way.

Dusk was falling as the front of the procession came into view with a flare of spinning firelight. The lead performers were painted and dressed totally in blue, the whites of their eyes stark against their painted faces. Some were beating drums with rhythmical precision, while others carried huge sticks of greenery that they whirled around them. Their pace was slow, full of import, but behind them came the tumblers and jugglers, tossing their fire sticks high into the air, and behind them was a troupe dressed all in red. The flames cast grotesque shadows, and Avery pulled her cloak around her and adjusted the draped hood over her head. In the end, they had all decided to dress up. They knew most people who watched would be costumed in some manner, whether it was just painted faces or full outfits, so Avery wore a heavy woollen cloak that she sometimes used for rituals, and El had painted her face white, outlining her eyes with bold makeup.

Now that the procession was closer, Avery stepped back into the shadowed recess of a shop front and for a moment she let the cleansing smoke wrap around her, bringing calm and clarity that strengthened her resolve. Then she sent the smoke out in a whirl of wind into the crowd. This time she said the spell louder, her voice drowned out by the drumming, and it carried the cleansing blessing far and wide. Opening herself up to the night, she felt Briar's presence, and then Reuben's, and with a smile she banged the pole of her besom broom onto the ground in time with the drums, feeling it resonate beneath her feet. Magic was already rising — potent and unstoppable.

Avery worked her way down the street, keeping to the back of the crowd, only pausing when she reached the quay. Here the procession would turn and make its way along the coast road to Spriggan Beach. Fire jugglers and drummers were already entertaining the crowds, lining the harbour and backed by blazing torches.

Avery waited patiently for the May Queen to finally arrive, surrounded by her maidens. The procession was like a river of blood with its own pulse, the Queen its beating heart, and as she appeared, the excited chatter became louder, and then dropped with an awed silence. She wore bold make-up that enhanced her fierce eyes, an elaborate crown piled high with flowers and ribbons, and her white dress was richly embroidered with tumbling leaves and blossoms. Avery blinked to clear her vision, dismissing the *something else* that burned beneath the very human form of the May Queen. Alarmed for a moment, she looked around at the crowd, but they were lost in the moment, craning to see the Goddess as she progressed in her majesty. Avery smiled, knowing their spell had a very good chance of working, and planting her smoking broom in a protected corner, wedged into the stone, she left the harbour and hurried to join Alex.

Avery spelled her way in through the side door of the theatre and waited for a few short seconds for her breathing to settle and her heart to slow. It was deathly quiet after the hedonistic noise only streets away, but the theatre was throbbing with a different kind of power.

Kit's power.

She quickly threw a witch-light above her and headed into the auditorium. As soon as she opened the door, the candlelight drew her gaze to the stage, where Alex had set up his summoning circle. For a moment Alex didn't see her, and she watched as he worked, his concentration absolute. He had tied his hair back high on his head, leaving his stubble-grazed jaw exposed. He had also taken his shirt off, and she was surprised to see an elaborate design painted on his chest and along the inside of his arms.

Avery had barely taken two steps towards him when Kit's malevolent spirit appeared before her, reaching out to squeeze his icy-cold hands around her neck.

She immediately dropped to her knees, shocked at how corporeal he was. Within seconds she started to choke, and she summoned her power, desperate to fend him off. But a blast of magic caught Kit from behind, and he vanished as quickly as he'd arrived, leaving her gasping for air.

"Avery!" Alex yelled. "Get in here. Now!"

She staggered to her feet and clambered onto the stage, and Alex pulled her into the circle, raising the protection again immediately.

"Shit! He caught me by surprise!" Avery's hands flew to her neck, already feeling it start to swell, and she quickly said a healing spell to ease the bruising. "Has he been like that since you arrived?"

"Sort of," Alex said ruefully. "I had a few minutes of blissful peace, long enough to start my protection spell, when he seemed to realise what I was doing. At that point, I had a bit of a problem getting it finished, but I managed to buy myself some time to get it done."

"You should have called me."

"No. It was important you did what you needed to out there." Alex took a deep breath and exhaled heavily as he looked at the series of circles before them. "As soon as my main circle was up, I was able to finish these."

Avery noted that within the large outer circle edged with candles was a complex series of interlinked designs, the centre one a double circle, the ring of which was filled with runes. A series of sigils was drawn in the middle, and she realised one of them was the same as the one on his chest. "What does that sign mean?"

"It enhances my power, and I'm going to need it."

A long, wooden stick was lying on the floor, carved with rudimentary symbols, and Avery frowned. "You need your staff?"

Alex grinned. "I rarely use it, but I decided I needed it for something that Kit won't like."

As if he'd heard his name, the air crackled around them and the temperature plummeted, and Kit appeared at the edge of the stage. He sent out of bolt of energy that hit the protective shield around them and bounced back.

"You won't get through that!" Alex shouted. "I'm a flesh and blood witch, and that makes me far stronger than you!"

Kit paced around them, as if looking for a way to breach the circle, silent and brooding.

Alex continued to goad him. "Have you noticed that Yvonne has gone?"

Kit shot him a look of pure loathing. "You were lucky."

"I was cleverer than you!"

"But are you?" Kit stared at Alex, an ugly smile creasing his face. "You haven't broken my spell, have you? I can feel it working right now. The cast are being eaten by it. I feel their anger and betrayal, even though they are halfway across the town!"

"In that case, you can feel the atmosphere in the town, too," Alex said. "They aren't so angry anymore. Their petty jealousies are disappearing. Your spell is failing."

Kit shrugged dismissively. "Not with the cast. It's too strong. It will take weeks to wear off." Kit sent another blast of energy towards them, but again his magic was deflected easily and he resumed his pacing. "Remember Yvonne? It was weeks before she killed herself. The spell continued to work all that time. And on Charles. It's the beauty of the interlocking magic."

"Keep congratulating yourself, Kit. You won't win."

Without waiting for a response Alex pulled Avery into the centre circle, swiftly picked up the wooden staff, and cracked it hard off the floor, uttering an incantation as he did so. The candles' flames shot higher and the runes blazed with fiery light as the protective spell around the double-edged circle snapped into place. With another crack of the staff, Alex dropped the outer protective circle completely, allowing Kit to come closer.

Avery looked at Alex, surprised. That was clever magic. What was he planning? Alex's power was so different to her own. She never attempted conjuring or necromancy. It was a skill she didn't possess and never would, but Alex did, and she'd noticed that his abilities grew stronger every time he tested them. And he looked sure of himself now.

Kit glanced warily at the floor. "Devil's traps?" His head snapped up. "You think I'm foolish enough to step on those?

Alex shook his head. "No. But you're weak enough that you won't resist them."He turned to Avery. "Sit in the centre of the circle, and lend me your magic when I need it."

Avery nodded, and quickly moved into place.

Alex cracked the staff again and again, and Avery felt energy thrum through her. She watched as with each crack, the other circles flared to life, the runes blazing, until the air around them was illuminated with runes that seemed to be projected from the floor.

Kit stepped back a pace, his eyes narrowing, as he tried to work out what Alex was doing. He must have decided that attacking was the best form of defence, because he unleashed a barrage of magic at the runes. They flickered momentarily, and then returned.

Alex ignored him and started an incantation, his voice becoming stronger with each word he uttered, and with every bang of the staff. The runes shimmered and glowed, and the marks drawn on his body blazed to life, too. It was at this point that Avery felt him draw on her power, and she willing joined it with his, watching with amazement as the runes started to multiply, seeming to tumble out of the air so quickly that they surrounded Kit.

Panic crossed Kit's face and he vanished, and Avery turned in alarm, her eyes darting around the theatre as she looked for him. But Alex didn't stop, and soon the fiery runes had not only filled the stage, but had filled the auditorium too.

In seconds they caught up with Kit. He manifested again, this time unwillingly. His spirit was in the middle of the theatre, caught within a spider's web of magic. The runes were binding him, crawling over his body and beneath his spirit-skin until he glowed from within.

"What are you doing?" Kit shouted, looking at his arms.

Alex continued to bang the staff rhythmically but stopped his incantation, and Avery was suddenly sure it was combining with the drums on the streets. "I am binding you to the spirit world, Kit. You will never be able to cross here again. You will never be able to roam the spirit world, either. Your spirit is now imprisoned for eternity."

Kit writhed as he tried to break his rune bonds, his face ugly with fury. "No! It isn't possible. My spirit is bound here—with the play!"

"We found the original copy, the one that anchors the others. Even as we speak, it is burning in the Beltane fire, part of the cleansing of White Haven. You are bones and dust, Kit Bonneville, and I now banish you from the Earth forever."

Alex uttered a final spell, and on the last word brought the staff crashing down. The crack resounded through Avery and the theatre, and the runes and Kit vanished with the sound of thunder, leaving them alone in candlelight. For a brief moment, the sigils drawn on Alex's body continued to glow, before vanishing completely.

Avery looked at Alex admiringly, her gaze running across his half-naked body. "Just when I didn't think you could surprise me any more, you go and do that!"

He stood with his arms outstretched, a teasing smile on his face. "Impressed?"

"Very." As they spoke, Avery felt rather heard a boom, and in seconds a wave of magic raced through her. Her fingers started to tingle, and the scent of herbs filled the theatre. "Did you feel that?" she asked as she stood up.

Alex nodded. "The cleansing spell—that wasn't what I was expecting!"

Avery's eyes widened. "What has El done?"

"Seems like it's the night for unexpected spells," Alex said, grinning. He pulled her close and kissed her. "Sorry, I might have smudged your makeup."

"I'll forgive you," she said, resting her hands on his chest. "I've smudged your sigils."

"I don't need them anymore. Let's get this cleared up and go and join the party."

"Can you cope with witch-flight? It will be quicker."

"I can cope with anything right now! I've just pulled off the biggest spell of my life."

When Avery and Alex arrived in the middle of the dunes on Spriggan Beach, the sound of drums and shouting filled the air.

"Come on," Alex said, grabbing her hand. "This way."

"What's going on?" Avery asked. "You're not sick!"

"I know! My adrenalin is keeping it at bay. And probably also my awesome magic."

Alex didn't wait, pulling her along behind him, and when they reached the top of the dune, Spriggan Beach was spread out before them.

The Beltane fire was blazing, and on a low stage a short distance away were the May Queen and the Green Man, seated on their thrones in a bower of flowers. Surrounding them was the rest of the procession—the May Queen's maidens, the fire-jugglers, drummers, tumblers, and acrobats, and other costumed characters. And all around them was the crowd, dancing and celebrating the night away.

"What the hell is El doing?" Alex asked, pointing down to the sand where they could see El leaping around like she was possessed. Her hair was flying and she was grinning from ear to ear as she kept time with the primal drumming.

Avery was unable to suppress a giggle. "It looks like she's dancing!"

"Holy shit. So is Reuben!"

Avery saw Reuben cavorting around the fire wearing his Herne mask, and then through a break in the crowd she saw Hunter wearing his wolf-head mask, and Briar next to him, barefoot and wild, her hair seeming to snake in the firelight like the Medusa.

"What are they doing?"

"Having fun!" Alex turned to her. "Can you feel it? All of that horrible, brooding undercurrent has gone!" He still had her hand in his, and he leaned forward and kissed her. "Come on, Ave, time to join in!"

Twenty-Eight

It was dawn by the time the party on the beach finally ground to a halt, but Avery and her friends were still there, clustered around a small fire, the curve of the dunes behind them.

Reuben was sipping whiskey, and his eyes were bloodshot. His mask was perched on the top of his head, the horns pointing up at an odd angle.

"You'll regret that later," El told him.

"I don't care." He lifted the whiskey bottle to his lips and took another slug. "Besides, a surf will get rid of a hangover."

"I'm with you," Hunter said, refusing to be outdone, and he reached out and took the bottle from Reuben, swallowing a healthy gulp. He shuddered. "Yep. That will do it. Alex?"

Alex grinned and took his turn, and when he'd finished, Avery laughed and reached her hand out, too. "It's cold. I'm taking the medicinal approach."

After dancing for hours around the fire, they had made their own small one, watching as the crowd diminished. They'd been sitting and talking for a while about the spells they had used to banish Kit and cleanse the town, and after the week they'd had, everyone felt the need to celebrate.

"I feel I've become nocturnal," Avery said, pulling her cloak around her shoulders. "And maybe slightly feral."

"I like feral," Hunter said with a wolfish grin. "Look at Briar. She's definitely on the wild side now!"

Briar rolled her eyes but looked pleased, self-consciously running her fingers through her tangled hair. "Bloody Green Man. He's nothing but trouble."

A shout interrupted them, and they looked across the beach, seeing Newton and Dan approach. In minutes they were at their side, and Dan nudged Avery out of the way, making himself space around the fire, while Newton did the same on the other side of Alex.

"You're still up?" Avery asked, surprised.

"I've been stuck at the station all night supporting Harry," Dan said resentfully, "while you have clearly been having too much fun!" Dark shadows were etched beneath his eyes. "Harry's wife was at home looking after the kids, but she was worried sick. It was the least I could do."

Feeling sorry for him, Avery passed him the whiskey. "You're a good friend, Dan."

He grunted. "He bloody owes me for this."

"Thanks for the call," Newton said. He took his jacket off and rolled his sleeves up as he reached his hands towards the fire. He jerked his head towards the beach. "This will take some clearing up."

The beach was strewn with litter, discarded masks, the remains of fires, and most of all the smouldering remnants of the main fire. The thrones had long gone, someone having hoisted them onto the fire to keep it going. The tide was coming in, and the soft *shush* of waves threatened to take the debris with them.

"Not my problem!" Reuben said, squinting into the distance. "We did our part. Besides, I can see the volunteer clean-up crew is already out." He pointed to a straggling line of people in the distance carrying large plastic rubbish bags. "How are the cast?"

"Confused and disorientated, and wondering what the hell they're doing in police cells." Newton looked puzzled. "How did you do it?"

Avery nodded at El. "The cleansing spell was her baby, not mine."

El laughed. "I won't bore you with the complexities, Newton, but essentially it was as Avery said—a cleansing spell. I just tweaked it. Sort of put a magical stick of dynamite under the Beltane fire and let it roll through the town."

"Well, it worked," Dan said as he wrested the whiskey out of Reuben's hands and took another swig. "It was like flicking a switch. The cast literally just blinked and looked around like they'd been in a trance."

"What about Emma and Josh?" Briar asked.

"Them too," Newton said. "Although, they'll both have some explaining to do to their partners."

"At least they're alive," Alex said. "For one horrible moment in the wood, I didn't think we'd stop them."

"And Kit?" Newton asked.

"I've bound his spirit with the biggest rune spell I could find. Bye-bye Granddad. Miserable bastard."

"Good," Dan said with feeling. "Harry doesn't know whether he's coming or going."

"How are your police colleagues?" Alex asked. "Did they take the redirection to White Haven well?"

Newton grimaced. "Not really, but I don't care. I don't think those cells have ever been so full. We had to put too many people in together, and it was highly irregular, but some of my colleagues have learned not to question me too much."

Avery shuffled, making herself more comfortable, and drew her knees into her chest. "What will you charge them with?"

"For most it will be a warning. For others, there'll be assault charges. Fortunately, the guy who was stabbed is doing fine. It was a minor wound and from what I can gather, he doesn't want to press charges."

El looked up abruptly. "He won't have had the benefit of the cleansing spell!"

"No, he won't," Newton acknowledged, "but I think the shock of being stabbed cleared his head—or so I gather."

Avery gazed at the sea, her chin on her knees. At the moment it was a milky grey colour, and the horizon was a pale green. The air was still, and the shush of the waves was hypnotic. "You know, I'm sort of disappointed that Lyonesse didn't appear."

Dan laughed. "Did you really think it would?"

"I thought it might! Those two days of fog were weird, and Kit's spell was so strong!" She shrugged. "I wasn't sure what would happen."

"I like the idea, too," Briar said as she looked to the horizon. "But to conjure a mythical island into being—well, wow, that would be something!"

Newton groaned. "I am *very* pleased that didn't happen! The play and Beltane have caused enough problems. I'm hoping that now it's passed, everything will settle down."

Alex grinned at him. "There'll always be something!" He paused for a moment, perplexed. "You know, I'm surprised we didn't see Shadow last night."

"I saw her for a while," El told him. "She was here with the Nephilim, partying away over there—" she gestured away to her left. "I think they left a couple of hours ago to finish the party at home. The boys wanted to fly!"

"You know, I feel really guilty," Avery confessed. "We've been so busy that I haven't called Genevieve, or checked in on Oswald!"

"If there had been a problem, we'd have heard," Alex reassured her. "And I'm sure Oswald managed to keep Ulysses in check."

Newton frowned. "Oswald is in Mevagissey, is that right?"

"Yes, why?" Avery asked alarmed.

"Oh, nothing much," Newton said, unable to stop a smirk. "Things got a little fruity over there on Beltane Eve. I believe they had to issue a warning to a very large guy who ran naked down the main street."

The witches looked at each other, mouths open, and Avery asked, "How big was he?"

"Are you asking about his height, or something else?"

Reuben threw his head back with a raucous laugh as Avery said, "I meant his height!"

"Oh, that." Newton said, looking cheeky. "Long hair, massive guy, pretty fit from what I hear! I gather the female PC's enjoyed that arrest."

"That was Ulysses! Was he locked up for long?"

Newton shook his head. "Long enough for him to calm down, and for someone to bring him some clothes."

Alex shook his head. "Poor Ulysses!"

"And how are you feeling, Alex," Briar asked, "after banishing Kit? That must suck."

He shrugged. "It did and it didn't. I never knew him. I wasn't emotionally attached to him. I'm more disappointed that one of my family members could do what he did. But, it is what it is, and I did what I had to do." He nudged Avery. "I'm surprised Helena didn't intervene!"

Avery frowned, his question provoking concern. "She's been quiet lately—which is actually worrying! I hope she's okay."

"She's a spirit!" Dan said. "I don't care where she is as long as she doesn't appear in the shop."

A giggle from above and behind them caused them all to look around, and at the top of the dunes behind them, they saw a couple holding hands and looking dreamily at each other.

Reuben sniggered. "There will be so many babies around here in nine months! Those dunes saw a lot of action last night."

"Will you miss Beltane, Reuben?" Avery asked him, laughing. More than anyone, Reuben had enjoyed the mischief that Beltane had brought.

"I think I will!" He winked. "There's always next year!"

Thanks for reading *Crown of Magic*. Please make an author happy and leave a review.

Vengeful Magic, White Haven Witches Book 8, is on sale now at Happenstance Books.

When lost treasure is discovered, supernatural creatures unleash violence across Cornwall.

Some things are meant to stay buried...

I have also written a spinoff series called White Haven Hunters. The first book is called *Spirit of the Fallen,* and you can buy it at Happenstance Books.

Newsletter

If you enjoyed this book and would like to read more of my stories, please subscribe to my newsletter at tjgreenauthor.com. You will get two free short stories, *Excalibur Rises* and *Jack's Encounter,* and will also receive free character sheets for all of the main White Haven witches.

By staying on my mailing list you'll receive free excerpts of my new books, as well as short stories, news of giveaways, and a chance to join my launch team. I'll also be sharing information about other books in this genre you might enjoy.

Ream

I have started my own subscription service called Happenstance Book Club. I know what you're thinking! What is Ream? It's a bit like Patreon, which you may be more familiar with, and it allows you to support me and read my books before anyone else.

There is a monthly fee for this, and a few different tiers, so you can choose what tier suits you. All tiers come with plenty of other bonuses, including merchandise, but the one thing common to all is that you can read my latest books while I'm writing them – so they're a rough draft. I will post a few chapters each week, and you can read them at your leisure, as well as comment in them. You can also choose to be a follower for free.

You can comment on my books, chat about spoilers, and be part of a community. I will also post polls, character art, share rituals and spells, share the background to the myths and legends in my books, and some of my earlier books are available to read for free.

Interested? Head to Happenstance Book Club.

https://reamstories.com/happenstancebookclub

Happenstance Book Shop

I also now have a fabulous online shop called Happenstance Books where you can buy eBooks, audiobooks, and paperbacks, many bundled up at great prices, as well as fabulous merchandise. I know that you'll love it! Check it out here: https://happenstancebookshop.com/

YouTube

If you love audiobooks, you can listen for free on YouTube, as I have uploaded all of my audiobooks there. Please subscribe if you do. Thank you. https://www.youtube.com/@tjgreenauthor

Read on for a list of my other books.

Author's Note

Thank you for reading *Crown of Magic,* the seventh book in the White Haven Witches series.

I had a lot of fun writing this! I love exploring the pagan beliefs and festivals, and Beltane was an absolute must for me. I'm not entirely sure where the idea for *Tristan and Iseult* came from, but once it was in my head, I couldn't let it go. I really enjoyed weaving the story with Beltane, and it is fittingly Cornish! The name Iseult is interchangeable with Isolde, so you'll see both depending which version you read.

I used the basic plot of Wagner's opera, *Tristan and Isolde,* for the play, and having spent quite a bit of time acting in my past - unprofessionally of course, I had lots of experience to draw on. I also watched a few videos of Edinburgh's Beltane Festival to get inspiration. I recommend watching some!

As usual, my characters continue to evolve, and it was great to see a bit more of Hunter and Dan in this story. I also wanted to explore El's and Alex's magic. In future stories we may see more of Alex's family, and probably the other witches, too. I'm already thinking about plots.

Thanks again to Fiona Jayde Media for my awesome cover, and thanks to Kyla Stein at Missed Period Editing for applying her fabulous editing skills.

Thanks also to my beta readers, glad you enjoyed it; your feedback, as always, is very helpful!

Finally, thank you to my launch team, who give valuable feedback on typos and are happy to review on release. It's lovely to hear from them—you know who you are! You're amazing! I love hearing from all my readers, so I welcome you to get in touch.

If you'd like to read a bit more background to the stories, please head to my website tjgreenauthor.com, where I blog about the books I've read and the research I've done on the series—in fact, there's lots of stuff on there about my other series, Rise of the King.

If you'd like to read more of my writing, please join my mailing list at tjgreenauthor.com. You can get a free short story called *Jack's Encounter*, describing how Jack met Fahey—a longer version of the prologue in *Call of the King*—by subscribing to my newsletter. You'll also get a free copy of *Excalibur Rises*, a short story prequel. You will also receive free character sheets on all of my main characters in White Haven Witches and White Haven Hunters—exclusive to my email list!

By staying on my mailing list you'll receive free excerpts of my new books, updates on new releases, as well as short stories and news of giveaways. I'll also be sharing information about other books in this genre you might enjoy.

You can also follow my Facebook page, tjgreenauthor. I post there reasonably frequently. In addition I have a Facebook group called TJ's Inner Circle. It's a fab little group where I run giveaways and post teasers, so come and join us. https://www.facebook.com/groups/tjsinnercircle

About the Author

I was born in England, in the Black Country, but moved to New Zealand in 2006. I lived near Wellington with my partner Jase, and my cats Sacha and Leia. However, in April 2022 we moved again! Yes, I like making my life complicated... I'm now living in the Algarve in Portugal, and loving the fabulous weather and people. When I'm not busy writing I read lots, indulge in gardening and shopping, and I love yoga.

Confession time! I'm a Star Trek geek – old and new – and love urban fantasy and detective shows. Secret passion – Columbo! Favourite Star Trek film is the Wrath of Khan, the original! Other top films – Predator, the original, and Aliens.

In a previous life I was a singer in a band, and used to do some acting with a theatre company. For more on me, check out a couple of my blog posts. I'm an old grunge queen, so you can read about my love of that here. For more random news, read this.

Please follow me on social media.

facebook.com/tjgreenauthor/

pinterest.pt/tjgreenauthor/

tiktok.com/@tjgreenauthor

youtube.com/@tjgreenauthor

goodreads.com/author/show/15099365.T_J_Green

instagram.com/tjgreenauthor/

bookbub.com/authors/tj-green

https://reamstories.com/happenstancebookclub

Other Books by T J Green

Rise of the King Series

A Young Adult series about a teen called Tom who's summoned to wake King Arthur. It's a fun adventure about King Arthur in the Otherworld.

Call of the King #1

The Silver Tower #2

The Cursed Sword #3

White Haven Witches Series

Witches, secrets, myth and folklore, set on the Cornish coast.

Magic Unbound #2

Magic Unleashed #3

All Hallows' Magic #4

Undying Magic #5

Crossroads Magic #6

Crown of Magic #7

Vengeful Magic #8

Chaos Magic #9

Stormcrossed Magic #10

Wyrd Magic #11

Midwinter Magic #12

White Haven and The Lord of Misrule: Novella

White Haven Hunters

The action-packed spin-off featuring Shadow and the Nephilim.

Spirit of the Fallen #1

Shadow's Edge #2

Dark Star #3

Hunter's Dawn #4

Midnight Fire #5

Immortal Dusk #6

Brotherhood of the Fallen #7

Storm Moon Shifters

Paranormal Mysteries set around the wolf shifter pack, Storm Moon.

Storm Moon Rising #1

Dark Heart #2

Moonfell Witches

This series features the mysterious and magical witches who live in Moonfell, the sprawling Gothic mansion in London. They first appeared in Storm Moon Rising, Storm Moon Shifters Book 1, and then in Immortal Dusk, White Haven Hunters Book 6, and features characters from both series. However, this series can be read as a standalone.

If you love witches and magic, you will love the Moonfell Witches.

The First Yule: Novella

Triple Moon #1

Printed in Great Britain
by Amazon

68d47d91-8397-411e-8068-c90fabc60f3aR02